T0354979

HIDDEN STAR

FAITH, FAMILY, FUTURE

ELLIE GERSTEN

iUniverse

HIDDEN STAR
FAITH, FAMILY, FUTURE

iUniverse books may be ordered through booksellers or by contacting:

iUniverse
1663 Liberty Drive
Bloomington, IN 47403
www.iuniverse.com
844-349-9409

ISBN: 978-1-6632-5257-9 (sc)
ISBN: 978-1-6632-5258-6 (e)

Library of Congress Control Number: 2023907959

Print information available on the last page.

iUniverse rev. date: 05/31/2023

DEDICATION

This book is dedicated to the women of the Inquisition who chose to continue observing their Jewish traditions with the threat of losing their homes, their families and their lives to pursue
Kiddush HaShem, for the sanctity of the G-d of Moses.

CONTENTS

1

REFLECTIONS

"No, no. Abuelita, Grandmother. Don't die." I was jolted awake in tears, sweaty and terrified. I saw my grandmother lying dead in her bed, with my crying family surrounding her. Could my nightmare be real? I had to call my mom. I knew Abuela was in poor health. As I clutched the phone, waiting for Mom to pick up, I paced back and forth. Before asking Mom how Grandma was, I could hear from her raspy voice that she had been crying.

She said, "The doctor told us Grandma does not have much time. He said she may have days left. How soon can you get home? She's waiting for you."

I said, "Immediately. I will come today."

My knees began to tremble, so I sat down. My grandma helped shape the woman I am. I immediately thought back to a writing assignment in fourth grade. I proudly showed Grandma the perfect score on my paper. She was impressed. Grandma loved how beautifully it was written and encouraged my talent by giving me a journal. She suggested that I write in it every day. A few days later, I ran to my grandma, eager to tell her how much I loved my journal and show her all the pages I had filled.

She continued to foster my talent. Next, she got me a rolltop desk for my bedroom, a dictionary, and a thesaurus. I remember how much fun it was going through the pages of the thesaurus, finding new ways to write words like *happy*—gleeful, joyful, cheery, merry, and many more.

I loved playing with words. It was my abuelita who steered me toward a career in journalism.

Another talent abuelita nurtured in me was cooking. Spending hour after hour in the kitchen, making food for the family, was pure joy. I can still see her instructing, with her finger pointing at me. "Don't add too much honey here. A bit more lemon juice there. Paprika is not just for color. Remember, you always need the bitter and sweet." She was part of my heart. Now I was going home to say goodbye.

I hung up with Mom and went to tell my husband, Jeremy. I took a deep breath and with a crack in my voice said, "Sweetie, Grandma is … dying. We have to leave town. I hope we can get there in time. Don't forget to pack your black suit for the funeral."

Jeremy shifted back and forth with a grimace on his face. He said, "Sorry, honey. I'm meeting with new clients at eight o'clock tomorrow morning. I can't leave tonight."

"Are you sure you can't?" I said. "It would mean so much to me. Why don't you fly out once the meeting is over."

Jeremy sighed. "I don't know if I can leave work now."

I shook my head, walked over to him, and gave him a hug. Then I put my hands on his shoulders, stared into his eyes, and said, "You know I feel family comes first."

I booked the next flight to Santa Fe and packed my bags.

As we drove to the airport, Jeremy made small talk to ease my worries. "Wow, Strella. There is no traffic on the highway."

I responded, "I really can't concentrate."

I felt numb, in a trancelike state, as I stared out the window at the cars zooming by. The only image racing through my head was my abuelita lying in her bed and how scared she must feel. I was comforted knowing that she was in her own home, surrounded by loved ones. She never liked hospitals. The putrid smells made her gag. Abuelita told me, "I want to be in my own bed when I die."

Jeremy hugged me lightly and spoke softly. "I hope Grandma will be okay. I love you."

I hugged him back as I slowly exhaled. I said nothing, then quickly moved through the airport to the gate and onto the plane. I made it to my seat and tried to visualized my favorite place, the creek behind my childhood home in Pueblo. Then I gazed down and noticed I had been wringing my hands and shaking my right knee.

A stewardess put her hand on my shoulder and asked me, "Are you all right? Can I get you a drink?"

"Yes, I'd like some water please."

The stewardess came back with a glass of water and some warm cookies. "Let me know if you need anything else."

I smiled at her.

As I sipped the water, I began to relax. Fortunately, the trip went lightning fast. Before I knew it, I had my bags in hand and saw a familiar face. It was my dad, with his arms outstretched waiting to give me a big bear hug. "There's my girl. It's so good to see you, Estrella."

In the car, at first, neither of us spoke, both lost in our thoughts. My fingers couldn't stop moving as I twisted and untwisted my hair. Dad broke the silence when he began reminiscing about Mom and her family. I knew my parents' love story, but I thought talking would be good for him.

Dad said, "I won a football scholarship to St. Mary's Preparatory High School. I still remember what a bundle of nerves I was on that very first day of school. I didn't know anyone, and most of the students were from very rich families. Honey, you remember that I grew up poor. Your mom—or as I thought of her, the fair Melina—who was in my English class, welcomed me to school. It was love at first sight. Mom was beloved, kind, and the most beautiful girl in high school with her long, black, curly hair and sparkling smile."

Dad continued, "One day, I mustered up enough courage to talk to your mom. I walked up and tapped her on the shoulder. When she turned to face me, I got tongue-tied and tried frantically to think of something to say. Finally, I asked, 'Is this room 204?' Mom pointed at the large numbers right on the door with a half-smile." Dad realized we were almost home and said, "I better stop daydreaming now and get you home so you can be with your grandma."

As we pulled up to my childhood home, I immediately ran over to the garden to glance at the sunflowers. It was as if they were smiling at me, happy I was home. I was glad to be there.

Mom greeted me with a hug and a kiss on my forehead. "It's so good to see you. Grandma just fell asleep. Why don't you get settled, and then we can go for a walk." I quickly went to Grandma's room, peeking in just to check on her. She looked different from my last visit but was peaceful as she slept.

Mom and I talked as we walked around the grounds. "Mom, what happened to Abuela?

She wasn't so sick the last time I was here. Why didn't you call?"

Mom answered, "The doctor changed her medicine because she was not steady on her feet and she became lethargic. I took her back to see him, and he changed her medicine again. This time, she felt better, but it didn't last long. Things changed suddenly. Remember, dear, she is almost one hundred years old."

I said, "I never thought of her as any age, she was just my abuela."

We continued our stroll all the way to the stables. I was excited to see that my childhood oak tree had grown. "Grandma and I planted this tree together." I smiled. "I love this ranch so much. This Spanish-style hacienda made of adobe is perfect. It is warm in the winter and cool in the summer. How long has it been in the family?"

Mom was deep in thought and said, "I know Abuelita Maria inherited the ranch from your great-grandmother, whose family had lived there for generations, but I don't know how long our family has owned it."

I said, "We have an interesting family. Should we head back to the house? Do you think Abuelita is awake?"

Mom nodded as we headed back to see Grandma.

I ran to Grandma's room. Opening the door, I stopped suddenly, surprised at how it appeared. This time, I took a long look at the room. It was different, resembling a hospital room instead of the palatial, sunny bedroom suite I had known and loved. It was now a room cluttered with pill bottles, half-filled glasses of water, a chair with stacks of photo albums on it, and a large oxygen tank. I remembered enjoying sitting at her vanity and playing with different types of makeup and perfumes when I was little. My favorite activity was putting on Grandma's lipstick. I would paint my lips and surrounding area with as much of it on as possible, not understanding how it was supposed to look, and called yipstick.

4

In the midst of this was my abuelita. She was so small, almost disappearing under the sheets. When I took my grandmother's hand, it felt like a child's hand, except it was frail and bony. Her hair was white as snow in a long braid.

She smiled when she saw me and said, "I've missed you, my dear."

"I've missed you too." I moved the blanket so I could have some room to sit on the bed next to her. "Grandma, do you remember the fun we had making woven blankets? We used the wool from our sheep to make the yarn. You had special looms made for my brothers, sister, and me since we were so young when we started to weave."

Abuelita answered, "Of course I do. This was the first blanket we made together. You all became obsessed with making blankets. The only problem was finding space to display them. They were everywhere—on the walls, counters, and finally their original purpose, as covers on our beds."

As my eyes glanced at the nightstand, I stared lovingly at the wedding picture of my grandparents with a *hamsa*, a good luck charm, draped over the corner of the frame. "Grandma, I never realized how much I look like you."

Grandma said, "Let me see. Sweetie, hand me my glasses please. I can't see without them anymore."

We looked at the picture together, pointing to the photo as we studied all the little details. I could see that I resembled Abuelita with her thick, curly black hair, olive skin, and the same mischievous smile. I knew I was pretty with my arched eyebrows, high cheekbones, and slender waist. I was a bit taller than her, standing at five feet six inches.

I continued, "Look how much the baby of the family, Marco, favored Abuelo, Grandfather Sam. He was tall, thin, and cute, with dark, thick hair and blue eyes."

Abuelita added, "Marco also has your grandpa's personality. Sam was such a practical joker, just like Marco."

I said, "Marco enjoyed imitating Grandpa. Grandma, you are still beautiful with your sparkling blue eyes and dimpled cheeks."

She smiled and held my hand. It was as if I was a little girl again. I felt protected under her watchful eye. I wanted to know more about her.

I asked, "Did you have a lot of people at your wedding?"

Abuelita nodded and said, "It was a very big wedding. Remember, Estrella, I had ten older brothers. It was one of the happiest days of my life. We sang and danced all night. It was the last time we celebrated together."

"Abuelita I'm glad to hear that. It's nice to know you have wonderful memories to look back on."

I reminded Abuelita of how silly she could be. "You always knew how to make me feel better. I still remember what you did when I came to you crying after falling."

Grandma said, "Yes, I remember."

I continued to reminisce. "You would take my hand and have me show you where I fell. Then you would smack the place with your hand and say, 'Don't hurt my baby!' Every time you did this, I smiled, feeling loved and protected. When I told my friends what you did, they thought you were making fun of me. I never felt that way. Thinking back to my school days, I remember how you greeted me and my siblings at the door with a big hug and lots of kisses."

Abuelita nodded. "It was a joy for me."

"Abuelita, you are still the best cook I know. One of my favorite things to eat are your *biscochitos* (sugar cookies). I enjoyed talking with you while I ate them."

Abuelita explained, "When you cook, you need to add salt whenever you make something sweet. It is an important step when cooking to help achieve a balance of flavors."

I noted, "This is why you are so amazing in the kitchen."

Abuelita said, "Thank you, sweetheart."

I nodded. "I've always enjoyed our time together." Since I didn't hear anything after a few moments, I whispered, "Grandma?"

Grandma responded with a loud snore.

I began to giggle and mumbled, "I'll let you rest." As I tiptoed out of her room, I stopped at the chair with the stack of photo albums. I took the one on top, gently closing the door behind me. It would be fun to see old photos.

I walked to the kitchen and said to my mom, "I had a really nice chat with Grandma but left once I heard her snoring. I'm so glad I'm here. It's good to see everyone. As I was leaving Grandma's room I saw an album. Let's look at the pictures together."

"That sounds nice. I'll make us some hot cocoa. Why don't you go out in the courtyard. It's a beautiful day, and I planted some new flowers by the tree. Let me know what you think. Remember to grab a blanket from the basket by the door. It's a little chilly outside."

I said, "You always act like such a mom! And don't forget to add marshmallows to the hot cocoa."

As I opened the French doors that led to the courtyard, I walked over to my favorite spot under the maple tree. I marveled at the beautiful flowers. It was a feast for the eyes—reds, greens, blues, purples, and yellows everywhere. I loved hearing the babbling sounds from the fountains. Mom soon joined me, carrying a tray of treats.

As we went through the photo album, the first thing we saw was a certificate from Israel.

Mom explained, "Grandma's cousin Camilla took a trip to Israel. I believe toward the end of her visit, Camilla had a heart attack and died there. It was a really sad time for Grandma since the two were very close. On the certificate, it says she was buried at the Mount of Olives. It looks like it is a really special place in Jerusalem."

I said, "I think I remember Grandma talking about her friend Camilla. I didn't realize they were cousins."

Mom continued, "To thank the Israeli people for their help, Mom always donated money for trees in memory of Camilla."

I turned the page and began looking through these treasured pictures. "Mom, look at Julio. He was so cute dressed as Joseph."

Mom added, "And look at my little Estrella dressed as Mary for Las Posadas. You and your brother did such a good job reenacting the journey Mary and Joseph took to Bethlehem."

I remarked, "We loved playing the roles. When I got older, my sister Consuela took over the part of Mary, and my little brother Marco took over Julio's role. It was quite an honor to play the holy family."

Mom told me, "Our family and neighbors followed the sacred procession. The couple was refused shelter in every home until, at last, they were welcomed in. That's when the fiesta began. We would sing and dance all night. Sweetie, these photos are great. Let's see more."

I said, "Oh, look at this picture! You're pulling my ear. Why did you do that?"

Mom chuckled, "It's a custom on birthdays. One pull for each year, plus an extra for good luck."

I remembered asking my roommate Karen if she had that birthday tradition. She told me that she had never heard of it. Her tradition on birthdays was to spank the birthday boy or girl—one spanking for each year, with one for good luck.

I said, "I remember this birthday! Abuelita always made the most unusual cakes. I was surprised when I cut the cake, because it was checkered inside."

Mom said, "The fiestas were complete with piñatas, the papier-mâché toy filled with candy and money. Each child had a chance to hit the piñata. Abuelita always had extra candy set aside. She didn't want to see anyone leave our home without candy."

As we continued to look through the photos, one image confused me. I asked, "Why does Abuelita look so sad in this photo?"

"Don't you remember? You used to go to the cemetery with her. It's a picture from El Día de Los Muertos, the Day of the Dead. Abuelita always placed pebbles and flowers on the headstones. She said prayers for the departed souls, passed each grave, and told us about our relatives who had left this world. It was a bittersweet day of remembrance."

I smiled. "You know, after all this time sitting and looking at albums, it is still one of my favorite things to do with you and Abuelita. Do you think she's awake?"

Mom said, "Why don't you check on her?"

With the taste of hot cocoa still in my mouth, I walked back to Grandma's room. There was nothing like Mom's cocoa. She always managed to seamlessly blend the bitter and sweet. It was the richness of the chocolate combined with the spiciness of the chili powder that made it so exceptional. This was a lesson Mom had learned long ago from Abuelita.

I was happy to see Grandma was awake and said, "Good to see you. I was remembering a folktale you told us about bitter and sweet."

Abuelita said, "Yes, it began with the silly swan named Salida. Losing and getting new feathers made Salida sob. She sniffled at the sight of her scruffy feathers. Salida complained to her mother, who explained that birds must lose their old feathers to get new feathers. Molting helps birds stay cool in the summer and warm in the winter. Salida surmised there was a need for the bitter to enjoy the sweet. The pain was losing the feathers, which was sad. The sweet was getting new, beautiful feathers that kept her secure. I used to love to make up folktales for you kids."

I exclaimed, "I knew it! I remember asking my friends if they knew that story. They always said no."

Laughing, Grandma said, "I had to find a way to teach you lessons, and I'm not done teaching you. What do you know about our family history?"

"A lot! You are a great storyteller. I know we came from a large family. Our ranch was passed down through many generations. We originally came from a prosperous family in Spain. You taught us to love our Spanish heritage. If there's more to learn, please tell me. You know I've always enjoyed hearing your stories."

Abuelita nodded. "Yes, I remember our talks as we looked at photo albums. I know family stories that go back hundreds of years—stories that are filled with joy, sorrow, and secrets."

I was intrigued. "Really. I didn't know that. Tell me a secret."

Abuelita asked me to come close so she could whisper something to me. I thought she would tell me that she loved me and wish me a good life. "*Somos Judios*. We are Jews," my grandmother said softly.

Confused, I asked, "What did you say?"

Abuelita repeated, "Somos Judios."

2

I DON'T UNDERSTAND

I said, "Grandmother, I don't understand. I'm confused."

With a burst of energy, she said, "Go to the closet. Look under the hat boxes."

I went to the closet and began to search. Grandma had many hat boxes. I asked, "What am I looking for?"

"It's a cedar box." She pointed. "To the left."

I carefully moved things around. Then I spotted what I thought was the chest. With a smile, I pulled it off the shelf and brought it to her. "Is this it?"

Softly she said, "Yes." Taped to the top of the box was an old rusty key, which Abuelita took and placed in the lock. "I can't turn the key. Please open the box."

When I opened it, I was taken aback. There was a silver amulet with foreign writing; a piece of gold metal about four inches long, with a diamond mounted in the middle; poetry; pictures; a package of letters tied with a faded blue ribbon; journals; other trinkets; and audiotapes. The letters and diaries were faded from age.

Abuelita told me, "These audiotapes tell the story of our ancestor, Doña Estrella Fuentes Gomez, who was the matriarch of our family. She represented hope for a better future. Our ancestors came from Spain to the New World in 1597. Since the journal writing is faded, I put her story on tape so you could hear what happened."

I asked, "What does this mean?"

"Our family left Spain during the Inquisition and settled in America, seeking religious freedom. Her story marks the beginning of our lives in America. I am speaking for her in these tapes, since she was unable."

"You know, Grandma, I'm shocked. I didn't know anything about this. Why is this the first time I'm hearing about her? You've told me so many tales about the family. Why is being Jewish a secret?"

"Estrella, our religion was hidden to keep us all safe."

"I don't know what you're talking about. Safe from what? Safe from whom?"

She took a deep breath. "When I was growing up, I saw a Jewish house of worship firebombed. My family later learned there were two children inside who were burned alive. My parents had wanted to openly practice the Jewish faith; however, after this horrific incident, they decided we must continue hiding."

I said, "That was a long time ago. Why didn't you ever talk to me about this?"

"My dear Estrella, before you were born, there was a madman who was on a mission to massacre all Jews. Unfortunately, he came very close and slaughtered six million of our people. This terrified me! Abuelo and I thought we would have a better life if we didn't tell our secret, just like our ancestors. I knew we had to remain in the shadows."

"Why are you telling me this now?"

"I want our traditions to live on after I am gone. I want you to know where you came from. Look through the box and listen to the tapes. This will help you understand our past. I am trusting you to honor our history."

Tears streamed down my face as I gasped to catch my breath. "Yes, I will."

Grandma said, "It is our tradition to pass down our history to future generations. By sharing this with you, I am fulfilling a promise I made to my grandmother almost seventy years ago."

I could see this brought a peaceful smile to her face. Fearing the end was near, I began to cry and said, "I love you."

She asked again, "Will you pass along our history?"

I nodded. "Yes."

We held each other's hands, looked into each other's eyes, and smiled.

"Goodbye, my dear grandmother. Thank you for making my life so happy."

Her hand dropped. It took a moment to realize that she was gone. I picked up her hand and kissed it. After nearly one hundred years of life, just like that, it was over. My heart sank. I was unable to move.

I was overcome with grief as I rested my head on her hand. I loved her so much. She had fought to stay alive until I arrived since she had a tender spot for me. I gently placed her hand on the bed and slowly stood up. With each footstep, I could feel my eyes welling up, and then the salty tears streamed down my face. I stood outside the kitchen and studied the faces of my family for a moment. I took a deep breath and wiped the tears away. I stepped into the kitchen and said, "She's left us."

Consuela stood, walked over to me, and gave me a big hug. "I'm sorry."

Uncle Mario put his hand on Aunt Mia's shoulder, who had just arrived from Spain, and said, "She was the best mom."

Mom said, "I'm glad she is with Dad and our three brothers."

It was heartbreaking to see my mom clutching Dad's forearm as he said, "Mom is gone."

Julio brought a pitcher of water and a box of tissues to the table and said, "It's important to drink some water."

Aunt Mia dabbed her eyes with a tissue and got up. "I have to call the family." Consuela asked, "Where is Grandma's address book? I can start making calls."

Mom answered, "Thank you, sweetie. Grandma's book should be in the top drawer of her nightstand. Take my book too. You know where it is."

Consuela returned from the bedroom and excitedly exclaimed, "I found Abuelita's book. Marco, look at Grandma's writing. How old is this address book?"

Marco shrugged and said, "It's old. They don't make books with such fine leather anymore. Oh, her initials in gold lettering—so sweet. Before you start calling the family, let me find the number for the funeral home."

Consuela began making calls to family and friends. The book was filled with notes along with postcards and pictures.

As a sign of mourning, Mom grabbed a ladder and started to carry it to the bathroom.

Julio yelled, "Mom, what are you doing? I can do it."

Mom answered, "Thank you."

Julio climbed the ladder to cover all the mirrors. He asked, "Mom, why do we do this?"

Mom shrugged and said, "It's tradition."

Consuela added, "It's to focus your attention on the departed and not on yourself."

I walked into the bathroom and said, "I remember we did this for Abuelo."

We went into her room and recited Psalm 23, her favorite. "The Lord is my Shepard, I shall not want ..." Later, there was a knock at the door. The funeral director was at the front of the house.

"I'm sorry for your loss. I am here for Mrs. Maria Spencer." We went out to the back patio while the men removed Abuelita's body. We couldn't bear to see her taken from her bed for the last time. When we returned, there was a beautiful red rose on her bed with a note from the funeral home saying memories last forever. I said, "That was a very thoughtful gesture."

Our family gathered around the kitchen table. It was hard to believe she wasn't there anymore. We were all in shock. To break the silence, I decided to share Grandma's secret with the family.

I hesitantly asked my mom, "Did you ever see a wooden chest in Grandma's closet?"

A big smile washed over Mom's face, and she said, "Why, yes. I loved that chest. It was always an adventure for me to see what was in the box."

I stammered a little and said, "Grandma told me about our family from Spain."

"Hmm." Mom pressed her lips together, thinking deeply. "I know it was her dream to revisit Spain. Why are you asking, *mija*, honey? Did Grandma talk about Spain?"

It was time to fill the family in on Abuelita's deathbed confession. "She told me we are hidden Jews."

My mom responded, "Huh, I'm not surprised. Your abuelita always made donations to Israel. I remember Aunt Mia told me that Grandma showed her some mementos and said our descendants were from a prosperous Jewish family from Spain that had to flee because of religious persecution."

Julio added, "Oh, this makes sense to me. Grandma told me to find a Jewish study partner in medical school, because they are very smart."

Mom said, "My friend Luna's ancestors were Conversos. She also has a pork allergy."

Marco said, "I didn't know Luna was allergic to pork. Is she Jewish?"

I said, "That's a good question, Marco. I don't know."

Consuela said, "I can always talk to my roommate Leah. I've been to her house to celebrate Jewish holidays. Something I do know about Leah's religion is they are not allowed to eat pork. In our family, we are allergic to pork."

Everyone smiled.

"Grandma had her ways of keeping us on our toes," I said.

Dad asked, "Why did Grandma keep this from us?"

I answered, "Grandma had a lot of fear after World War II that Jews in America would be killed."

Mom explained, "Luna's secrets were part of being a Converso. I believe it goes way back to the Spanish Inquisition. People feared death for observing Judaism openly."

Marco said, "I'm curious. I think I'll take a Spanish history class next semester. It would be nice to have some answers."

Julio smirked. "That would go nicely with your beer studies and Partying 101. I know that our little brother would ace those classes!"

Marco laughed. "You're right."

I felt such a sense of relief telling my family about the secret. I was thrilled to know it was not a big deal.

I left the room to call Jeremy. "My abuelita di … di … died." It surprised me how overcome I was saying those words. "The funeral is tomorrow," I added, my voice cracking. It was one of the hardest things I had ever had to say.

He said, "I'm so sorry. She was a great lady. Did I hear you right? The funeral is tomorrow? That's not a lot of time for people to make arrangements."

I simply said, "This is our custom."

"You know how much I love you, but I can't get there that quickly."

"What do you mean? You have to be here. I need you."

Understanding my disappointment, he promised, "I will be there."

I felt his business opportunities were more important to him than helping me deal with my loss. Trying to salvage any good feelings for him, I said, "I will see you when you get here."

I was hurt, and he knew it, but he didn't seem to care. Making money had become his passion. I wasn't surprised that he didn't want to be at the funeral. He didn't like to face grief.

The next morning, I got dressed. I sighed and said, "This is now going to be my funeral dress."

Most of those at the funeral were young since Abuelita had outlived her contemporaries. Many were our friends from school who had kept in touch with Abuelita long after we graduated. They had felt close to her since they were children.

Next to the grave of my abuelo was the burial site for my abuelita. My abuelos planned to be together in death. Our family priest blessed her soul and comforted my family. The worst part of the day was when I took a handful of dirt, accompanied by dirt from the Holy Land, and threw it into the grave. Hearing the thud as it hit the pine box gave the feeling of finality. Forever my grandma was gone. Our stories would keep her spirit alive.

Consuela and I walked around the cemetery. My sister said, "Oh my, Estrella. Come over here. This is the grave of our uncle Mateo."

I said, "I remember Mom talking about her eldest brother. Would you look at that, Consuela? He was only twenty-two years old when he passed."

Consuela added, "Grandma showed me a picture of him. He was so handsome. Now he is reunited with both his parents."

I said, "I had no idea there were so many of our family members buried in this cemetery. Can we all say a little something about Abuelita at home instead of at the funeral? After all, that is where she felt the happiest."

Consuela nodded. "It's a good idea." Just then, our brothers joined us. Julio agreed, "That will be fine."

Marco nodded. "Yes, let's do that."

We went back to the house for something to eat and to share stories. I couldn't shake the disappointment I felt about my husband, though he was with me. This was a very critical time in my life. I said, "I need some comfort, Jeremy."

Jeremy gently held my hand and walked me to my bedroom. He closed the door and started to kiss me passionately.

I shoved him off me. "What are you doing? That's not what I mean by comfort, Jeremy!"

He said, "I don't know what you want from me. You wanted me to come, so I'm here. You wanted me to comfort you. That's what I was trying to do."

"You are physically here, but you are not with me emotionally. Don't think I didn't see you sneak away to speak on the phone."

He clapped his hands together and said, "Fine, Estrella, you win. I will leave."

"That would be best. I'll tell my parents you had to leave. We can talk when I'm back in a few days."

I walked into the kitchen and said to our house manager, "Raquel, I'm glad I found you. Please help Jeremy. He needs to get back to LA tonight. Can you make the necessary arrangements?"

I said to my uncle, "I hate the reason for this, but it's nice we can be together, almost like a family reunion. You know it has been years since I spent this much time with our family." My siblings and I acted like kids again. The four of us reminisced.

Then Marco blurted out, "Get 'em."

We all started to holler in laughter.

I screamed, "Oh shit! I can't stop laughing. Guys, we have to hold it together. People will think we are crazy."

Consuela nodded. She had been laughing and crying so hard her black mascara streamed down her face. Giggling, she said, "You're right."

Little Marco now resembled a bright tomato. Ever since he was a baby, anytime Marco laughed, you could always tell just by the color of his cheeks. "If I keep on laughing, I'm going to pass out!"

Julio added, "I know what you mean. We can do this. We just have to stop laughing. I'll turn my back on you. It will help if I don't see you."

Aunt Mia asked, "What's going on over here?"

I was able to say, "It was the bubble fight. Ha-ha."

That's when Aunt Mia understood why we were laughing so hard. She recounted the battle she had many years before. "Grandpa did the same thing with your mom, uncles, and me. It was the best backyard bubble fight of all time." Aunt Mia joined in laughing with us. Finally, we were able to go back to the mourners.

In the living room, Consuela told the others how fortunate she was to have many beautiful memories of Abuelita. "I watched Grandma sew sundresses by hand. I thought I was special because she made them just for me."

Marco nodded in agreement. "She was good at making us all feel special, but I could never get away with charming her into giving me an extra piece of cake or buying me more toys like I could with the rest of the family."

Mom added, "You had the whole family wrapped around your little finger, except for Grandma."

Marco continued, "One day after hearing no from Abuelita, I gave her my saddest face and asked her why she didn't love me. She roared in laughter and said, 'Of course I love you. Marco, I was you! I was the baby of my family. I know all of your tricks because I played them long before you were here.'"

Julio pointed out, "Marco, you were not the only one who couldn't get away with things. When I got in trouble at school, Grandma and Grandpa made me feel terrible. They gave me the longest lecture of my life, telling me how disappointed they were. I immediately changed my behavior at school just so I could avoid hearing another speech like that from them."

I added, "Our grandparents had a special way of bringing out the best in us, didn't they? Abuelita Maria was a fortunate woman because of her approach to life. Her attitude was everything. No matter what happened, she dealt with it and remained positive. It was her wish to celebrate her one hundredth birthday, only shy of six weeks."

Marco interjected, "She was worried she would not reach one hundred. I told her a little fib. 'You are one hundred,' I said to her. I could tell this satisfied her."

I added, "It always made her happy to know she had achieved her goals. She was quite the businesswoman, but I did not know that until I interned for her over the summer. The grandma I knew up until that point was full of hugs and kisses. Now the grandma I saw in those meetings was savvy, a no-holds-barred businesswoman. It surprised me."

Mom said, "Many times, she was the only woman in meetings."

Aunt Mia noted, "For those meeting, she was dressed impeccably. Melina, do you remember how she did her hair?"

Mom nodded. "Yes! She put her hair in a braided circle on the top of her head, resembling a crown, which presented a more dominant look."

I said, "Years later, when I started working, I had a newfound appreciation for her. She commanded respect and attention in boardrooms full of men and got it—much like at home."

Aunt Mia told us, "She was a shrewd negotiator, but at home, she was full of fun."

My childhood friend Lucinda added, "She mentored me. I learned so much from her."

I could see Lucinda was tearing up, so I commented, "Doing business in a man's world is not easy today. I don't know how she did it. Many times in my professional life, I had to deal with being treated differently since I am a woman." I wanted to say more, but I couldn't because I flashed back to the moment when I saw her die. I got choked up and couldn't go on.

Aunt Mia began to speak. She told the mourners her love story. She was shopping in the downtown center of Santa Fe. Suddenly it began to rain so heavily it drenched her in minutes. Aunt Mia ran to get out of the shower when the heel of her shoe broke. As she was falling, Uncle Eduardo caught her. Auntie thanked him for helping her, and then they went to a café to warm up and enjoy a hot drink together.

They spent the next three hours talking, realizing they liked each other. The only problem was Uncle Eduardo was leaving that evening, with plans to return to Spain. They spent his remaining time in town together, deciding to correspond. After two years of writing beautiful love letters, they fell in love. Both families agreed to the marriage. They decided to make Spain their home because Uncle Eduardo was needed to help run the family's business. Aunt Mia, accompanied by her parents, brother, and sister, took the long journey to Spain. The trip made memories for a lifetime, and it felt like a lifetime getting across the Atlantic Ocean.

There was silence in the room until my friend Lucinda blew her nose so loudly that it sounded like a car backfiring. Everyone laughed and began to tell their stories about grandma.

3

BITTER AND SWEET

The days passed quickly. There was a flood of food and conversation. Being in the house brought back many happy memories. Abuelita would have been pleased to know how we were honoring her life. Toward the end of my stay, the house began to empty. The only people who remained were Grandma's immediate family. As we sat at the kitchen table enjoying the start of a beautiful new day with cups of coffee, we began to reminisce again.

Marco said, "It's so quiet. I hadn't realized how many people were here and how noisy it was until this very moment."

Consuela nodded. "I know what you mean. Can you imagine how noisy it was when Grandma was growing up?"

Julio shook his head. "Wow, I don't know how our great-grandparents did it with ten boys and one girl."

Uncle Mario quipped, "I remember your great-grandma Evangelina joked how the family decided to break tradition by having a girl, so they had your grandma Maria as their last child."

Mom chuckled and added, "All her brothers, parents, aunts, uncles, and extended family doted on baby Maria, and she relished all the attention and power she commanded."

Aunt Mia remarked, "Your grandma grew up with so much testosterone in the house she knew how to take care of herself! I remember hearing stories from my uncles about how their little sister could arm wrestle, dig ditches, and climb trees faster than any boy in town."

Mom said, "Abuelita also was a champion at throwing horseshoes."

Uncle Mario explained, "When it came time for Mom to marry, the family knew she had to find someone who could handle her rough-and-tumble brothers. Fortunately, our boxing-champion dad could do that. Dad told me that many times in the beginning of their marriage, he demonstrated his fighting abilities with his brothers-in-law. They would make bets to see who the best fighter was. Dad always won. The best boxers trained him in England."

I remarked, "I didn't know that about Grandpa Sam. He was born and raised in New York, right?"

Aunt Mia explained, "He always had a thirst for adventure, and just like Mom, being the youngest, he got his way. He knew how to get along with his siblings and had a special place in his parents' hearts."

Julio teased, "How does it feel being royalty? Aunt Mia, did you ever get to wear any of the crown jewels?" He laughed.

Aunt Mia answered, "No, silly, we are not really royal. Your great-grandpa William was a duke, but his title went to his firstborn son, our uncle Philip."

Uncle Mario said, "Anyway, I always thought Grandma's wealthy Spanish family was more interesting."

I said, "Okay, tell me if I have the story right. Grandpa Sam was born in New York. His family divided their time between Madrid, Spain, and New York City. Like his brothers and father before him, he was educated in England at Oxford, earning a degree in business. Instead of following his family's footsteps and working in the New York area, he longed to go west. He would take trips to dude ranches in Texas on summer breaks. It was the beloved adventure of young, wealthy men—hunting buffalo, going on cattle runs, and spending hours fly-fishing."

Dad said, "Estrella, how do you know so much?"

I proudly proclaimed, "I wanted to be a reporter, so one of my favorite things to do was to hear stories from Mom and Grandma."

I continued, "After experiencing the wonders that the west had to offer, Grandpa longed to leave the busy life of New York City behind him. He broke the news to his family, who consented—provided he agreed to an arranged marriage. A matchmaker found a lovely young girl living in the southwest of the territory of New Mexico, named Maria, your grandma."

Aunt Mia added, "They had a wonderful courtship, exchanging letters for over six months. In that time, they discovered how much they had in common, like their love of nature, the unspoiled beauty of the west, and their shared heritage."

Uncle Mario pointed out, "Dad told Mom how much he loved her independence. According to Dad, women in Spain didn't act like Mom."

Mom remarked, "She returned his compliment by expressing how charming he was. They married in the family's hacienda and had a happy life together, filled with lots of fun and joy. They were hardworking people and expected the family to work on the ranch."

Marco laughed as he explained, "We always hated doing the stinky chores like cleaning the troughs. Well, at least until Abuelo showed us just how much fun that could be. I accidentally poured too much soap into the feedbox and got upset and started to cry. Quickly, Abuelo saw this and, with a twinkle in his eye, took the soap bottles and poured a whole gallon in each of the troughs, filling them with water. He looked me in the eye and said, 'Let's play.'"

I said, "I will never forget staring at the bubbles as they overtook the troughs and spilled onto the ground. We didn't know what a prankster our grandfather was. Abuelo then grabbed bubbles with both hands and put them on his head. He ran over to Abuelita, kissed her cheek, and put some bubbles on her head."

Marco said, "He bent down to me—I was still very upset—and gave me a kiss on my cheek, grabbed a bucket of bubbles, and poured it on my head."

Consuela added, "I remember thinking, *Oh no! Marco's gonna be even more upset*. I was so relieved when I saw your smiling face and heard you squeal with delight."

Marco laughed as he said, "Get 'em! It was the battle cry that led to one of the best backyard bubble fights of all time."

I said, "Marco, Abuelita, and Abuelo each took a bucket of bubbles, ran after us, and poured the soapy bubbles on our heads. Abuelo took out water guns from our toy chest, which made our bubble war more spectacular. Before we knew it, the backyard was full of bubbles."

Mom said, "When your dad and I came home, we were greeted with buckets of bubbles. I immediately knew who had started the fight. It was Grandpa."

Uncle Mario said, "Dad did the same thing with Aunt Mia, Uncle Mateo, and your mom long ago."

Mom added, "I laughed and gave my dad a soapy hug."

4

LIFE GOES ON

Mom lamented, "Things changed as Abuelo got older. He started to act peculiarly. One day, Grandpa came back from a horseback ride with a sunburned face. I was surprised because Abuelo always insisted that we all put on a hat anytime we went horseback riding. So I asked him where his hat was. He told me he never wears a hat."

Uncle Mario added, "Another change was his storytelling. Dad started to tell a story, then stop and walk away. He forgot what he was doing."

Dad pointed out, "Abuelo didn't take his pills, even after Grandma reminded him. She had to stand next to him and watch him take his meds to ensure he had swallowed them."

I remarked, "I think the strangest thing was when he began to speak with an English accent. We all were starting to worry about him."

Dad continued, "You are right, mija. Grandpa began to call me Mateo, despite his son's death long ago. Also, that special twinkle in his eyes had disappeared. It was getting scary. We feared for his safety. Especially after that terrible horseback riding incident. I'll never forget that day he told Abuelita to expect him back in an hour."

Mom continued, "When he didn't return, we assumed he had lost track of time at the stables. Hour upon hour passed, with no sign of Abuelo. Your dad formed a search party to look for him. It wasn't until seven o'clock that we found him. His one long outing became eight hours."

Dad shook his head and said, "He was sitting next to the creek, skipping rocks with a big smile on his face, unaware people had been looking for him."

After that, my parents, uncle, and Abuelita sat down and discussed a care plan for Abuelo. After many doctors' appointments with several neurology visits, finally, there was a diagnosis. He had dementia. There needed to be some changes. Abuelita ensured he had the best care, including taking him to a memory-care facility. There was no mention of putting him into a rest home. Abuela would never have allowed that.

Mom recounted, "Abuelita felt incredibly fortunate that she had the means to have round-the-clock care to keep her husband at home."

I said, "The memory center Dad found for Abuelo was a terrific support for the whole family. Grandpa enjoyed singing, doing art projects, dancing, physical therapy, and going on outings. He went there five days a week, spending four hours each day. He always had a smile on his face when it was time to go to the care facility, happily proclaiming, 'I have to go to school!'"

Julio remarked, "Before choosing a team to care for his father-in-law at home, my dad interviewed several nurses. One of his favorite, Gina, resembled Abuelita Maria when she was young, with dark black, curly hair. Grandpa called her 'my sweet Maria.'"

After a routine checkup, Grandpa's doctors discovered he had stomach cancer and end-stage dementia. He did not have long to live. My mom called her sister Aunt Mia in Spain with the news. Aunt Mia and Uncle Eduardo were in our home within the week. Upon their arrival, Abuelo changed back to his old self.

I said, "When Grandpa Sam saw his beloved daughter Mia, the sparkle returned to his eyes."

He said, "My darling Mia, I have missed you." I remember Consuela took many pictures of my grandparents, Aunt Mia, Uncle Mario, and the baby of their family, our mom, Melina.

Uncle Mario lamented, "There were three missing in those photos. My three brothers."

Aunt Mia remarked, "I sometimes forget Mom and Dad had six children. Two died when they were little, and Uncle Mateo died years later."

Mom added, "It was such a miracle, having Dad come back to life when he saw Mia. Once again, he regaled his grandchildren with stories from his youth. He had a rousing game of poker with his son and sons-in-law. No one could leave the table until Dad won and collected his winnings."

Aunt Mia continued, "Dad danced the flamenco, proudly using his castanets, smiling during the entire dance. Mom was thrilled to be dancing with her husband again. It was a wonderful sight to see. I felt fortunate to witness this miracle. Regrettably, it didn't last long. Two days after his fantastic performance, Abuelo passed away in his sleep."

I told the family, "Abuelo experienced a death rally that happens to some people just before they die." We were grateful for that last glimpse of how our abuelo lived his life. I recalled with great fondness our game nights with family and friends.

Once a month, our home turned into a meeting place for people to sing, dance, and talk. Laughter and cigarette smoke filled the dining room along with bottles of tequila. I recounted to Grandma once, "Your friends always became extra giggly after a shot of tequila." Uncle Mario played the guitar and broke into songs about the glory of Spain. The night would last until the wee hours of the morning, when guests stumbled home. Those who lived far away were taken home by one of the servants. Friends who remained in our home enjoyed Abuelita's breakfast of *torrijas* (Spanish-style French toast).

After Grandma's passing, Uncle Mario and my parents found it hard to live in the hacienda. I knew we would all do better as time passed. We would need to keep busy. It was a difficult task to go through Abuelita's closet along with my mother. The wardrobe was large, almost the size of a room, and exquisitely decorated with crystal chandeliers. It had cedar shelves that gave off a pleasant smell when you entered. It was painted bright blue with mirrors as the backsplash. Since Abuelo's death, Grandma wore only black dresses but kept her fancy clothes from years before. The gowns were beautiful. Other things like sweaters, skirts, and scarves were all in black. She had an extensive collection of blankets that we made. Each of us took back what we had made for her. She had saved them all. We donated everything else to our family-run charity. The women were delighted to get the wonderful wardrobe Grandma had left. They had never seen such well-made clothes.

It was a collection of almost one hundred years of my grandmother's possessions, which we had a hard time giving away. Mom couldn't do it. I had to sort through all of her things. There were her candlesticks she used every Friday night. She would light candles, put her hands on her face, and sway back and forth, not saying a word. I remember, as a child, imitating her by swaying my body.

I came across what appeared to be a costume—a bright pink taffeta, floor-length dress, with pearls sewn into the bodice and a long, flowing cape. Over the hook of the clothes hanger was a beautiful rhinestone tiara. I asked my mom, "Is this a costume?"

Mom answered in a whisper, "It's for St. Ester's Day." I remembered the holiday, parading around in dresses fit for a queen. I hadn't celebrated the holiday for many years.

I asked Mom, "Why don't we have the parade anymore?"

Mom said, "It's no longer a holiday because Father John, our young parish priest, said it wasn't a Catholic holiday and stopped the celebrations. Ester wasn't even Catholic."

We always spoke in whispers when we talked about St. Ester's Day. *That's so strange*, I thought. I felt that it had something to do with our Jewish heritage.

On the last night I was there, I walked outside the hacienda to catch a breath of fresh air. I loved the night sky and looked up to see the stars twinkling. My abuelita had said, "My dear Estrella, little star, you will always know that I watch over you whenever you look up." Grandma always looked up and faced life with strength. It made me smile. Whenever looking at the night sky, I felt protected. Speaking to her would help me get answers to my questions. She was my guide. Even in death, my abuelita found ways to help me. I knew she would be with me for the rest of my life, to answer my questions. She was and would still be my lifesaver, my rock.

A few days later, it was time to go home, back to life with Jeremy and work. I wanted to be with my family in Pueblo. I didn't want to go back to LA right then. For the first time since I left for college in LA, I wanted to stay with my family, yet I knew I couldn't. I needed to be in a cocoon, protected by my loved ones, licking the wounds that had appeared with the loss of my granny. I packed my things and got into my dad's car.

Driving to the airport, once again we sat in silence. Dad began to speak about his relationship with my abuelitos. He said, "Your grandparents allowed your mom to attend her first high school party that was coming up at school during her first year. She wanted to go because her friend Heather begged her, not wanting to go alone. Unbeknownst to the girls, the boys spiked the punch with alcohol. Many of the boys started acting like jerks. Annoyed, Melina stepped out of the school to get some fresh air. Around the same time, I also stepped outside to take a break from trying to fit in.

"Scott, one of the boys from school, was drunk, and he came over to her and touched her. Melina pushed and slapped him, telling him, 'Get away!' Scott, infuriated, grabbed her shoulder hard, tearing her dress, and said, 'Why, you little bitch!' She smacked him again. Just as he reached his arm back to hit her, I grabbed it and pushed him away. I looked over at Melina and saw tears streaming down her face and a rip on her dress. Without thinking, I punched Scott in the face. Then I took my coat off and handed it to your mother. I asked Mom to call her father.

"I sat with Mom until Abuelo came to pick her up. To distract her, I told her stories about the names of the constellations. When your abuelo pulled up, Mom thanked me for my help and handed back my jacket. That's when Abuelo saw that her dress had ripped. Your grandfather got out of the car, took hold of me by the scruff of my neck, and demanded to know what happened. Knowing he was about to smack me, your mom quickly explained. She told him, 'Dad, it was Scott who got fresh with me.' Your grandfather was embarrassed and said, 'Thank you for helping my daughter,' and offered to take me home. Melina was his youngest daughter and favorite child, so he became a lion protecting his cub when he saw the ripped dress.

"Principal Douglas called me to his office on Monday morning. He told me, 'You are expelled from school for starting a fight with Scott at the party.' Mr. Douglas said that the school's reputation was in jeopardy if word got out that a scholarship student behaved poorly at school. I felt devastated leaving the principal's office, and I saw your mom waving at me. She wanted to thank me again for my help at the party. I said, 'I was glad to help you.' She saw the sad look on my face and asked me, 'What's wrong?' That's when I said, 'I have to leave school. Mr. Douglas kicked me out for hitting Scott.' Melina said, 'Oh no, you're staying in school! You did nothing wrong.'

"Your mom marched into the office and picked up the phone to call Abuelo. She asked her dad to come to school because she needed his help. Abuelo got there quickly and had a closed-door meeting with the principal. After their meeting, the principal called me back to tell me the good news; I could continue school. Abuelo then asked the principal what he was going to do about Scott.

"He told Abuelo, 'Scott will be suspended from school for one week.' Abuelo said, 'That's not good enough.' He continued, 'You must suspend Scott for the rest of the year. When he returns, he cannot take any classes with my daughter, or there will be severe consequences.' The principal started to protest but stopped midsentence. After seeing Abuelo's face, he nodded and said, 'Of course.' I thanked both Abuelo and Melina for standing up for me. The principal told me, 'You are back in school. Don't do anything like that again.'"

Dad continued, "A couple of days after the party, your mom asked me to come back to her house after school to work on a class project together. My eyes popped out of my head, on my first visit to the hacienda. I was overwhelmed. The house was so big I couldn't believe it. I'd never been around rich people before. I was quite nervous. To my delight, your grandparents were very welcoming. As our courtship continued, I went to her house after school to do homework most days. I worked hard to get good grades, wanting to excel in school.

"Your grandparents trusted that I would be respectful. They took pride in showing me around the ranch. One of the gardeners was about to throw out some plant food because he thought it was spoiled. 'Please do not waste the food,' I offered. 'The garden can use this for mulch.' Your grandparents let me help in the garden from that time forward, listening to my suggestions.

"One day when I was working with Abuelita, she began to tell me about her family. She told me, 'I had five children before Melina was born. Two of my boys died during the great influenza epidemic that consumed the world—Marco on October 6, 1919, and Mathew passed away on January 15, 1920.'"

Grandma went on to tell my dad about the anguish she felt losing two babies within a couple of months of each other. Sadness consumed everyone until her miracle baby came to the family on January 15, 1923, when Melina was born. "The veil of grief lifted with the birth of my darling daughter," she said.

Grandma said that when she looked at Mom for the first time, she saw the essence of her two lost children in her baby's eyes. Finally, she was on the mend. "My daughter is more precious to me than anything I own," Grandma told him. She said, "Melina was the perfect child. Whenever I asked her to do something for me, she always said, 'Sure.'" Abuelita continued by saying, "Our family is devoted to each other. That's the way it is, and that's the way it will always be."

He told me that he said to my grandma, "Please do not judge me by my family's behavior. I know I come from a troubled home, but I try to care for everyone. I hold Melina in the highest regard; I promise to be good to her. I have many good people in my family, like my widowed aunt Ruth and cousin Gabby. I try my best by doing yard work for my aunt, cooking for my family, and taking care of my little sister. I get good grades in school and work hard as a football player for my team."

Dad smiled as he told me how their encouragement helped boost his self-esteem and comfort level—coming to love each other. My grandparents consented to their marriage. The only challenge was waiting until they were eighteen to marry. Dad often said that joy entered his life when he met Mom. His little sister, Elisa, fit into his new family too.

My dad loved his little sister unconditionally. Since there wasn't any money to buy Elisa things, my dad carved a toy horse from scraps of wood he found. Elisa loved it and proudly displayed it on her dresser. She adored her big brother.

A tragic accident changed his family forever. It was a cold, rainy night when Elisa and her cousin Gabby were driving on the highway in an old truck. Driving conditions were so poor Gabby could barely see in front of her, so she pulled over onto the shoulder to wait for the rain to stop. Both girls expressed a sigh of relief, knowing they were safe. Gabby turned the radio on, hoping the music would calm their nerves.

A few yards behind the girls, a driver was desperately trying to stop his car. He pumped on the brakes to no avail and turned the wheel frantically, trying to avoid hitting the truck in front of him. The tires screeched, and there was a smell of burnt rubber filling the air. Boom! Crash! Glass shattered, breaking into a million pieces.

My dad was sitting next to Elisa in the hospital room, holding her hand. Gabby survived. Tragically, Elisa did not. She had been thrown from the vehicle and never regained consciousness. My dad's father became irate after hearing the news from the doctor. He threw chairs, started yelling, and required restraints. He looked at my father with hate and said to him, "It should've been you. The wrong child died." Those words marked the end of their relationship. That evening, my dad went back to his home, packed up all his belongings and Elisa's toy horse, and headed to Aunt Ruth's home. She welcomed him with open arms.

After the death of my aunt Elisa, my dad fell into a deep depression. Lost without his baby sister, Dad told me it felt like he was in an eternal mourning period. He also wondered why my mom would still want to be with him. Feeling like an albatross, Dad told Mom, "We should call off our wedding so you can find someone else to love."

Firmly, Mom said, "No."

She told him they would deal with their loss together as a family and agreed to move the wedding from the summer to the fall of that year. Initially set for July, they would change it to November. A delay would give them more time to heal. My mom was also heartsick over the death of her soon-to-be sister-in-law. She loved the idea of having a little sister. They enjoyed being together and were about to look for bridesmaid dresses for Elisa.

Mom was there to support him. This unwavering support solidified their bond. My grandparents also helped my dad find constructive ways to channel his pain. They took him fishing and shooting and loved him like a son. One of the most challenging experiences of my dad's life also made him appreciate his new family even more.

My parents married on November 8, 1941. Less than a month later, the world changed after the tragic event of Pearl Harbor when the Japanese bombed the US fleet in Hawaii. America declared war. My dad enlisted in the navy the next day. Soon he would go by Seaman Recruit Benjamin Pérez. To my family, he would always be Benny.

Abuelo Sam, Abuelita Maria, Uncle Mario, and my parents drove to Albuquerque, New Mexico, where my dad took the train to San Diego, California. They all had an emotional goodbye. Dad had to swallow hard to get rid of the big lump in his throat. Mom tried her best to fight back the tears when she said goodbye to her love. Their final goodbye was a tender kiss on the lips. After his basic training in San Diego, Dad served in Italy. Years later, Dad would joke about waiting years to marry Mom, only to have a little over a month together before being separated for five years. What an inspiring story. I began to tell my dad my story, including meeting and falling in love with Jeremy.

Since I was young, I had planned to be a journalist. Now I held the ideal position as an editor and writer with a column and a byline for a prestigious magazine. I had found my niche. It wasn't always that way. Things started to change for me when I went into my Psychology 201 class at USC.

I was in my second year. I remember seeing this handsome young man out of the corner of my eye. I swooned as he found a seat in the back of the class. I was surprised to be so attracted to him. I told one of my classmate, Dianna, "I'm going to marry him someday."

She replied, "Don't you think you should meet him first?" Different from any boy I had ever known, he intrigued me. Jeremy Schmitt was tall, blond, and well built, with blue eyes that sparkled when he looked my way. My insides fluttered when I looked at him. The next day, I sat in the back of the class. I had put my books on the chair next to me. I took the books off the chair when he entered the classroom, hoping that Jeremy would sit there. He did.

One fateful day, my books fell on the floor with a loud crash during class. I was embarrassed, quickly bending over to pick them up. My hair fell on my face. Gently, he brushed it aside. When our eyes met, it was magical. We smiled at each other. He whispered, "Let me get that for you." After class, we began to talk. I told him about my life living on a ranch in New Mexico. He asked, "Do you have any chickens?"

I told him, "Why, yes we do, and I have names for many of them.

The type I like the best is the Ameraucana. They lay eggs of different colors—blue, green, pinkish, cream, and dark brown. It's fun giving the extras to our friends." Jeremy thought that was cute.

I explained how excited I was living in California, with plans to go to the beach and learn to surf. When Jeremy heard I had never gone to the ocean before, he planned a trip for us. We traveled on the Pacific Coast Highway with the top down on his new Corvette convertible. I loved feeling the wind on my face. I hated how fast he drove, darting between the lanes. It made me nervous. He enjoyed seeing me squirm in the seat and chuckled at my discomfort. Our destination was Venice Beach, also known as Muscle Beach because of all the muscular men who exercised there. I told him, "I can see why it's called muscle beach." Being a native of California, Jeremy grew up surfing all the big waves. I couldn't believe how vast the ocean was until I saw it. I rapidly became smitten by both the water and Jeremy. We had a wonderful day together. I said, "Thank you so much for the best day of my life."

He answered, "There's more coming your way."

A few weeks later, Jeremy taught me to surf. We decided to spend as much time together as we could, including going to civil rights marches. We believed that all people deserved to be free. I wore a colorful tie-dyed shirt, bell-bottoms, and a peace sign necklace. Jeremy's shirt read, *Give peace a chance*. Lifting our signs proudly in the air, we shouted cries for freedom. It was an exciting time. We were a young couple in love.

Aside from our love of marches, we had many other things in common. Dancing and singing to the twist was a favorite pastime. I loved the blues as much as he did. B.B. King was our most beloved blues artist. We were not the least bit interested in team sports. Our mantra was that each day is an adventure to be enjoyed. We wanted to see the whole world before settling down to life with a family. When apart, we felt lonely. It was exhilarating staying up all night talking to Jeremy.

Our daily routine included dancing to the Doors and singing our song, "Come on, baby, light my fire." We met in the afternoons to talk about our classes. Our little world existed just for us. After school, we would go shopping for food, then back to his apartment to fix dinner under the light of the lava lamp. That's how we spent our lives together in college.

5

GETTING TO KNOW HIM

Jeremy, like me, went through a transitional period after he left home for school. He found freedom to do as he wished instead of being under his mother's thumb. It was like opening Pandora's box. Jeremy changed. He began experimenting with women, liquor, and drugs. Before he met me, Jeremy spent his days rebelling against his mother, dating women of all backgrounds. He joked, "It's so much fun to get a rise out of Mommy dearest."

Jeremy reveled in driving his mother mad. He told his mother, "I'm in love with Estrella."

His mom was furious with this news. She cried and said, "I won't give you one more cent."

He stood his ground, telling her, "I don't care."

After seeing a photo of us together, she told Jeremy, "She's too dark, and her features are too ethnic to be beautiful. What's more, she's too ambitious in her career to be a good wife." Jeremy didn't agree.

After another amazing evening with Jeremy holding me close, he said, "Come with me for brunch to meet my parents."

I said, "I'd love to, but you know your mom doesn't like me, and that's without even meeting me."

He said, "Don't worry about her."

I wanted to please his mother. So excited the day of the brunch, I must have tried on all of my dresses to see what looked the best, giving myself a pep talk as I got ready.

We were greeted by their maid, Celeste, who brought us into the living room, where Jeremy's parents were seated, cocktails in hand. A beautiful Italian opera played in the background. I noticed how his mother held her drink. She had her pinkie finger extended out. It looked so odd. They both got up and introduced themselves to me. With a scowl on her face, Jeremy's mother began to ask me questions about myself, speaking to me in a haughty manner, slowly and loudly. Kat asked, "Do you like living in this country?"

I answered, "Of course. I've lived here all my life. I'm from New Mexico, not Mexico."

She sweetly told me, "Please do not be too overwhelmed by the grandeur and size of our house." She let me know that it was very cozy, explaining they got a great deal on their home and had done well in the stock market but were not wealthy. She told me, "There is no trust fund for Jeremy." That was an odd thing to say. I felt she told me this because she thought I was a gold digger. My family didn't act superior to other people.

After she spent what seemed like hours drilling me to find out about myself and my family, I was seething with anger. Inside, I wanted to run away. I remember tapping my foot nervously under the table and shifting back and forth in my seat.

Jeremy told his mother that I lived with my uncle, grandparents, brothers, sister, and parents. She went on to ask, "Was it hard living in such cramped quarters?"

I politely explained, "There was more than enough room for all of us, as I didn't grow up in a house but a family compound with several buildings on our ranch, which was around one hundred acres. My family home has a pool, tennis court, art studio, stables, and barn." She gasped. I suspected she thought I came from a needy family. My only saving grace was being from a wealthy family, which impressed her. I wanted to tell her that I had a trust fund, but my family never liked listening to braggers, so I held my tongue.

Kat wanted to know what my hobbies were. I told her, "I enjoy the sport of western dressage, horse dancing. We have a special breed of horse called the Lippizana. I competed in western dressage, where the horse and rider progress with structured and focused training together, without speaking."

Kat responded by saying, "That's different!"

Cameron, his dad, was not like his wife. He was interested in everything I had to say. I enjoyed meeting him. Kat made me feel uncomfortable. She asked a lot of questions that I felt intruded upon my privacy.

We sat down for a lovely brunch complete with pancakes, shrimp, lobster bisque, bacon and eggs, and champagne. I told Kat that I was allergic to the pork and the seafood. Surprised, she asked, "Are you Jewish?"

I answered in a huff, "Of course not. It's a family allergy."

After Kat met me, she was determined to make our relationship as problematic as possible but in ways not evident to Jeremy. Before we married, Kat even fixed him up with the "right kind of woman," who looked like her. Tall, thin, blonde, blue-eyed women from wealthy Protestant families were the only acceptable mates for her beloved son. She arranged to see Jeremy for mother-and-son lunches without letting him know another guest was coming, one of her picks to be his next girlfriend. Kat was brilliant. She and her fix-up would be seated at the table before her son arrived.

When he arrived, Jeremy sat down, surprised by the additional guest. Kat introduced them and then found a reason to leave, like remembering she had a manicure in five minutes. Asking for forgiveness, his mother apologized. "My darlings, I have to go. Please enjoy your lunch. It's my treat." Jeremy was stuck at the table with a stranger for lunch. He did not realize it was a setup until he told me what had happened. I explained that Kat had planned the meeting to find him a new girlfriend. His mom was the most clever family member, though Jeremy and his dad felt they were.

It was my turn now. My family wanted to meet my boyfriend. During spring break, my parents were very welcoming to Jeremy and seemed interested in what he had to say about investments, always of interest, which was what my honey was studying. He stayed for three days and then went home to Pasadena, California.

My parents sat me down to speak to me about my relationship with

Jeremy. They told me, "Our own marriage had difficulties in the early years, even though we were both Catholic." Mom said, "I was annoyed when we first were married because your dad would cut a napkin in half and only use half at dinner."

She continued, "Another upsetting thing was when Dad cut the toothpaste tube to squeeze out all the paste because he came from an impoverished family. There were food differences too. One of Dad's favorite dishes was chicken tamales. I had never even heard of this food. Abuela and I learned how to make them." My parents tried to explain how differences can be hard to overcome. The one thing that unified them was their shared faith. My parents were afraid that Jeremy and I had too many things that separated us. We came from different places, we looked very different, and our faith was very different, being that Jeremy is Protestant.

Jeremy was from a completely different background, from the language to the Christmas traditions to the food he ate. Though they liked him, they asked me to stop seeing him and focus on dating Hispanic men. I was furious and surprised by their objections. I told them, "You never discriminated against my friends from different backgrounds before, so why are you doing it now?"

My parents explained marriage is not the same as friendship. They said, "Marriage is forever. Friends may not be. A person doesn't invest their lives in friends, as they do in a marriage."

I told them, "I love him and will marry him." If they objected, I would never speak to them again.

Horrified about losing me, their darling daughter, they made a deal. They told me, "If you stay with Jeremy until you graduate, and still feel the way you do today, we will let you marry him." There was one condition. They said, "You can't live together until that time."

I was huffing and puffing in anger. I said to them, "You are being unfair, but I accept your terms." I was determined to prove them wrong. We would stay in love and get married.

Just before our senior year, Jeremy and I took a once-in-a-lifetime trip overseas with some of our closest friends. We wanted to see Europe before college ended and real life began. At the train station in Florence, a group of Gypsies surrounded us on their hands and knees, saying, "Please, please help us."

My heart ached seeing people so hungry. I opened my bag and searched for food. I smiled and said, "This is for you," as I handed an old woman an orange and a sandwich. I bent down and handed a chocolate bar to a little girl and told her, "You are so pretty." The little girl and I exchanged smiles.

Disgusted, Jeremy looked at me and asked, "Why did you give that little peasant girl the chocolate I bought for you?"

I stammered as I said, "Jeremy, I'm sorry. I saw this little girl looking sad and hungry, and all I had left to give was the chocolate bar. I didn't mean to upset you."

He shrugged. "I was surprised, but you know, Strella, you should not give food to beggars. They're dirty, and you don't know where they've been." I didn't like seeing that angry side of Jeremy.

Our trip to Europe was long, including taking planes, trains, taxis, cars, and buses. Finally, we reached our hotel in Florence, Italy. Jeremy turned on the TV to have some background noise while unpacking. He was busy looking at the city map and his travel book, thinking about what sites to see.

Suddenly Jeremy stopped what he was doing and focused on the TV. He cocked his head and had a curious look. After a few minutes, he burst into laughter. My boyfriend told me what was so funny. So tired, he started to watch the show and got very confused when he heard people speaking Italian instead of English. Then he realized that he was in Italy, so they would be speaking Italian. Jeremy could not control his laughter. "I forgot we were in Italy and couldn't understand why they were speaking Italian!" I joined him laughing.

Jeremy and I had a remarkable time in Florence. We marveled at the Ponte Vecchio (Old Bridge), built in the Middle Ages. Ideally situated over the Arno River, this pedestrian bridge is home to many shops. Tourists can buy jewelry, art, and antiques. Jeremy was determined to buy me something. We stopped in what felt like every jewelry shop on the bridge—until my boyfriend found the perfect gift for me, an 18-carat gold necklace with a star on it for my name, which means star. I saw a pretty, six-pointed one and said, "I like this one."

He was shocked. "That's a Jewish star."

I said, "But this is the one I want." He bought me a five-pointed star instead.

Another overwhelming site was the Uffizi Gallery. I remarked, "The walls are covered with paintings. There's hardly any room between the pictures." It was hard to concentrate on a painting because there was so much artwork. It flooded our minds.

Another exciting find was gelato. Gleefully, we found bins and bins of every gelato flavor throughout the city. Tasting the different flavors turned into a game. We remarked to the vendor, "It's so hard to decide our favorite, but we liked chocolate fudge the best. The pistachio was a close second."

We waited in line to see Michelangelo's *David*, which felt like an eternity. The line seemed to be miles long, and maybe it was. I had a sinking feeling in the pit of my stomach we would never see the statue. It was well worth the time spent waiting when we got to view the sculpture. It was perfection. The tour guide said, "When Michelangelo saw the marble, he saw David appear. He just chiseled away the pieces of the stone he didn't need. The material used by Michelangelo was a poor-quality marble. Several other sculptors had tried to use the marble before he did but had difficulty working with it, so it was left unused."

Now onto Milan. Weary travelers, we tried to get off the train. Suddenly, we could hear a loud whoosh, followed by a sea of passengers boarding. There was no way we could exit—lots of pushing and shoving so that we missed our stop. Extremely annoyed, Jeremy swore at the people, calling them lousy "Wops!" Someone understood what he said and was offended. A burly Italian shoved him hard against the door, which cut his lip. At the next stop, we pushed our way off the train. I glanced back at Jeremy and had to do a double-take. His face was bright red with anger. He swore he would never return to Italy.

He needed to calm himself. I thought if we went to a pub, he would settle down. I asked the bartender, "What do you recommend?"

With a big grin, the bartender poured drink after delicious drink of Negroni, a strong cocktail. "This is just what he needs," I suggested. It was potent. The bartender enjoyed watching us drink the Negroni. I felt dizzy after the first sip. The more you drink Negroni, the more you want it. We could not stop laughing. Anything anyone said was funny.

The drink was so tasty that my boyfriend told the bartender, "A round for everyone in the bar." Suddenly, Jeremy had a lot of new friends thanking him and slapping him on the back. After a couple of Negronis, Jeremy loved Italy once more. I was relieved that the drinking helped. I had never seen Jeremy so relaxed.

Our next magical stop was in Barcelona, Spain. The Spanish people were dark and hairy, which surprised my boyfriend. He commented, "They look like Jews with their big noses." Hearing these words offended me.

I reminded him, "My family was from Spain." Embarrassed, he quickly apologized. I hadn't realized how prejudiced he was until that trip. It bugged me. However, I dismissed any negative thoughts about Jeremy. *After all, I'm not perfect. Why should I expect him to be?*

Another highlight of the trip was visiting the beaches. I was stunned. Women of all sizes and shapes were topless. It was cute seeing little topless girls holding their topless mothers' hands. I'd never seen so many women's breasts. Jeremy pretended he didn't care, but he couldn't keep his eyes off the parade of women passing by and mumbled to himself, "Mama mia!" Near the beach was a wide walkway filled with restaurants, called Las Ramblas. We stopped at one for lunch—a lovely place to take a walk with my honey.

Many kinds of seashells on the beach washed up from the sea. I noticed the ones that I had seen in our home. They were small, white, and cylinder in shape with ridges. They resembled white Good & Plenty candy. My granny had picked them up the last time she visited my aunt and uncle. She told me, "These seashells are magical. Keeping them with you will bring you good luck." I placed a handful of them into a paper bag, planning to give them to Abuelita for her collection. I loved surprising her with little gifts.

The best part of Barcelona was seeing my family. Aunt Mia, my mom's older sister, took out her wedding pictures. I gasped when I saw the first photo of Aunt Mia. "You look like a princess."

Aunt Mia said, "Thank you, mija. My parents had a diamond tiara made especially for me. It was beautiful. I wore the tiara on top of my lace mantilla."

I asked, "Why was the wedding in Barcelona?"

Uncle Eduardo explained, "My grandparents were very old and too weak to make the long voyage to the States. We planned on raising our family in Spain and felt this was the perfect place to begin our marriage."

Jeremy added, "It looks like you made the right choice. These pictures are spectacular. You can't find a cathedral like this in the States."

Uncle Eduardo bragged, "In my family, we have a tradition—to keep the celebration going after the wedding for seven days. I will never forget at one party we had an ice sculpture of two swans kissing."

As I flipped through the pages of the album, I said, "Mom looked lovely with her long pearl necklace, bracelet, and ring. She wore her fashionable gown with a bow in her hair."

Uncle Eduardo interjected, "All the men wore top hats, and I believe my groomsmen wore pink flowers in their lapels to go with the pink bridesmaid dresses. Is that right, honey?"

Aunt Mia nodded. "Yes, that's right."

I said, "Wow, Uncle Eduardo. I am impressed you have such a good memory."

Uncle Eduardo smiled. "It was one of the happiest days of my life. How could I forget?"

Aunt Mia remarked, "We all wore long, white, lambskin gloves. Everyone dressed in the style of the day. It was pure elegance. Your grandma wore a lovely high-waisted gown from a well-known designer in Paris. It was accessorized with a beautiful diamond necklace and matching bracelet."

I said, "What a beautiful family. I remember hearing Mom recount how lovely Aunt Mia looked when she was coming out of the cathedral after her wedding, with the bells ringing and a procession marching along the cobblestone streets. It really was an incredible feast for the eyes."

The wedding party then came out to cheer, throwing rice at the young couple, as did spectators watching the amazing event of the season. It was a sight to see. The pictures demonstrated how happy everyone was congratulating the wedding couple. They were as delighted that day as they were now. I marveled at their wonderful marriage. They loved being together and missed each other when they were apart.

I saw a picture of the family standing in front of a huge white ship named the SS *Espania*. This confused me, and I asked, "Did you travel all the way to Spain on a ship?"

Aunt Mia nodded with a big smile. "Just about. At first, we were in a car. Next, by train, and finally, we traveled by ship. That was the only way to get there. We couldn't just get on a plane like you can now."

I said, "I didn't realize that. What was the voyage like?"

Aunt Mia said, "Oh, mija, it was magical. Each day, chefs prepared the most sumptuous meals served on delicate bone china and sterling silver cutlery."

I said, "I am sure the first-class suites were elegant."

Aunt Mia explained, "Yes they were. I remember not knowing what to expect since I had never been on a ship before. And I still remember your mom and I giggling the moment we opened the state room door. In my mind, I thought it was gonna be something far less glamorous. I was pleasantly surprised. There were fresh flowers and crystal vases everywhere, a sitting room, a balcony, and a bedroom. So many nights, your mom and I stayed up until the wee hours of the morning talking, too excited to get any sleep. It was wonderful."

I said, "I had no idea. It was a trip you'll never forget."

Aunt Mia said, "Oh yes, our cabins had their very own butlers. Each night, we enjoyed listening to the big band music playing on the deck. Your mom, abuelita, and I dressed in evening gowns, and the men wore tuxedoes as we danced the nights away. There were plenty of activities to keep us busy from dusk till dawn. We dined with the captain many times."

Jeremy asked, "When did you get married?"

I said, "It was during the war, right?

Uncle Eduardo said, "Actually, it was just before the war. We got married in 1938."

Jeremy asked, "Was it hard living in Europe at that time?"

Aunt Mia noted, "It wasn't so bad here in Spain. It was not like the rest of Europe."

Uncle Eduardo closed his eyes, took a deep breath, and explained, "Europe was on fire. Millions of people were killed, including my little brother, who was a part of the underground resistance. He couldn't stand by while Jews, gypsies, and communists were being executed."

Aunt Mia added, "No group was more vulnerable than the Jews. Six million died during those war years. The world changed to bitterness and tears." Her storytelling changed to speaking about her little sister.

Auntie was a great storyteller. She loved her little sister, and when they were together, they acted silly. I had pictures of my mom and her sister sleeping on the couch when they were little, holding hands in the most adorable matching dresses celebrating Saint Ester's day. Both girls were wearing lacey, ruffled white dresses with crowns on their heads. They played and ate so much candy they were exhausted. My cute little mom was about two years old, and her big sister was around nine. My auntie's family saw the pictures and broke out in laughter, never having seen photographs of their mother at that age. It was a lovely evening.

Jeremy enjoyed spending time with my relatives. He didn't have many relatives since his parents were only children. My honey said, "I find all the noise and laughter in the house grand." In his house, there was no noise.

My relatives invited us to stay with them. All of their children were married, living independently, so there was plenty of room—one room for me and one for Jeremy. Around midnight, I heard a scratch at the door. It was Jeremy. I told him we had to be very quiet. He stayed for as long as he felt he could, most of the night, and left just before the sun came up. I found it exciting to sneak around in my aunt and uncle's house. I hoped we didn't make too much noise and disturb them.

It was hard to leave this wonderful city. The trip to Barcelona was a memorable holiday; I felt very connected to the land and people, and I found myself daydreaming. What was life like for my Spanish family hundreds of years ago? This city would turn out to be one of my favorites. Clean and inviting, the beaches called to us. After seeing so many spectacular fountains in flower-filled courtyards, I couldn't believe my eyes. Lively music played throughout the city. It was like having a free concert every night.

The jewel of the town was a unique-looking church called La Sagrada Familia, still being built today. The famous architect Gaudi designed the church. All wonderful trips must end, but the magic didn't. I thought about our trip often.

On the last day of our journey, Jeremy got down on one knee and said, "Marry me. Please be my wife." He presented me with a beautiful blue diamond ring that he secretly bought on the Pont Vecchio.

So excited, I jumped for joy and gleefully said, "Yes."

Then I called my parents to tell them the good news. They said, "We are happy for you. When do you want to get married?"

I told them, "We don't know yet, but it would be after graduation."

Before I knew it, I was back in school, working nonstop on the school paper in addition to my studies.

During our holiday break, my parents had an engagement party for us and invited Jeremy's parents to stay at our home. It was lovely. All of our family was there, which numbered over one hundred people. To prepare his parents for the party, Jeremy told them that the party would be casual and just a few hours long. When his parents came into the house, they felt embarrassed because everyone was dressed formally.

Kat said, "Jeremy told us the dress was casual."

I said, "All that matters is that you are here to celebrate with us." Kat and Cameron, both only children, became overwhelmed with the commotion, singing, dancing, and drinking but seemed to have a good time after imbibing some tequila. My family made a great effort to welcome my future in-laws.

I told the crowd, "Jeremy and I would like to thank everyone for coming tonight to celebrate our engagement, especially my new future in-laws, Kat and Cameron, who came from Pasadena, California, to join us. Thank you for being here. As a way of giving everyone a little special treat, I asked my beloved cousin Enzo to sing a serenade. Enzo is an opera singer from Italy."

As Enzo began to sing the audience swooned.

Aunt Gracie whispered, "This is so beautiful."

Cameron and Kat looked dumbfounded.

Kat said, "I never had a private concert. I didn't realize it would be so loud."

Cameron remarked, "Yeah, that was really something."

Their reaction was less than what I thought it would be. I was hurt. My parents and I had put in so much effort to make sure that everyone had a great time, especially my new in-laws. I wondered, *Will I ever win them over?* I quietly said, "I'm sorry if the music was too loud."

My dad announced, "Everyone, please join me outside now."

We assembled together, looking up in the dark sky. Suddenly, we saw flashes of red, blue, purple, green, and white fireworks covering the sky, accompanied by music. It was spectacular!

Uncle Mario yelled, "Ooh, aw!"

Marco shouted, "The best fireworks I ever saw."

The crowd cheered, but the Schmitts just stood there with their mouths open. I couldn't tell their reaction.

It was getting late, so my older relatives began to leave.

As Uncle Juan left, he remarked, "I can't remember being so happy at a party. Can't wait for the other children to marry."

My dad chuckled and replied, "I need some time to recover from this party."

After the celebration, Jeremy's parents left, thanking my family for their hospitality.

The next morning, my parents made a special effort to share one of our holiday traditions with Jeremy. Mom said, "Jeremy, we have another surprise for you. We're so excited to have you stay with us. I thought it would be fun to make some of our holiday food together since we're gonna be family soon. Have you ever made a tamale from scratch?"

Jeremy shrugged and replied, "No. Is that what we're going to be doing?"

Mom answered, "Yes. Making tamales for Christmas took all day. Estrella's great-aunt Ruth taught us how to make them. Everyone has a station around the kitchen table, with all the ingredients ready to make the tamales."

Marco shared, "Jeremy, we have fun singing and laughing all day."

I said, "Making them always transported me back in time. I still remember sitting on a stool, eagerly awaiting my assignment in my oversized apron when I was little."

"Jeremy, you will place the tamales in the pot. That's going to be your job," instructed Mom.

We all agreed that nothing could replace the taste of homemade tamales. Consuela remarked, "We always found it hard to sleep the night we made tamales. The smell permeated the whole house and made us hungry. We were eager to eat our creations."

I added, "The next day, we all sat down to eat with a great sense of accomplishment, knowing each of us had a hand in making the food we ate."

Jeremy said, "I can't wait until tomorrow."

My grandparents remarked, "Making tamales with the family was one of our favorite things to do together."

Then I blinked. College was over. I will never forget how excited I was to graduate. My family came out to celebrate with me.

Julio remarked, "I bet you feel important putting on your cap and gown."

I answered, "Yes, I do. I worked hard to finish my degree with honors."

My family made me feel on top of the world since I was the valedictorian. In my speech, I encouraged my classmates to work for a better tomorrow. After the ceremony, many people came up to me to let me know how my address moved them. My family and I went to lunch to celebrate my accomplishment. I was on cloud nine. Dad made a toast, saying, "You are the oldest child in our family. You have encouraged your brothers and sister to work hard. Thank you for being such a wonderful person. We are all very proud of you."

The months flew by as I was busy finalizing the details for our southwestern wedding. As special as it was to put on my cap and gown for graduation, putting on my wedding dress brought a song to my heart. At our traditional Latino wedding, my mother-in-law expressed dismay that the wedding ceremony was outdoors.

She told me, "I longed to see Jeremy married in the Church of the Beatitudes." Both Jeremy and his mother were appalled when they learned that a whole lamb was roasted in a pit dug in the ground with heated coal and wood overnight. "This is bizarre!" exclaimed Kat. She found ways to insult me and my culture.

Cameron, Jeremy's dad, had a completely different attitude, saying, "What an exciting way to cook."

After Jeremy got tipsy, he began to enjoy himself. He smiled from ear to ear when we danced the flamenco. Abuelita took out her father's castanets and happily danced to the music. Abuelo had his castanets, so he danced along with his wife. My abuelita taught my sister, brothers, and me the dance, so we joined them on the dance floor. Seeing them dance made me happy. Excellent dancers. The party continued until sunrise.

My new mother-in-law was polite and charming to my parents. Unfortunately, Kat didn't speak to me the entire day. One of my cousins saw her in the bathroom and greeted her. "We are family now," she said. Kat scowled, said nothing, and quickly left the room. Fortunately, I hadn't heard the comment. The next day, we left for our honeymoon.

Our honeymoon was in the Bahamas. It was ten glorious days in a little cottage by the sea, sunning, surfing, and making love. The room was beautiful, so much more than I could have imagined. We received a large bouquet of red roses, French champagne, and Belgium chocolates, and we were treated to a violinist in a private dining room—all from hospitality services. I felt like Queen Estrella with my knight in shining armor, Jeremy. It was heavenly.

Regrettably, Jeremy did not see our room the same way. He was angry. He told the manager this was not the room his mother had arranged. It was supposed to be a full ocean view suite, not a partial view. Jeremy was also disappointed by the quality of the robes in the room. It took a lot of coaxing and rum to get him back into honeymoon mode. After dinner, we spent the rest of the night together. I couldn't get enough of my man. A simple touch made me tingle.

Jeremy started to complain again about our room as we were checking out. He was so boisterous I was embarrassed, but he got what he wanted, a discount on the bill. I dismissed his loud behavior as sorrow at leaving our paradise for the real world. However, that was not a good reason for misbehaving. As always, I let it go.

I couldn't wait to show Abuelita pictures from our honeymoon. We talked and laughed like always. Then I asked my wise abuelita for advice about getting along with my mother-in-law. She happily shared her favorite quote from Khalil Gibran. "Some give with joy, and joy is their reward. Kindness is a gift to yourself because it makes you happy, and the person who receives your happiness makes them happy too." She then went on to tell me about her mother-in-law and father-in-law who, even though they both had some Spanish heritage, had a lot of differences. It was her mother-in-law's generosity and warmth that won the family over. Every time she had to buy someone a gift, she made sure to find out what they wanted and gave it to them. Everyone grew to love her in time, becoming their favorite relative. It was because of her loving disposition. When she died, her husband's family was distraught. I promised Abuelita I would make the same effort as my great-grandma.

6

FINALLY, I GOT A JOB

About a month after we returned from our honeymoon, I received a letter asking for an interview for a writing position at a well-known magazine. I could barely contain my excitement since this was one of the top magazines in the country, with headquarters in New York City. I spent a week putting together a portfolio to highlight my work in college as the editor of our newspaper. I liked showing off my accomplishments. It was exciting to go to the Big Apple since I'd never been to New York before. Seated next to see me on the plane was Eric, a dear friend from school. What a surprise!

We had worked together at the newspaper and had taken many journalism classes together. I enjoyed chatting with him. I showed him my portfolio and said, "Do you remember when we worked on this article?"

He was amazed and said, "I didn't prepare for the interview." We were so different. I couldn't understand anyone who wouldn't prepare for an interview.

I wasn't worried that Eric was also interviewing for a job with the magazine. I figured there would be many positions open. No problem; my credentials were impeccable. I led our study group and was the editor and writer for the school's newspaper. As the top-ranking student in the College of Journalism and the valedictorian, I had an impressive portfolio. My work ethic allowed me to achieve my goals.

I put on my new black suit and black pumps, ready to shine during the interview, which I did. I was impeccably dressed. The interview went perfectly. I told myself, "This is my job." The only question that surprised me was when the editor, Mr. Edwards, asked me, "Are you married?" When I said yes, the next question was "Are you planning to start a family soon?" I found the question strange, but I answered no. Since this was my first interview, I was puzzled. I wondered if that was a typical inquiry.

Eric and I arranged to meet for coffee to discuss our interviews, feeling really excited about working for such a well-respected magazine. I told him, "I forgot how much fun it was spending time with you." Since we were having such a good time together, we had lunch and then decided to take in some of New York's amazing sights together.

I was overwhelmed by the skyscrapers. They were so tall it was hard to see the sky. It was a little scary. We visited the Empire State Building and had time to go to the Museum of Modern Art, even managing to squeeze in a musical on Broadway. It was *Grease*. I loved the songs and sang them with Eric on the plane ride home. We had a wonderful time together.

A week later, I got a call from Eric. He said, "Estrella, I got the job. We will be working together once more." He assumed I heard the good news, that I would be working for the magazine with him. Eric was shocked to learn I hadn't heard anything. A few days later, I got a rejection letter. The news broke my heart. I replayed the interview in my mind and wondered if my being a newlywed influenced their decision. Many questions raced through my head. Did they ask the male candidates the same questions? It made me suspicious.

It was the first time I had not achieved my goal. I was upset and wondered why I didn't get the position. Months later, Eric wrote to tell me about a conversation he overheard. He said, "Estrella, you didn't get the job since they knew you would quit after a year to start a family." I thought, *Are you kidding me? All this because I am a woman.* I started singing Helen Reddy's song, "I am woman, hear me roar," because I needed encouragement. I was getting worried about being a woman in the man's world of journalism. I prayed that a magazine would see my accomplishments and want me in their organization. It took me two more weeks to get another interview.

The next interview I had was at a woman's magazine based in LA. I did a great job on the interview and was offered the job on the spot. I knew I was competent to do great work. The woman's magazine did not consider me less of a candidate since I was a woman. They told me, it was an asset to be a woman for this job. Finally, they saw my worth. I was happy to get the job and vowed to do my very best.

Around the same time, Jeremy had good fortune too. On his first interview, he landed a position in finance at the corporate headquarters of a leading bank in LA. What luck! Quickly, Jeremy found a mentor, Marshall Winston II, the vice president. Marshall saw himself in Jeremy. He said he would make Jeremy a rising star at the bank. My honey was very excited about his future. The two bankers spent a lot of time at the country club, chatting with clients. There were also many cocktail parties I attended. It was at these parties where I noticed a habit of Jeremy's that drove me crazy. While he was talking to someone, his eyes would dart around the room, looking for someone more important to talk to next.

At first, Jeremy was offended by comments Marshall made, like when he blamed the Jews for promoting the advancement of civil rights. The people Jeremy marched for were the same people his boss ridiculed—women and minorities. As time went on, Jeremy's behavior changed. My husband found these comments funny. Jeremy forgot all that he'd worked to eliminate, such as prejudice against minorities. Then he started spending more money on clothes, watches, and sunglasses. He wanted nothing but the best. The very things he once thought were ostentatious he happily bought for himself. That really upset me!

He came home very excited and said, "I bought a new car!"

I was confused. "You have a car. Honey, what are you talking about? You didn't buy a car!"

He picked me up and spun me around, saying, "Oh yes, I did, Strella. I bought a brand-new red Corvette with financing."

With financing were words I hated to hear. "Large items bought with financing cost much more than the sticker price. I learned that in Accounting 101." I told him I made it a point to save my money until I was able to pay for things without financing.

I laughed but felt like crying. "Sweetie, what are you talking about?

You didn't buy a car without discussing it with me! Especially with financing. That car will cost us a fortune. We need to budget to make sure this is something we can afford."

Jeremy shrugged. "I'm the only child. My parents will give me whatever money we need. Relax! Let's go for a spin." I took several deep breaths, realizing that, as a new wife, I needed to pick my battles, and this was not worth a fight. But I was worried. *Is this a pattern of behavior I will have to struggle with from now on?* My family was much more conservative about spending. I never even thought of relying on my parents for a frivolous purchase like an expensive sports car. We were hard workers and didn't overspend.

7

TRYING TO BOND

I had the drive to be the best at whatever I did from an early age. It could be anything, including

needing to sell the most cookies in my Girl Scout troop, winning blues ribbons in western dressage riding competitions, and taking the top prize at the spelling bee at school. Most of my effort went into my passion for learning. The nuns praised me for my academic achievements when I was in Catholic school. I worked tirelessly and received a four-year merit scholarship to USC. My parents decided to endow the school with a room in a new building because, though I earned the scholarship, my family did not need the financial assistance.

I thought back to my first days in Los Angeles. Wow. LA. I was thrilled to go to school in that exciting city. Looking forward to trying new things, it was my first college party. I really lucked out with my roommate, Karen. We were excited to experience college life together. We looked completely opposite. My roommate had long, blonde, curly hair, twinkling green eyes, and a ready smile. We instantly became friends from the first day we met. She always looked out for me. Born and raised in Southern California, she felt it was her duty to take me under her wings. She joked, "You are a fish out of water," since I'd never been to California before.

I'll never forget how excited and nervous Karen and I were as we got ready to go to a college party. We got there and were immediately greeted with a couple of drinks. We chatted with some girls, friends we had made in our dorm.

Then Karen shouted with excitement, "Heather! What are you doing here?" She turned to me and asked, "Is it okay if I talk to my friend for a little bit? I promise I'll be right back."

I smiled and nodded. "Absolutely. I'll be fine. I'm having a great time."

After Karen left, out of the corner of my eye, I spotted a very cute guy. The two of us exchanged smiles. Then he walked over to me. I remember feeling a flush in my cheeks.

He said, "Hi. I'm Chad. What's your name?"

I answered, "It's nice to meet you, Chad. My name is Estrella."

He smiled. "Wow. I've never heard the name Estrella before. It's beautiful, just like you."

We continued to flirt, and then I found myself less interested and more annoyed with Chad. He was trying to impress me with a story about how he knew how to take charge.

Chad explained, "My parents were away, and I was in charge of managing the household staff. It was going well, except when I had to deal with those stupid, lazy gardeners from Mexico. They could barely understand English or speak our language. I don't know why we don't just put them all on a bus and send them back to Mexico."

I was shocked. A little voice came into my head from my grandparents, reminding me to be proud of who I am. I loudly proclaimed, "I'm Hispanic, and I speak English."

A surprised look appeared on his face. Then he said, "Oh, I thought you were Italian, not one of them. It's too bad if I offended you, but your people need to learn the language. Why don't you teach your people to communicate in our official language?"

I was speechless. I could feel my face burning red with anger. I had to run out of that party before I started to cry. As I opened the door to leave, Karen and I exchanged a glance. I could see the worry on her face. She was concerned as she mouthed the words, "Are you okay?" I shook my head no. Then I left.

Karen ran after me to find out why I was upset. Between my tears,

I told Karen what had happened and asked her, "Why do people hate me for being Hispanic? I am no different. I don't understand."

Karen just hugged me and said, "You'll be all right."

Growing up in a rural town, I hadn't experienced prejudice. Living in a big city with people from all walks of life was the first time I realized how people saw me and said hateful things. Such a difference! LA was nothing like I expected. I thought it was going to be all fun and games. In reality, it was a lot of prejudice against minorities, including women. I didn't realize the bubble I had grown up in Pueblo. I knew I was fortunate to have a family that supported my aspirations, but I had no idea how the world saw me, a rich, curly-haired, olive-skinned Hispanic girl.

After interacting with Chad, I knew I had to create a cultural group with people like me. I did this with the new friends I made in school by posting a sign on the bulletin board in the main dining room. It read, *A new group is forming for feminists.* I had heard so many stories about women who felt like they were on society's periphery. They were looking for a group to call their own. We created our own identity. Our group aimed to empower educated, successful, career-minded women to express themselves through writing. Once a month, we met to talk. We spent the first fifteen minutes discussing family, school, or work. In reality, it was longer than that. My job was to stop the chitchat, or we would never get anything done. Then we read our latest poems to one another or whatever we were writing. I remember feeling relief to be a part of a group finally. Most women in my group were single, but a few were married with children. I loved our meetings. It made me feel connected. We all felt the same way.

Another high point during college was meeting Karen. I was fortunate to have her as my roommate. She was easygoing and funny. We found ourselves laughing so much that our sides hurt. Also, she was sensitive to my feelings. Not too long after the Chad incident, Karen wanted to lift my spirits.

We decided to go shopping downtown, where we came across a strange-looking store. Skulls, witches, and a smoke-filled cauldron filled the window display. It looked spooky. Karen said, "Do you want to go in?"

With a smile, I said, "Why not?"

As we entered, passing through the beaded doorway, it felt weird. I wondered if something would jump out at me. We got a whiff of patchouli oil as we wandered through the store. Many neat things in the shop piqued our interest, like the enormous, multicolored, scented candles, artwork, and jewelry. My eyes focused on a cute red-beaded bracelet. Behind the counter, a hippie girl with her long braided hair and flowing white dress helped us. She said the bracelet was for protection and good fortune. We decided to each get one as matching friendship bracelets, feeling we could use more good luck. The clerk put each bracelet in a box that had the word *Kabbalah* on it. Even though I wasn't familiar with Kabbalah at that time, I felt it would be important in my future.

As enjoyable as it was for me to remember how excited I felt going to LA for college, nothing could take away how I felt now returning to LA. I didn't want to be there. My abuelita was gone forever. There was no escaping the sadness that stung deep in my heart. The burden of what she confided in me hung over my days like a thundercloud. What did it mean?

I knew my abuelita would want me to be there for my parents and also for Uncle Mario, who was distraught. Abuelita was the most important person in my uncle's life. Now, he had no one else except my parents. From stories gathered through the years, it seemed that my uncle had been a strikingly handsome man in his youth, with a swagger like a movie star. The young girls enjoyed talking and flirting with him, but he only had eyes for Rosaria, a sweet girl from a nearby ranch who wanted to be a nun. She felt her calling when she was five years old. Rosaria fell into a boarded-up nonworking Indian well. Miraculously, Rosaria was rescued by a stranger. The stranger took the frightened little girl home and told her that Jesus had sent him to find her. To repay Jesus for saving her life, she would have to make a sacrifice, which was to serve the Lord, though she loved Mario. Knowing this, Uncle Mario still tried to convince her to marry him. It was no use; she went to a convent to live out her life. Uncle Mario was heartbroken and never married. He wrote to Rosaria, but she never wrote back. He even went to see her, but she wouldn't see him. It was unfortunate. He never loved again. I wished more for my uncle.

Back in LA, I forgot to set my alarm clock for work the next day. "Oh no!" It did not go off. What happened? No alarm! That wasn't like me at all. What do I do? I usually double- or triple-checked my alarm. I was pooped after a night of cramming for a presentation I had to make that day. Jeremy thought it was funny and told me not to worry, but I was frantic. *Oh man, I'm in trouble,* I thought. I was frantic, nervously rushing to work as fast as possible to get out the door. I was never late for work. I told myself to focus on getting to work and not blame myself now. I got ready in ninety seconds flat, went to work, calmed myself down, and ran into a meeting, happy to know that I wasn't late.

When I looked down, I stopped breathing. In my haste to get to work, there were two different shoes on my feet. Worse than that, the levels of the shoes were different, so I walked with a limp. The left shoe was a red pump, while my right was a brown sandal. I didn't have time to go home to change my shoes. I had to make the best of it. The rest of the day, I tried to strategically put one foot over the other to hide the mismatched shoes, hoping that no one would know I was wearing two different shoes. I thought, with a smile, I could get away with it, as I tiptoed on my right foot, pretending both shoes were the same height. When I stood up to make my presentation, I stood on the tiptoes of my right foot to compensate for the difference. As I returned to my seat, I almost fell.

I sat on one foot to avoid anyone seeing my faux pas, hiding my feet under my desk. I did anything I could think of to prevent anyone from seeing my shame. My friend Kristine whispered, "Are you okay?" I guessed my ability to hide my feet wasn't working. Kristine told me, "You look nervous. I saw your mismatched shoes. Let's go for a drink after work today."

After a long, embarrassing day, it felt like a good idea. We settled in at the local bar, both getting a beer. Feeling unsteady, I went to the bathroom to wash my face. As I got up, I spilled my drink. Kristine smiled and said, "Chaimi did it."

I said, "What did you say?"

She repeated it. I was appalled. I told her, "You just said a Jew spilled the beer."

She was insulted, saying, "I did not."

I said, "Calling someone Chaimi in that context is a derogatory term for a Jew."

She apologized, saying, "I'm sorry. I didn't know you were Jewish."

I told her, "I'm not. It's just a terrible thing to say." Things weren't going well.

I felt something had to change. I knew a vacation was in order. It was always an excellent opportunity for Jeremy and me to reconnect. I needed some time to absorb all the shocking information my abuelita shared with me. Jeremy and I had planned to visit Hawaii for years, but with our schedules, we never had the time to do it. I learned from Grandma's passing to make the time you have count. We needed to take this vacation now. We'd share a well-deserved respite and spend precious time intertwined in each other's arms, something our busy lives in LA didn't allow for very often. Just like the trip we took to Europe before starting our senior year of college.

I wasn't feeling well, so I made an appointment to see my doctor, something I hadn't done in a few years. I told him that my grandmother died and that I was not feeling well. After the exam, he called me into his office and told me the wonderful news. He said, "Estrella, you are pregnant." I was shocked. Jeremy and I had talked about having children, but we wanted to wait awhile. Dr. Lawler said, "There's no need to wait; the decision had been made." I was excited to know that we would be blessed with a child. Now it was time to tell my husband. I thought I would wait until we were in Hawaii.

The following week, we were on the beautiful north shore of Maui, Hawaii, lying on a blanket, soaking up the sun. I gazed at him as his face turned up to the sky.

My man and I spent a beautiful afternoon wrapped in each other's arms. Just what I wanted and needed. It was the perfect time and place to tell him about the baby.

I said, "Honey, you know how I said I've been feeling tired?"

Alarmed, he asked me, "Are you okay?"

I smiled and said, "I am better than that."

He looked at me curiously and asked, "What do you mean?"

I shouted, "We are having a baby!"

Jeremy's jaw dropped. He said nothing. When he was able to gain his composure, he turned to me and yelled, "How could you let this happen?"

I was shocked. "I thought you'd be happy."

"We were waiting."

"Sometimes things cannot be planned."

He said nothing and left.

Overcome by his reaction, I packed my things and headed back to our suite. I thought, *He'll get over this feeling.* Jeremy returned several hours later and was still unable to talk about the baby, but we were able to talk about where to go for dinner. Going to a bar was the answer. When the band began to play, I asked him to dance. Reluctantly, he accepted. It was a slow dance, and I melted in his arms. I felt the tension in his body relax. We were going to be okay, though he still couldn't talk about the upcoming event. My husband didn't adjust well to changes. Time would help him deal with the blessed event.

When we returned to LA, it was business as usual, except that now I had a warm feeling in my heart. I was thrilled to become a mother. Jeremy stayed away from talking about the baby—until I began to show. He was fascinated with the bump in my tummy and said, "Look at your belly. It's getting so big."

I giggled and said, "There's more. Give me your hand." I placed his hand on my stomach. After a few moments, the baby kicked.

Jeremy jumped and asked, "Are you okay?"

I nodded. "Yes, sweetie, I'm wonderful. Our baby just wanted to say hi to her daddy."

Jeremy grinned from ear to ear and said, "I'm your dad."

After that first kick, Jeremy was hooked. He would just sit there and stare at me. I'd never seen him so happy. We were now united in our love for this child. He accepted the fact that we were having a baby.

My parents were thrilled. Our baby was the first grandchild for them. It helped temper the sadness they felt loosing Grandma. They went to Toys R Us and wanted to buy everything in the store. Just a few more months, and we would be together celebrating our new addition. My siblings promised to take turns visiting. I would hold them to that.

Determined to continue working until the birth, I was exhausted by the end of each day but feeling great. My pregnancy was a breeze. I would take a year off. My plans were to take care of my baby during her first year of life and then go back to work. Thanks to my family's generosity, I could afford to do that.

Everything was in order. We painted the baby's room purple because it was my favorite color. The curtains were multicolored, with all of the letters of the alphabet in upper and lower case. We got the finest crib and changing table from my parents and an antique rocking chair from Jeremy's parents. It was the same rocking chair that Kat used when Jeremy was a baby.

Jeremy proudly exclaimed, "We are ready to greet our baby. I can hardly wait." The time flew by quickly.

Just before the baby was due, Jeremy had a financial conference in San Francisco and asked me if I felt comfortable being without him for a few days. I told him, "Of course, silly. I'll be fine." When he left, I was surprised at how lonely I felt. We were together most of the time, and I found that I missed him. Then I remembered my abuelita's box. I thought, *This would be a good time to rummage through it.* I picked it up, opened it, and found a letter addressed to my great-great-grandmother Evangelina Luna. I opened it and began to read. It was in Spanish, dating back to 1790. My Spanish skills were good enough to understand the words. The letter was from a distant cousin in Mexico City. In the letter, her cousin Madelina Luna told her about a trial at the Palace of the Inquisition. She wrote that her friend was accused of practicing Judaism and was sentenced to death by fire. In the letter, she warned Evangelina to be careful. She pleaded with her cousin to keep the secret and not share it with others.

I was so disturbed by the letter that I threw up and quickly called Consuela to let her know about the letter. Consuela insisted, "Put the letter in the box and put it away! There is nothing you can do about this. You will only make yourself sick. The Inquisition is over." Once again, my sister had come to my rescue.

I said, "You are always right. I'll put it away." I placed the box under my bed and lay down. Fortunately, I began to feel better. I wouldn't look at it again. It was upsetting.

At work the next week, my water broke, though I was two weeks early. I was so embarrassed by the puddle on my chair that I quickly ran to the elevator, got in, and went down to the lobby. Fortunately, the guard saw my dilemma and knew what to do. He immediately called the fire department as well as Jeremy. He told my husband to meet me at the hospital. He was nervous and excited about the birth of our baby. The time had come, but the baby wasn't quite ready to come into the world. She was happy in her home and didn't want to come out.

It took sixteen hours of labor to produce this remarkable being, my daughter Maria, named after her great-grandmother. Baby Maria was exquisite, with dark blond hair, blue eyes, chubby cheeks, and lovely shaped lips—the spitting image of Jeremy. I felt such overwhelming joy I couldn't stop smiling. Jeremy felt the same way.

I checked her fingers and toes. I told Jeremy, "She is perfect." I smiled at her, and she smiled back at me. My heart was bursting with pride. We brought her home and put her in her crib. We didn't leave her room. We just stood there watching her sleep. Jeremy said, "Thank you for bringing Maria to us."

Mom and Dad came to meet their new granddaughter two days later. Mom said, "She is perfect. Mija, your father and I found a wonderful night nurse to help you and Jeremy."

I said, "Mom, that is so generous of you, but we don't need a night nurse. Jeremy and I are two capable adults; we can handle our baby by ourselves."

Mom responded, "I know you can, but Maria needs the best care. And having too well-rested parents is going to give her that. Remember, I raised four babies."

Mom stayed to bond and help me out with Maria. We couldn't stop staring at our bundle of joy. It was more entertaining than any show on TV. We were focused on each movement she made. We laid her on the floor and sat marveling at her.

After Mom left, Jeremy's folks came and were pleased with their new addition.

Kat loved the fact that Maria was fair skinned and was relieved to note this to me. "Thank God she looks like our family." Under her breath, she muttered, "I would have hated it if she looked Hispanic."

I ignored her comments and walked away. Nothing anyone could say would spoil how I felt.

After their visit, Consuela came to help. It was wonderful having her with us. I decided to leave my baby for the very first time with her aunt Consuela. I got a haircut and came home feeling like a whole new woman. As I entered the house, my blissful state of being was shattered when I heard Maria screaming at the top of her little lungs. My heart sank as I was heading to the baby's room. Once I entered, I saw my sister sitting on the rocking chair asleep, with a book lying on her stomach. Maria was in her crib, snot flowing from her nose, with tears streaming down her face. I quickly swooped up my baby to comfort her. Then I shook my sister awake and shouted, "What's wrong with you?"

Startled, she answered, "What are you talking about?"

I told her, "The baby was screaming. Why didn't you pick her up?"

Shrugging her shoulders, she said, "Sorry. I didn't hear her."

I walked out of the room and continued to soothe Maria. After she calmed down, I calmed down. I thought, *I wonder, if the cries of a baby aren't your baby's, can you always hear the cries?*

Unable to stay angry, I walked back to the room and hugged my sister. "I'm sorry for yelling. Being a new mom is hard." Then we laughed.

The best part of the day was singing to Maria after bath time. I sat in the rocking chair singing a beloved song from her great-abuelita Maria, De Colores, a folksong brought to the Spanish-speaking world from sixteenth-century Spain that had a cheerful and upbeat melody. "De colores de colores, se listen los campos en la primavera ..." (The colors, bright with colors the mountains and valleys dress up in the springtime ...)

Time marched on, and Maria grew more beautiful every day. Jeremy and I loved making her laugh. We enjoyed all of the attention from visitors. Marco and Julio relished being first-time uncles and pampered her.

I told them, "I knew you'd be great uncles."

At five months, Julio took baby Maria out of her crib and said, "You are Spanish, and it's about time you learned the flamenco. Your great-grandmother Maria, who you were named for, taught us this special dance. We waited until you were a big girl and now think it is time for you to learn the family dance."

I said, "You know, Julio, I know Maria's advanced, but she can't stand yet."

He responded, "It's never too early to learn the flamenco."

Julio handed the baby to Marco, who put her on his lap as they watched Julio dance for them. Marco took her hands in his and clapped the beats of the flamenco. My baby was squealing with delight as she giggled and drooled, loving the attention from her uncles. The adults in the room could not stop laughing as they watched Maria's first dance lesson.

We were settling into a routine with feeding schedules in the middle of the night and sharing all of our parental duties, especially diaper changes.

Sometimes Maria was so fussy that we brought her in bed with us. One morning, I woke up to laughter from Jeremy and Maria. Jeremy had clapped her hands together, which made her giggle.

Each time he clapped her hands together, he said, "Clap, clap, clap."

Each clap brought a giggle to Maria's lips.

I loved seeing them play. I loved my little family.

Out of the blue, I got an invitation from my coworker to come to lunch with our former editor as well as the owner of the magazine. I was delighted to catch up with my friends and coworkers again. It was far too long since I had seen them. I chuckled as I got dressed because it felt so strange to look like a professional again.

Ms. White, the owner of the magazine, said, "Estrella, the reason that we're getting together is because we have an exciting assignment for you. Our market research discovered that our readers want a story from the perspective of a first-time mom."

I said, "Well, it is a roller-coaster ride being a mom."

Ms. White continued, "We want you to write a monthly column about motherhood. We'll go over the details later. What do you think? Are you ready to get back to work?"

I thought, *What a loaded question. Am I ready to get back to work? Yes, I love what I do. No. How can I leave Maria*" I answered, "Yes! I have a lot of great topics the readers would enjoy. I've been journaling throughout Maria's life and even before she was born."

I was so excited for Jeremy to come home and share my news. I was going back to work and writing about motherhood. I anxiously stood by the door, waiting for him to come home. I couldn't stop fidgeting. The door opened, and I greeted my husband with a big hug and kiss. "I have some exciting news!"

His jaw dropped, and he asked, "Are you pregnant again?"

With a giggle, I said, "No, but I do have some good news about work. I've been asked to write my own monthly column on motherhood. Isn't that wonderful I'm starting work next month! Isn't that amazing?"

He bit his lower lip and shook his head. "I thought you were going to wait to return to work until Maria was at least a year old. I assumed you'd be like my mom and not want to leave Maria for a job. How could you agree to this without talking to me?"

I was stunned. "I'm sorry, Jeremy. It's just an amazing opportunity. Of course I don't wanna leave Maria, but I'm excited to write my story. Besides, what's wrong with showing her that her mom can have a successful career?"

He shrugged. "I'm really disappointed that you made this decision before we talked about it. We will find a way to make it work, but I can't discuss it with you now."

I said, "Thank you, Jeremy. You'll see this is going to be good for our family."

Jeremy was a bit distant from me, but in time, our happy little family resumed. As the days grew closer to my return to work, I found it harder to think about it. I was bonding with my daughter, loving her, singing to her, bathing her, and brushing her bright, beautiful hair. I don't remember being more satisfied. My husband felt the same. We loved her cooing sounds. We were complete.

Only four more days to go before the rat race would begin. I was feeling sad. The joy of caring for Maria full-time would go to someone else. Linda would start in the morning to get used to the schedule.

When I put Maria down for the night, I held her longer than usual. I nuzzled and kissed her on her forehead and placed her in the crib with her little lamb beside her. She smiled and blew me a raspberry. I remember saying, "Good night, my love. Don't let the bedbugs bite." Just a silly saying I had never said before.

When I got up in the morning, I was surprised that I had slept so late. Jeremy must have taken care of Maria earlier. I began to walk to her room and met my husband at her door. We walked in together, greeting her.

I said, "Hello, my sweet angel. Mommy and Daddy are here," in a singsong voice.

Maria was in the exact place I had put her the night before. I picked her up and saw her rosy cheeks had turned gray.

I turned to Jeremy and said, "She doesn't look right."

As we stared at our baby, my heart and breathing began to race.

I exclaimed, "She's not moving, Jeremy!"

I grabbed my baby and felt her neck. No pulse. We put her on the floor and started CPR. I could hear Jeremy on the phone. "Hello, my baby is not breathing! We need help!"

The paramedics got there quickly and took over.

In the ambulance, I prayed, "Jesus, help my baby." We accompanied our child to the hospital. We sat there waiting, wringing our hands. When the doctor came out of the exam room, he sat down beside us and said, "Your baby is gone."

I couldn't comprehend what he said. I asked, "Where did she go?"

He quietly said, "She died."

I cried, "No! No! No! She just had her monthly checkup. She was a perfectly healthy baby."

The doctor explained, "I am very sorry. We think Maria died of SIDS, sudden infant death syndrome. We don't know why this happens."

We sat with our baby, holding her and kissing her until we couldn't anymore. I hollered, "Why my baby?" We were distraught.

Going back to our home was difficult that night. We couldn't go into her room. Our families came in for the funeral, which was conducted by my local priest. Burying our baby was the hardest thing I had ever done. We suffered when we saw the little coffin. I hoped she would be with Abuelita and all of the relatives who had passed.

I was in a state of shock and couldn't do anything. I couldn't cancel our nanny. I couldn't call my work. Jeremy took over and did those things for me. I needed time to adjust to my new life without my Maria. She had been with me just a little time, but she would always be part of my heart. I'd never forget her.

I wallowed in my grief and took more time off of work. I knew I had to busy myself to keep the pain at bay. I cuddled my baby's toy lamb and couldn't eat or sleep. I pushed myself to get back to work. There was always a lot to do at the magazine.

Jeremy took time off from his job too. His grief turned to anger and then violence. During his time off work, he went into Maria's room, looked around, and began to pull the curtains down. He ripped them up and put them in the garbage can. Then he disassembled the crib, put all of her clothes in a bag, took the changing table, and set them all outside on the curb. The only thing he left intact was the rocking chair. He sat in the dark, rocking in the chair. I yelled at him for being so destructive. "Destroying things won't bring her back. What's wrong with you?"

He said, "We are not having another child." I didn't believe him. He, too, was in a great deal of pain. It would take time for the raw wound to heal, but it never would completely. Going to counseling would help us cope. There was a special group for parents of SIDS babies.

We needed counseling. I was surprised how many couples were in the room when we first started. You'd think in this day and age, with all of the advances of medicine, deaths of babies would be nonexistent. It was all a big mystery. We became friends with some of the suffering parents. It helped at first to cry together, but after a while, it was just too painful.

In time, we went back to our lives before the baby. Our family and friends helped by calling and taking us out for evenings of fun. Jeremy was adamant about not having any more children. He said, "We will not have another to rip our hearts out." I loved being a mother and looked forward to trying again.

Things had settled down after a year, so I suggested that we take another beach vacation. This time, I wanted to go to the Cayman Island. I heard that the water was calmer and warmer than in Hawaii. The island was less crowded and more peaceful too.

Once again, we were sunning ourselves on the beach, enjoying being together. Then I remembered my abuelita's box and said, "There is a family secret I want to share with you."

He replied, "You can tell me anything." Leaning his chin on his hand, he smiled as he asked me what it was.

"She told me that I am a descendant of Spanish Jews."

He stopped what he was doing and said, "What?" A shocked expression came over his face. I hadn't expected that reaction.

I tried to explain to him that my ancestors were Conversos (forcibly converted Jews) who went to the New World. I told him, "On her deathbed, my grandma revealed it to me."

He wanted to know if that meant that I was a Jew. I was shocked by the question, answering that I wasn't. He questioned, "What are you?" I was annoyed by the question. He turned away. Then he turned back to look at me. The expression on his face shocked me. He was upset.

I said, "I am no different."

Now, almost instantly, I detected a change in his attitude. He stuttered, saying, "Are you sure she said that? Are you sure she said *your* family? She was ancient, you know."

"Yes, I'm sure. Abuelita gave me letters, mementos, and audiotapes of the story of my ancestor. Her name was Estrella too."

He was looking at me sideways. I queried him, asking what the matter was. He said that he couldn't believe it. "You casually mentioned to me that you are a descendant of a Jew. That's the problem!" Jeremy said with disgust, as if I was not even human.

I replied, "I found out just before she died."

My hubby annoyed me. He answered in a still, small voice, "I know that, but you dropped a bombshell on me, knowing I would react. I need time to absorb the news."

I persisted, saying, "Jeremy, you may even have Jewish ancestors."

He yelled, "I'm not one of those people!"

I said, "You may be. I am the same woman you married, whether I have Jewish blood or not."

He was quiet. Then he said, "You are not who I thought you were."

I said, "You are not who I thought you were either." When I put my hand on his shoulder, he didn't caress it like he always did. Then he moved away from me.

Back in LA, I couldn't stop thinking about the man in my life in a different light. Many troubling thoughts came to mind. It was always easy for me to forget about them, which I did. My brain erased anything ugly. Now I remembered it all. I was upset. How could I let Jeremy's prejudiced remarks go? We were not even married when he began saying those negative things about different ethnic groups. From an early age, I learned discrimination was wrong. Everyone was my friend.

At my cousin's quinceañera, her coming-out party, Jeremy went into a tirade, telling me how silly it was to have such an extravagant party for someone so young. He thought it was a stupid tradition. Since my cousin was so happy, I thought, *Why not have a party?* In my family, young ladies had a coming-out party at fifteen. The girls in his family had debutant balls at seventeen. The traditions to honor the girls in our families were almost the same. There was little difference. Jeremy was such a hypocrite.

I loved going to parties and hosting them as well. Since I had such a hectic life, I found it easier to prepare cheese boards for my guests rather than making an entire meal, so I was able to entertain a lot. My life was too busy for anything too elaborate.

I invited my in-laws many times, but they always had other plans. I kept trying to connect with Kat but to no avail. Jeremy's family and I loved to ski in the winter. Last year, Jeremy and I visited my in-laws' vacation home in Aspen, Colorado, to celebrate Christmas with them. I was looking forward to spending more time with my mother-in-law. A couple of weeks before our trip, we had dinner with my in-laws. I thought Kat and I were starting to bond for the first time. Kat was complaining about Cameron's colorblindness. She said, "He wore an olive-green tie with a red shirt. It looked like he was dressing up as a clown." She looked at me for the first time when she spoke to me. Something was different.

I thought I was finally making headway with her. I offered her some advice, "Why don't you label the color on the inside of Cameron's clothes? Choosing colors in the grey scale is an easy way to have clothing complement each other." I continued explaining my fashion opinions, telling her that I loved colorful clothing. "There's only one color I refuse to wear. It's the color olive green. I hate it." Kat seemed quite interested and smiled at me. Her smile could be dazzling. She had perfect white teeth and great cheekbones, and her blonde hair was always perfectly coiffed. Could I have broken the ice queen? I wondered. I hoped I could connect with her.

At last, I was going to be accepted. To keep this level of goodwill going and to further ingratiate myself to her, I made sure I sent my mother-in-law the most tasteful gift. She collected Lladró figurines, so I bought her a figure, a delicate piece of a young boy reading. I thought it would be unique. It would remind her of Jeremy's passion for reading, which she encouraged when he was little. The little boy even looked like her sonny boy.

On Christmas morning, I woke up eager to greet the day. I was on vacation with my family in a beautiful setting. I felt so lucky. The family room was gorgeous, dressed with tinsel and beautiful, twinkling colored lights. A pleasing aroma filled the air of apples, cinnamon, evergreen, and hot chocolate. Gazing out the large picture window, it looked like a postcard. I saw snow-covered mountains and green trees that sparkled in the sunlight with a dusting of white. Gently and slowly, snowflakes fell to the ground. Under the big blue spruce Christmas tree were the gifts, perfectly placed. Curled ribbons sat on top of the wrapped presents. We gathered around the tree, singing Christmas songs as we sipped spiced eggnog. What beautiful gift did Kat buy me? I wondered. I was so excited that I tore into the wrapping paper. I opened the box I recognized from a very pricey boutique and felt my heart sink. My gifts from my in-laws were all in olive green. There was a beautiful hand-embroidered pashmina (shawl) in olive green, lambskin gloves in olive green, and a wallet in the only color I hated. I gave them hugs and thanked them for the lovely presents, knowing I would never use them. I planned on giving the gifts away once we got home. I felt defeated, but I thought I'd try again to bond with my mother-in-law.

8

REALITY SETS IN

One more time, I made an effort to win Kat over. I suggested we go down the slopes together. Jeremy and my father-in-law decided to take a different trail, leaving me plenty of time to connect with my mother-in-law. During our ski adventure, I hit some ice. I skidded and tumbled down the slope. Rattled, I slowly tried to get up. "Uh, oh," I groaned. It was painful to put weight on my left ankle. Kat was lovely and said she would leave me and get some help, promising to return. Kat said, "Just rest and stay calm."

I remember thinking that maybe this accident would bring us closer together. Perhaps I would have an amicable relationship with my mother-in-law since she was so sweet when she saw that I fell. I waited and waited and waited some more. As I was waiting, the sun was setting, and it was freezing. When the snow started to fall, my patience was gone. I was scared, alone, and cold. I tried to pull myself up again, but my ankle was hurting. It wasn't going to be easy to get down the mountain. I started to yell for help. "Help! Help! I need help!" No one came for me.

About twenty minutes later, help arrived. Henry, from ski patrol, heard my cries for help. He lifted me onto the snowmobile and brought me down the mountain. As we drove to the lodge, I asked him if there was a report of my accident. He told me, "There were no reported injuries in the area." He was simply on patrol.

After hearing this, I was devastated. Tears began to well up in my eyes. How could she leave me stranded in pain on the mountain? Did she hate me that much? What would I say to Jeremy? I wanted to pack my bags and leave, never to see Kat again.

Henry made sure the medic checked me out. The physician provided me with some much-needed crutches. Before entering the lodge, I took several long, deep breaths, wiping my tears away as best I could. I limped into the clubhouse on the crutches. There they were, laughing in front of a roaring fire. Kat drank a hot toddy with outstretched legs, resting on an ottoman.

When she saw me, she was shocked. I was livid. I couldn't believe that my family was sitting there instead of looking for me. "What are you doing here? I was stranded on that mountain! Why didn't you send help for me?"

Kat stuttered, "Oh, oh, my dear, I forgot. I apologize for not getting you help."

Saying nothing, I limped away, needing to rest.

Jeremy quickly got up to help me to the car. During the car ride back to our cabin, I started to cry. I couldn't hold back the tears. Jeremy asked me, "What happened?"

"Your mother saw me fall and told me she would send for help."

Jeremy was in disbelief. He explained that his mother told him and my father-in-law that I had met some friends on the slope and wanted to catch up with them. I told him that it was a flat-out lie. Jeremy did not believe me. According to him, his mother never lied.

He said, "She's an older lady. Maybe she just got confused."

"I do not think she was confused! I hate your mother." I had nothing more to say. We drove back in silence.

The next day, we headed home, still not speaking to each other. I went to my doctor, who took x-rays. The doctor told me I had a severe sprain. He said, "You need to remain on crutches for several weeks." My doctor gave me some pain meds since I was hurting so much. I was grateful.

How could I get past my anger toward Kat and Jeremy?

Jeremy infuriated me! My husband made excuses for his mother's atrocious behavior. At times, he could be the most considerate person, but other times he was a brute. I knew I had stayed too long in my marriage.

I didn't feel abused. My husband never hit me. I realized later there were different types of abuse. I didn't know that it was abuse when someone spoke to you in a nasty tone, saying horrible things. The idealistic young man I first fell in love with no longer existed. Jeremy used to bring me flowers. He spoke passionately about civil rights issues and would never break any of our beloved treasures in a fit of anger. This new Jeremy was a workaholic, materialistic, and racist.

I needed to talk to Consuela. Like always, Consuela was the calming voice of reason.

"Kat bought me gifts in the only color I hated. I can't believe that upset me. Nothing compared to being left to die on that mountain. Kat showed her true feelings toward me. Trying to please my mother-in-law is over," I confided to my sister. Consuela pleaded with me to give her the benefit of the doubt. She reminded me of our favorite folktale as children. The moral of the story was you need bitterness in your life to enjoy the sweetness fully. I told Consuela, "I don't know what I would do without you. Thank you for being the voice of reason. I promise to think about what you told me."

I felt I was to blame; I hadn't accepted the signs. From now on, I would have my antennas up for any evidence of personal disdain, no matter how slight. Now it was a two-sided attack on me. I couldn't deal with all this hate by myself. I needed help.

I hadn't been able to sleep well since my abuelita and Maria died. Troubled by what my grandmother had told me, I began having disturbing dreams. One morning, I awoke from a fitful dream. My grandmother was in my room, sitting on my bed. I was happy to see her, and she was delighted to be with me. Abuelita told me, "Estrella, you must search for something." I couldn't understand it. I kept asking her what she wanted me to find, but she didn't answer. A vision of a wooden box kept appearing and disappearing. I sprung out of bed in a cold sweat. Did my dream mean anything? What was the story about the chest? I wanted to investigate but couldn't. Not yet.

If losing my abuelita and my baby wasn't bad enough, there was a family secret I couldn't face. Deeply wounded, I felt isolated and rejected by Jeremy. I thought I was beginning to come to terms with it. Then I would think that my life was upside down again. I had a whole new stigma to face. I was a female. I was a Hispana. Now, in the eyes of my husband, I was a dirty Jew!

Then there were terrible nightmares that would not subside. Jeremy consumed my thoughts, so much so that he invaded my dreams. Walking in a beautiful garden, a monk in a hooded garment approached, asking us to kiss the cross to show that we were believers. Jeremy did, but I couldn't. Suddenly, out of the woods came a group of monks shouting and cursing at me. Jeremy joined the crowd. His clothes instantly changed to a monk's habit. I ran as fast as I could to get away from him. Just as he was about to grab me, I woke up panting, hardly able to catch my breath. The nightmare replayed in my mind every night, making me feel attacked. Jeremy took every opportunity to accuse me of lying. Sadly, the reality of my situation was worse. Our marriage was in trouble, if not over.

Jeremy told me, "I suspected you kept things from me." Even when I swore that I knew nothing about my ancestors, he wouldn't listen to me. Jeremy told me, "You lied to me, and you slept with Eric on your trip to New York City." He harangued me every time he saw me saying, "You knew you were a Jew, but you didn't tell me. I don't know who you are anymore." Then he told me that I didn't act like a typical wife, like his mother. He said, "She would greet my dad at the door with a drink and dinner ready."

I laughed when I told him that I had come home from work long after he got home. "Where's my drink and dinner? Shouldn't you do that for me?" He didn't like that.

Jeremy's behavior changed. He cut up the photos from our honeymoon. Then he hid our wedding album. Next, he took the 18-carat gold necklace with the star he bought for me in Florence and hid it. One evening, while arguing, he picked up my favorite blue vase, the one that had been in the family for hundreds of years, and threw it against the wall, shattering it. I screamed, "Are you crazy? That's not yours. Throw your own shit around! That was from my grandma."

He yelled, "If you don't want your things destroyed, stop lying to me."

"What the hell are you talking about? I don't lie. I haven't lied about anything."

Jeremy insisted, "You lie! You lie all the time. You lied so I would marry you, so my mother would approve of you, but she doesn't." I ran to the bedroom, slammed the door, and turned the radio on full blast. My goal was to escape my thoughts. It didn't work. I saw the parallels between my ancestors hiding their identity and my husband accusing me of doing the same.

When Jeremy's daily tirades became unbearable, I would take out the contents of my abuela's treasured box and tenderly looked through them. They brought me comfort, but I couldn't listen to the tapes. No, not yet. It wasn't the right time. Too much was going on.

I was distraught after our fight. I left the house, got into my car, and sat gazing at the fountain in our courtyard. I sighed, listening to the babbling sound of the water while staring at the beautiful terra-cotta pots filled with flowers. I loved the Spanish-style arches that framed each doorway. Driving around the neighborhood, I waved at the children playing hopscotch on the sidewalk near our condo. With my windows down, I passed by a Chinese restaurant, smelling the delicious food. I also passed by the park where Jeremy and I would take walks together; it was filled with flowers, green grass, and meandering trails. I was feeling melancholy while playing my favorite Joni Mitchell tape; her words helped me. I knew I was not alone. "I am on a lonely road, and I am traveling. Traveling, traveling, traveling. Looking for something. What can it be?" I calmed down.

Then I saw a quaint-looking bookstore with a star on its bright blue door, named Starry Books. I heard the bell chime as I entered and instantly got a whiff of sage. I felt comfortable listening to the babbling water of a small fountain on the counter next to the old brass cash register. Standing behind the counter was a man with a skull cap on his head. He asked me, "Can I help you find something?" I told him I wanted to look around. He said, "Take as long as you like."

I spent the next hour wandering around the store, finding my way to the spiritual section, where I grabbed the first book I saw. After a few minutes of reading, I knew I had to buy it. It was a book on Kabbalah. As I read it, I remembered my abuelita's words. *You must add the bitter to appreciate the sweet.* I learned that Kabbalah is a Jewish spiritual practice. I remembered my shopping trip with Karen, my former roommate, where we each bought a bracelet that had a connection to Kabbalah. I wondered if Abuelita got her saying about bitter and sweet from this ancient practice. The saying brought a smile to my face. On my way home, I felt strong. I was ready to take on challenges. Jeremy and I were going to be okay.

As I entered our home, I had a newfound determination to make things work. Stepping into the house, I heard the crunching sound of glass under my feet. I quickly realized the floor was full of broken glass. My lips quivered when I saw our wine glasses smashed on the floor. These were wedding gifts from my aunt and uncle in Spain. I asked him why he broke the glasses. He told me, "Our wedding was a mistake, and I didn't want anything around to remind me of the day we married." I was appalled but thankful that it was the glasses and not me that was destroyed. I never had any thoughts of being hit by him.

From that time forward, he became noncommunicative. Shortly after Jeremy smashed our wedding gift, the phone rang. Jeremy picked it up and slammed it down when I walked into the room. I asked Jeremy who it was. He said it was the wrong number. A moment later, the phone rang again. This time, I grabbed the receiver. It was my sister, Consuela. She was confused and asked, "Why'd Jeremy hang up on me?"

"We aren't getting along. Hanging up on you was his way of punishing me." Things were not always that way.

Could I trust my memories? His kisses were irresistible. He knew where to touch me to make our lovemaking so sweet that it made me melt. I reminded myself to stop living in the past. It was different from when we first met. We were not the same now. Or was he someone that I made up? It was like night and day. We were inseparable initially, spending most of our free time together. Jeremy would do anything to make me happy. He used to love to surprise me. He would say, "Happy Tuesday," with a bouquet of long-stem red roses, or my love would bring home food from my favorite Chinese restaurant. There were other times when he showed me how much he loved me, like when I had a big deadline approaching and was up all night working. He would rub my back to ease my tension. The following day, before I awoke, Jeremy ran down to the bakery around the corner from our condo and brought back a large cup of coffee and a sesame bagel.

Now Jeremy would work late, come home, shower, get a quick bite to eat, and sleep. We didn't talk to each other anymore, and we didn't make love. The anger took hold of him, and he wouldn't let it go. My disappointment in him possessed me too, and I wouldn't let go. Jeremy's personality became very perplexing to me. Over time, his alienation intensified. I realized that Jeremy and I needed to discuss how this knowledge of my background seriously affected our marital relationship. When I asked him how he felt about me, he hesitantly told me, "I learned to be proud of my heritage and only my legacy from my mother." What this meant was she hated minorities, which meant she hated me. The Aryan race was the only race that mattered. It was difficult for her to adjust to me, but my Jewish ancestry was too much to bear. My husband felt the same. He felt ashamed of his reaction, but that's how it was. Jeremy spent most of his childhood and adolescence doing what his mother wanted him to do, including going to a German-language summer camp. He was in the choir at church. He even considered becoming a minister. I, too, had plans for my future.

We had planned on buying our first home. Not a house with a white picket fence, it would be a smaller California version of an adobe-style house, with four bedrooms and three baths. It resembled my childhood home. Everything in the LA area was more expensive than in New Mexico. Here we were, two highly educated people with great jobs. We did feel fortunate because we were together. Then the thought of children. I had the perfect plan. Now just a thought because of the death of our daughter, Maria. I figured we could wait another two years to start our family again, even though there was a lot of pressure to start a family now. We would have a boy first and then a girl. They would be bright, good-looking, and well-behaved children. We would speak English, German, and Spanish in our home. I was going to have everything I ever wanted. I wasn't used to having things go badly. I was not spoiled but had been indulged by my family. I was relieved that we didn't have any children but still missed my dear baby Maria. That would have made things so much more complicated. How could my life fall apart? I was puzzled by all that had happened.

To stem the tide of our estrangement, we tried counseling. Jeremy begrudgingly gave one-word responses to questions our doctor asked. After two sessions with Dr. Ben-Ami, I knew it was useless. He wasn't going to talk to her any more than he would to me. My husband, who I thought was my soul mate, was trying to understand and accept the revelations of my heritage. The prejudices of his past were too strong. All of our hopes and dreams of a future together had been dashed. I was angry! What seemed like an ideal marriage to me turned to mud. I always looked at life through rose-colored glasses. It was hard to see things as they really were.

My favorite relative had a past that I learned about moments before she died. The family I thought I knew wasn't the same anymore. Just like when a window breaks when a rock hits it, what happened shattered my seemingly perfect life. My abuelita and my husband, the people I loved the most, were gone. My abuelita left this world, revealing a secret hidden for years. My husband walked out because of that. As I reflected on our marriage, I realized it was more than the Jewish issue. Other things didn't mesh. Jeremy decided he would focus on my being a descendent of Conversos. It would be easier for him to use that instead of the many other things that were wrong in our marriage.

Jeremy and I were not the perfect couple after all. So many questions came to mind. Why all the secrecy? Why should a little thing like my Jewish background make such a difference? Why couldn't Jeremy have adopted his father's accepting attitudes? Cameron wasn't thrilled about the Jewish revelation, but it didn't hit him like a ton of bricks. My husband and mother-in-law didn't even know a Jew but couldn't handle the knowledge that my ancestors long ago were Jews, buying into the scapegoat mentality. Anything wrong was the fault of the Jews.

I didn't think it at the time, but upon reflection, I realized that Kat's actions on that mountain were the best thing she could've done for me. Freed from my constant compulsion to gain her approval, I no longer struggled for her love, friendship, respect, and kindness. I knew deep down I would never get them. I had been consumed with how to win her over. Now I was free. I had seen her relaxing and laughing at the lodge. I no longer cared what she thought of me. For the first time in our relationship, I asked myself, *What do I feel about Kat? Do I like her? Do I respect her? Do I aspire to be her?* The answer to every one of these questions was a resounding "Hell no." Kat's behavior allowed me to finally look in the mirror and ask myself what I wanted from this relationship. I also did this with her son. Quickly, the divorce proceeded since there weren't any children. We were finally free of each other.

About a month after I signed my divorce papers, I got a call from Alice and Danny. Danny and Jeremy worked together at the bank. The four of us had become great friends, even taking a vacation together. They called to see how I was doing and felt I should know that they had received an invitation to a party Kat was giving. I could have lived without that knowledge. They were trying to be nice but really missed the mark. In big red letters, *Celebrate My Son's Freedom!* Kat was so excited about our divorce. I thanked my friends for their concern. I told them, "I don't care. I truly mean it." I looked up to the sky, laughing and grinning from ear to ear. *How does Abuelita do it?* She was right again. In life, you need the bitter and the sweet.

Now that my marriage was officially over, I needed to move on. I'd been in my condo for seven years. I had many happy and sad moments in that place. It was time for me to separate from my past. It was over. Time to create new memories—hopefully only happy ones. I had to get rid of many things that kept me in the past. I remembered how hard it was to give away my grandma's things. Nothing could compare with giving my own things away.

I stood in my living room, surveying everything I had, surprised by how much stuff I had accumulated over the years. I had to be organized and decided to separate things in three piles. One to keep, one to give to charity, and one to throw away. The plan worked except when it came to pictures. That's when the plan failed. I found myself pining over what was. It was time to put them aside. Maybe Consuela could help with that.

My little sister, Consuela, was my go-to person. The heart and soul of our family. I relied on her a lot. We spoke every Sunday and wrote letters to each other at least once a month for years, starting when I left for college. She comforted me during the living nightmare, especially during the last two years of my marriage. I told her about my plans to move closer to the beach, and she cheerfully informed me, "Julio, Marco, and I are going on a surprise sibling trip. We are flying in to help you move to your new place." So touched by the offer, I started to cry. My family came through for me. That's how we always were for each other—what a relief. I was not looking forward to the move, but I could endure it with my sister and brothers by my side. I was anxious to see them. The meeting at the airport was exceptional. I'd never felt such love for my siblings as I did at that moment. They had stopped what they were doing to help me. Feeling grateful, I decided we would have a memorable visit with lots of fun.

Having my sister and brothers with me in California was just what I needed. I must have suggested they move out west ten times during their visit. When they arrived at my door, armed with boxes, tape, markers, bubble wrap, and a rented truck, I was pleasantly surprised by their thoughtfulness. My amazing siblings quickly moved me out of my condo, helping me pack things up to give away to charity.

We worked all day, so we were pooped when we stopped. The first night in my new place, we were so tired we could barely move. I fell asleep on the floor, Consuela had the couch, and Julio fashioned a bed out of two chairs, one to sit on and the other for his legs. The only intelligent, comfortable member of our moving crew was Marco, who collapsed on my unmade bed. I told my sister, "He always knew how to make the best of a situation."

The next day, Consuela helped me organize my bathroom and closets. Julio stocked my kitchen with delicious junk food and healthy food since Abuelita taught us the importance of eating right. Marco took me shopping for everything else I needed, He told me, "Don't forget to get a trash can. Somehow it disappeared in the move."

Now that the packing and unpacking were complete, I got to play hostess and show them around my town. The first destination I took them to was Disneyland. Though we were adults, we immediately became kids and played all day in the land of make-believe, taking pictures to remember the time together. It was grand. I bought my sister and brothers Mickey Mouse hats as a memento of the time spent together, with their names engraved on the brims. The next day, we drove to see the handprints and footprints of famous people on the Hollywood Walk of Fame. We ran around to see the names of people we knew. Julio exclaimed, "Look how small Cary Grant's hands were and how large Charlton Heston's were." Mickey Mouse was the first animated character to get a star. Marilyn Monroe was a top hit. Seeing the stars of old with my sister and brothers was a ball.

On the trunk of my car, Marco wrote the words *wash me*. My vehicle was indeed filthy. Smiling, I motioned for them to come with me, and we proceeded to the automatic carwash. We all sat quietly in the car until it began to move inside. Instantly, we were all transported back to a fond childhood experience. We screamed, made strange noises, and sang as loud as possible. The critical part was no one heard us. When the car got off the rails, we stopped screaming. With a smile, Marco commented, "That was a lot of fun, reliving our childhood escape."

We had such a great time staying up late talking, watching movies, seeing the sights, overeating junk food, and sleeping only a few hours a night. There was just too much to do during their visit. I didn't think about Jeremy once, which surprised me. So preoccupied with my siblings, he never entered my mind. He had been my world not long ago. Without my family, this move would have been horrible. I thanked them all for helping me through a painful part of my life. I told them, "Your presence allowed me to begin my next steps in discovering who I am and our history."

Julio said, "It was a pleasure helping you out." Since my moving was complete, I could focus on looking into my family's history.

Now I felt ready to hunt for the truth. I had to know more. It was time to examine what my abuelita had been hiding. I took the box out again and stared for a while. What secrets lay within? I took a deep breath and opened it. Inside was a treasure trough of ancient memories.

A smile immediately came to my face as I looked through the pictures. There was a picture with writing on the back saying, *Maria, at ten years old, dressed for St. Ester's Day, March 1889.* I was amazed, never thinking of her as a young girl. She looked darling in her St. Ester Day costume. I saw another picture; a beautiful church showed Abuelita wearing her Sunday best. I saw a handwritten recipe for torrijas made with stale bread, eggs, milk, cinnamon, honey, and citrus. I closed my eyes and imagined my abuelita serving me this treat. She would remind me to include the secret ingredient, a dash of cardamom. I thought, *Yum. I can't wait to make it.*

Next, I began to read the labels on the tapes and stopped at the tapes labeled Estrella. The first tape I selected said, *Estrella part I.* Placing it in the tape player, I took another deep, long breath and pressed play. I asked myself the question. *What will I discover? What will I learn? Will I feel good or bad about what I hear?* I turned on the tape and listened.

9

MEETING MY ANCESTORS

Silently, we crept down the creaky, wooden cellar steps. We knew not to speak. We had done this before but never in the middle of the night. In the corner of the cellar, under boxes of books, was a small trapdoor. Under the door was an additional flight of rickety stairs that led to a second dank cellar room. Opening the heavy door, we could see our prayer room. In it was a table draped in velvet cloth, surrounded by chairs. On the table were old, worn books, written in our ancient language. Those who entered through the trapdoor began to fill the chairs slowly, yet some remained empty.

Many of the young members of our community were no longer there. They had gone to New Spain to find religious freedom. We missed them. My husband, Jose's favorite cousin, Pablo, decided to leave Spain for the New World ten years earlier after the devastating loss of his wife, Helena, and their daughter in childbirth. He vowed never to marry again. In his most recent letter given to us by courier, Pablo regaled us with tales of his adventures, success in business, and some freedom not experienced in Spain. He then encouraged us once again to join him. After reading the letter, Jose had a sparkle in his eyes. I knew this look meant my husband had an idea. Jose wrapped his arms around me and asked, "Is it time for us to leave Spain? Pablo has a new life in a new land without fear of the Inquisition. Estrella, wouldn't it be wonderful to light the Shabbat candles without hiding them?"

We were all taking a chance observing our honored traditions in the prayer room. We used the prayer room many times. Each time we went into the room, there was a possibility of exposure. In 1492, expelled from Spain, Jews decided to leave or stay hidden. It was a difficult decision my family had to make. They chose to stay. My ancestors struggled to live with their choice, living two different lives, one life as New Christians and another as secret Jews. It was a dangerous undertaking. If we practiced Judaism, we could fall prey to terrible punishments followed by tortuous deaths, which is why it had to be observed in secret.

I stopped the tape. There were more details I learned about the Inquisition. To eradicate Judaism from Spain was the goal. I read about tortures meted out to those who had returned to Judaism during the Inquisition in my history class in college. I never imagined any family members living through this fear. One was the *strappado* (pulley). The victim's arms and legs were strapped to weights and attached to ropes. Then the victims were raised and lowered, stretching them painfully to death.

Another form of torment was *toca* (water torture). Forced down their throats was a piece of linen. Water was poured into their mouth and nose, causing semisuffocation. The most common torture was the *port*, a system of tying the victim to a rack with rope continually tightening it. This method cut through skin and ultimately through bone. Many confessed when they heard the cracking of their bones followed by excruciating pain.

Those practicing Judaism secretly dealt with brutal punishments if discovered. Even those who were devout Catholics were suspected because their ancestors were Jewish. This knowledge terrified New Christians. Some were so traumatized by these stories they often had nightmares about being captured and tortured. I closed my eyes and shuddered when I thought about what people went through to practice their faith. These were punishments my ancestors faced. I returned to the tape recording.

The story continued.

We chose to lie to others outside our walls about our faith. We remained true to our faith, at least as much as possible in our home. When the expulsion began, my family started to build the prayer room, this place of worship, with their own hands—kept secret from our most trusted servants. Since the men were not craftsmen, the work was challenging and time-consuming. Little by little, it took shape. Our ancestors created the room with great effort, each generation adding beauty to it. The room was a treasure trove of ancient artifacts. There were two large, gilded menorahs (candelabras) on each side of the bimah (platform). A beautifully carved rosewood cabinet held the Torah scroll (the five books of Moses) exquisitely decorated cover with rich purple velvet embroidery. Above the cabinet was a tablet with hand-carved Hebrew letters that spelled out the words *dai leafnay me atah ohmed* (know before whom you stand). Each time I entered the prayer room, I was struck with awe at being in this secret place and fear of being discovered. I had the same feeling when I uttered, "Adonay es me Dio" (The Lord of Israel is my Lord). The synagogue walls had images from the Bible created by our family throughout the generations. High-backed chairs were upholstered with a floral pattern.

It was a place of great solace for Córdoba's wealthiest families, the Fuentes and the Gomez family. Once a city of great Jewish learning, it was the birthplace of one of the greatest rabbis, Moses Maimonides. People describe our city as the ornament of the world. Córdoba during the Middle Ages was the most exciting, prosperous, and enlightened city of its time. To the present day, the Great Mosque remains a monumental testament to the architecture of the Moslems, a testament to the most outstanding achievements of the time.

Jose, my dear husband, can trace his ancestry back to the expulsion of the Jews in AD (Anno Domini) 70 from Jerusalem. After destroying the Second Temple and the Jewish army, the Romans forced their captives to Spain and other places along the Mediterranean Sea. From the beginning, the Gomez family survived and prospered in Spain. They were involved with kings and nobles, always on the winning side. The dictates of the family crest are faith, family, future. We took pride in honoring our motto, though it was hard to live them because of the Inquisition.

What a painful time in my family's lives. I was mesmerized by what I heard on the audiotape. I had to stop the tape player and digest what I had just heard. Both my ancestor and I had to deal with heartbreak. Coming from a well-respected family, my ancestors enjoyed a prosperous life but feared the Inquisition. They had decided to stay in Spain, not leave like many of their co-religionists. It was a hard decision to make, but they felt they had to stay in Spain. Here they had position and wealth.

I had a flashback to my history class but could not remember the details as I was listening. I searched my closet, looking for my college box, where I kept some papers and notes from USC. With excitement, I thought, *Yes, I have it.* I was reading my notes from class when I saw that as many as three hundred thousand Jews may have left Spain, with many going to Portugal. They were welcomed there because of the money they brought. The Jew tax of eight ducats collected from each person filled the royal coffers. Things changed.

I was hooked and eager to know more. At the library, I discovered a section on Jewish history during this time. To solidify a claim to the Portuguese throne, King Manoel proposed marriage to Princess Isabella of Spain, the daughter of King Ferdinand and Queen Isabella. Princess Isabella accepted the proposal on the condition the king remove the Jews from Portugal. Though King Manoel did not want to lose the wealth and skills of the Jews, he promised the Spanish king he would banish the Jews from Portugal. In 1497, a mere five years after the expulsion from Spain, the Iberian Jews were forced to find new places to live or go underground. They spoke many languages and were involved in commerce. Aided by relatives in other countries, they flourished in the import and export business.

At the time, Spain was sending ships to the Americas. Columbus, though Italian, sailed for King Ferdinand and Queen Isabella of Spain. There were rumors that Columbus was a secret Jew, though little evidence proved true. Some felt that was the reason he had Conversos on his ships. Jews were expelled from Spain on the day Columbus sailed for the New World. It was another sad day for Jews.

Converso money built the shipping vessels to explore new lands. Destroyed by the Spaniards, the wealth of the Aztec Empire came to

Spain. Gold and silver were the rewards for the king and queen for their investment. Quelling the jealousies of others, the Conversos always helped the community. Whenever a new church bell was needed or new clothes for an orphan, the Conversos were there to help.

My ancestors generously gave money to those in need with open hands and hearts. The community knew whom to turn to for donations. The Jews felt that giving money kept everyone at ease in doing business. Otherwise, they thought they would have suffered.

I turned on the tape player once again. I needed to learn more about my family's history. Estrella talked about her son's Bar Mitzvah and the pride she felt when he told her, "Today, I am a man." Estrella Gomez's story continued.

My son, David, was a perfect child. He was perfect just because he was born alive. Jose and I tried to have children before David was born for five years. The thought of our three stillborn babies still stung our hearts when we allowed ourselves to think about them. I always dreamt of having a big home filled with the noise and laughter of many children. After each baby died, my heart ached so deeply that I thought I would never smile again. My husband, Maria, Francisco (my devoted servants), and charity work brought me back to life. David was not like any other children. He began life with a piercing wail that left everyone in attendance laughing and crying simultaneously. Whenever David wept, I had one of the servants pick him up immediately. We never wanted our child to be unhappy. We were so grateful to the Almighty for the gift of a healthy child that anything David wanted, he got. He was not spoiled, growing to be a sensitive, kindhearted young man. David felt a duty to make his parents proud because his siblings could not. He pleased his loving parents in the memory of the ones lost. When he saw someone in need, he would help. My son was secure and confident.

David had long, lean limbs and was almost as tall as his father. The young girls would giggle when David walked into a room, whispering to one another about how handsome he was—resembling his father with black, curly hair and blue eyes. He had my smile; it would light up a room when he entered.

Today was a special day. It was David's Bar Mitzvah, my only son. He stood, thirteen years old, in front of the table covered with a beautiful cloth. For the first time in front of the elders and our community, David felt many powerful emotions, nervousness, and pride. He uttered his first words in Hebrew, "Boruch atah Adoshem Elohanu Malech ha'olam ..." (Blessed are you, Lord, King of the universe ...). He was reciting the beginning prayers for his Bar Mitzvah.

It was hard hiding our faith. As the years went by, we observed fewer and fewer customs. However, one of our proudest traditions was celebrating a Jewish boy's acceptance into our faith. That is how David found out about our heritage. As his twelfth birthday approached, we told David about his heritage and explained that he would have a Bar Mitzvah. David prepared tirelessly to learn Hebrew with his uncle Xavier, my older brother, for the following year. Xavier learned Hebrew when he attended seminary school. As time went on, my son developed pride in his faith and proclaimed *l'dor v'dor* (from generation to generation). Nothing was allowed to interrupt our celebration, except the sound of the prayer room door opening unexpectedly. Everyone held their breath, fearing authorities were there to take us away. Those seconds waiting to see who would come through the door felt like an eternity. The door opened. Panic raced through our minds; ruination and death were facing us. Looking at the doorway, we didn't see anyone. Our eyes drifted down to see Valentina (my adopted daughter). Relief washed over us.

Valentina was a curious child. She crept down the stairs to investigate the musical sounds she heard because someone had left the trapdoor ajar. She was scared when she came upon the group in our hidden prayer room. We were shocked to have our veil of secrecy ripped away after all these years.

I quickly took Valentina's hand and escorted her back to her room. I put her back to sleep and kissed her forehead. She asked, "Did I do something wrong?" I assured her everything was fine. After David completed his readings, everyone praised him, and he went to bed a happy young man.

The elders stayed to discuss how easy it had been to discover our prayer room. They thought it was a sign from God to leave Spain for the New World, where we would be free to practice our faith. It was our turn to go. Jose conceded the point and told the community leaders he would like his most trusted servants, Maria and Francisco, to know their secret and join them on their journey.

The elders questioned the servants about leaving Spain. Francisco, our head servant, explained how kind and generous we were to him; he felt part of our family. He said, "It would be an honor to help them begin anew. We will go to New Spain with them."

One more detail. Words that hung in the air like a fog. They told our trusted servants that we were Jews. Waiting for Francisco's response, everyone was silent. He nodded and said, "I know." He told the elders he never said a word about it to anyone. When servants asked him why there was no cooking on Saturday, Francisco always had a reason. It was the same when candles were lit on Friday night, followed by me standing in front of them, swaying back and forth without saying a word. To the Christian eye, we had the strange custom of turning the picture of Jesus around to face the wall before lighting the candles, and we ate a cracker-like bread in the spring. Unlike other Spaniards, when someone died, we hurried to bury our dead within a day. We did not even have a prayer service that neighbors could attend. When church officials asked about the Gomez family's practices, Francisco had the servants promise not to tell, out of loyalty. I never told Francisco if he was right or wrong in his thoughts about our faith.

After listening to Francisco, any reservations by the older members of our family disappeared. The family, including Francisco and Maria, would follow the other explorers and find our way to New Spain. We talked about leaving, but now it was thrust upon us. Pablo was there to help us adjust to our new life. We would be free to practice our beloved religion. One of the pillars of our faith is charity, which I've always embraced. That is why Valentina is in our lives.

It has been two years since Valentina joined our family. It began one evening. Jose and I took a stroll and saw a dirty little girl hiding by a tree and peeking out to see if we were looking for her. Filthy with ragged clothes, I was compelled to help her. She touched my heart the second I laid eyes on her. She was too scared to speak to us but, in time, told her story. We learned that her parents died several months earlier, and the church had placed her in an orphanage. She ran away one evening after being beaten. A few days later, tired of living on her own, she went back to the orphanage and begged to return. The nuns slammed the door in her face. After this, the waif was back on her own, starving, cold, and frightened, until we saw her. We decided to take her home and care for her.

As Valentina began to tell us about herself a little more each day, we learned how many children were on the streets, on their own. It was terrifying to think about what faced them. The orphanages did a lot of good for the community, but it wasn't enough. There were also unforgivable acts of cruelty, like shutting Valentina out. Meals sometimes were taken away from the children who did not obey the rules. All this from a place meant to care for children. I knew we had to do something. Our family motto is faith, family, future. We had to abide by that. Jose promised to do something about the fate of these innocent children.

When we brought Valentina to our home, her eyes became as big as saucers; she had never seen such a large hacienda. She couldn't believe the grandeur. I asked the servants to set a place for her in the dining room. They were puzzled because the little girl was so filthy. They asked if I meant the kitchen. I smiled and told them that I wanted her in the dining room. I needed to make our little guest as comfortable as possible. Then I asked the servants to make up the room next to David's for her. I wondered if they could find a nightgown for the little one and prepare a hot bath. Tomorrow, I told them, we'd discuss having some clothes made for Valentina.

After quickly eating three full plates of food, I stopped feeding her. I felt she would get sick if she continued eating. The servants were in disbelief that this little girl could eat so much. I gave her a long, hot bath, cleaning away all of the dirt on her tiny body. Valentina was ready for bed. I showed her to her room, and she smiled and lay down on the floor. I told her the bed was for her and tucked her in. Valentina hadn't slept in a bed since her parents died. She was so frightened I couldn't bear to leave her. I sang her a lullaby until the little one fell asleep. A maid entered the room and told me she would stay with her so I could leave. I shook my head and motioned her away. Sitting on a rocking chair, I stayed with her all night.

I always felt sad that David didn't have brothers or sisters. When Valentina became part of our family, joy filled my heart. I loved watching my children play together. Bringing her into our lives gave us more than we could have given her. God had granted us this beloved child. It was my duty to help her in any way I could. One of the maids taught me how to braid her long, light brown hair, which I loved to do. I put a red bow in it since this color was on our family's crest.

Valentina was now eight years old and flourishing, learning to read and write. She was a well-behaved little one, always trying to please me. She wanted to make me happy, just as I liked pleasing my mother.

Since becoming a mother, my relationship with my own mother had become very close. I couldn't bear the thought of leaving Mama, perhaps forever. There was no consoling my mother. "Mija, don't leave me!" she screamed.

"I must," I answered. "Mamacita, we will get our community started, and then you and the others can come too." She cried out. Mama told me that she would not live that long because she was old and sick. I pleaded with her that it was not true, that we would be together soon.

I pleaded with the elders to allow us to stay. My father took me aside and said, "You must go to the New World. It is for you, our family, and our community." He promised to follow us soon. He said, "Our hopes and dreams are that our people will celebrate the religion of our fathers in a free land. Please do this for all of us."

Jose turned to Luis, his younger cousin, put his hands on his shoulders, and asked him to run the business since he had apprenticed with him for years. He told Luis he had faith in his abilities. Luis was nervous about taking on such an enormous responsibility, but the love and respect for his cousin made him accept the challenge. He wanted to make his older cousin proud of him. I asked Sophia, Luis's bride, to supervise the kitchen staff. She, too, felt she couldn't do the job as well as I did, but I convinced her that she would be fine. She had to find her way of doing things.

Again, I had to turn off the tape player. I could feel my ancestor's broken heart. How hard it must have been to leave everything behind. I continued to see Dr. Ben-Ami, my psychologist. She was trying to help me sort things out. Since she was Jewish and Israeli, I thought she would understand my new situation better than most. I learned that many Holocaust survivors had suffered from the brutality of war, were now living in Israel.

Some whose parents were Holocaust survivors from Europe or the Mediterranean decided to throw their Jewish religion out when they reached the American shores. They lamented, "It was too hard to be a Jew." They wanted an easier life for themselves and their children. Usually, their children discovered their past when there was a death in the family. Deceived by their family, they now had a stigma hanging over them like a cloud. Some had felt they were different from others all their lives. Dr. Ben-Ami had other patients who had recently discovered their Jewish past and needed help accepting it. I was unique because she never had a patient with a five-hundred-year-old secret. She helped others grapple with the new complexities of their lives. Some were adopted at birth and just found out that their birth parents were Jewish.

With the help of Dr. Ben-Ami, I began to understand that my marriage had many problems. There was a lot more than the Jewish revelation. My husband and I saw the world very differently. I am grateful my abuelita told me about our past because it allowed me to see Jeremy as he was, finally, not who I wanted him to be. We just didn't fit. The fights we had about my Jewish ancestors were not the only reasons we didn't get along. I had to hear what my ancestors were going through. I needed to know what would happen to them next. I was compelled to learn. I went back to the tape.

10

FAREWELL, ESPAÑA

Our decision to leave Spain made us pack hastily. The next ship was due to leave Cadiz in four weeks, and we needed time to pack our belongings and get there before the ship sailed. Since the days of the exodus from Egypt, our people could load our things up quickly and leave instantly. Amid happiness and sorrow, my family began to prepare for our trip to Cadiz. However, not everyone was happy with the decision for us to leave.

David took his grandmother's hand and led her to another room to comfort her. She cried on his shoulder, and he wept too. He had never been anywhere but Córdoba. Quietly, my mother gave David something bright, shiny, and heavy with a stone on top of it. David took it, smiled, then kissed his grandmother's hand. Her heart melted when she was with her favorite grandson.

The packing was supervised by Maria. It was time to leave for the journey of a lifetime. Saying farewell to family and friends was unbearable. Saying goodbye to España was impossible. It was our home. The land where three faiths had flourished during the Golden Age of Spain would no longer be ours. The place where Christianity, Islam, and Judaism made advances in all segments of life was not to be where we would bury our dead. It was heart-wrenching to see the pain in the faces of my family. I wished I could take away their pain instead of causing it.

It was hard for me to listen to that part. I cried when I heard about Estrella leaving her relatives since I had recently lost my dear abuelita. I remembered her saying we must experience the bitter to enjoy the sweet. I heard about my ancestors' painful experiences. Where was the sweet?

Before leaving, Jose had us all sit down to hear his plans for our departure. He spread out a map to show us where we would meet if any one of us got into trouble. Jose gently explained that we never knew what could happen on the road. He had several places on the maps to meet if we got in trouble or lost. He repeatedly told us we had to take care of each other. If anyone ever got separated, these designations were where we must go. We would wait for each other as long as it took to get together again. He spent hours going over the terrain and travel plans on the maps with the whole family. Everyone was involved. Everyone was clear on what they must do. Jose arranged for gems to be sewn into everyone's clothing, including little Valentina's.

Each of us received a map with marks showing where we would meet if something happened to anyone. Jose continued to practice what we would do if we became captured until we could say it in our sleep. He would ask us questions as if he was an interrogator. When everyone knew what to say if necessary, Jose felt satisfied. He smiled when he knew that we were all prepared.

The journey was difficult. Ruthless bandits patrolled the road to Cadiz. They were looking for people to rob and kill. As the first nightfall approached, we stopped at an inn. We retired to our rooms after dinner. I was terrified and didn't sleep, pacing the floor, worried about capture. We found our servants eating breakfast at the dining room table when morning dawned. We knew how loyal Francisco and Maria were, but fear consumed me. I was worried about getting to our destination safely. I expressed my gratitude to my faithful servants, who were surprised by my concern.

Francisco spoke on behalf of Maria and himself. "Dona Gomez, there is a Bible story about a woman named Ruth. She married a Hebrew killed in battle along with his brother and father. Ruth's mother-in-law, Naomi, having nowhere else to go, decided to return to the land of Israel, where her family lived. She was despondent when she had to say goodbye to Ruth and her other daughter-in-law, whom she had come to love. Ruth, refusing to leave Naomi's side, said to her loving mother-in-law, 'Wherever thou goest, I will go, wherever thou lodges, I will lodge, your people shall be my people and your God, my God.' My dear Dona, Christians believe that Ruth is our ancestor. She was an ancestor to King David, and he was the ancestor of our Lord, Jesus. I believe that I am Jewish too. Your people are my people. Jesus is our Lord, but he practiced your faith." The family was speechless.

I wondered why Francisco didn't tell us about this before. I inquired. He told me he forgot the story told to him so long ago. He continued that it came back to him in a dream the night before. Maria quickly added that she was loyal to our family as well. She felt so welcomed in my home that the children were her children. "I would do anything for any of you."

Maria came to work for my family at fifteen, and I turned a year old. Maria was lovingly cared for by her grandmother after her parents died. Sadly, at fourteen, her grandmother also passed away. After that, she was on her own, finding work at a pub, living in the basement in a small room no bigger than a closet. Men would always grab her, touching her body and pulling her on their laps. One evening, a knife fell out of someone's coat. She quickly walked over and kicked it under a table. Once the pub was empty, she retrieved the knife and kept it for herself. From that point forward, she always carried the sharp blade with her. Sleeping with it under her pillow brought her comfort. She felt she had a fighting chance to survive an attack. That is just what happened. One evening while throwing the trash out, a drunk man grabbed her. Maria quickly retrieved her knife, pressing it on the man's throat, ordering him to let go of her. The stranger stumbled back, feeling his throat. After seeing blood on his hand, he ran away. Francisco witnessed this and ran to see if she was all right. Maria, still very shaken, held out the knife and told him not to come any closer. Francisco stopped, putting his hands up, telling her he was only checking to see if she was all right. Yelling at him to leave, she told him she could take care of herself. Surprised by her actions, he left. His life was very different from Maria's.

Francisco grew up at my family's estate. He came from a long line of mayordomos (heads of the household). He spent his whole life watching and learning from his father about managing a large staff for a powerful family. Fun was not a part of Francisco's life growing up. His father taught him that service to the master came before anything else. Francisco knew that our estate was looking for a scullery maid and asked his father if they would consider a girl who worked in a pub. With some convincing, his father allowed the young woman to come in and discuss working for the family.

Along with the head cook, Señora Herrera and Francisco went to the pub to find the young girl. They approached Maria, who was hesitant to speak to them. Señora Herrera knew how to talk to young girls. She explained that working for the family could give her a safer life. Maria longed for safety. She agreed to speak to the mayordomo. As they were heading to the estate, Señora Herrera and Francisco told Maria who she would talk to and how to present herself. Before meeting with the mayordomo, Señora Herrera brushed her hair and wiped the dirt off her face. Señora Herrera found a clean dress for Maria to wear and looked her over to see if she was presentable for the meeting. Giving her a big smile, the señora told Maria she would do a good job. Maria was nervous but spoke clearly to the mayordomo, immediately making a good impression. So thrilled, she had to tell Señora Herrera.

Maria ran back to the kitchen to find Señora Herrera to share the good news. She told her excitedly, "I got the job." Señora Herrera gave her a big hug and had one of the scullery maids show her where she would be sleeping. In time, Maria felt safe and developed a close bond with Señora Herrera, who taught her how to cook. The two became family. Maria was the child, and Señora Herrera was the mother teaching her everything she knew. Since her grandma died, Maria hadn't felt at peace. She was happy to have a home again.

While working, scrubbing the floor, Francisco would pass by Maria, always smiling and greeting her. She responded cheerfully back to him. Several days passed without Francisco smiling and saying hello as he walked passed her. Maria realized she looked forward to seeing him each day.

When I was little, I played near Maria, cleaning the floor. I stumbled, fell, and began to cry. Maria ran over to soothe me. "Don't cry, little one. Maria is here for you." From that day on, I never wanted to let Maria

Ellie Gersten

go. I always asked for her. I loved Maria because of her sweet-sounding voice that matched her good-natured attitude. Before long, she was my nurse, who loved to teach me dances, like the flamenco from her gypsy culture. We would raise our arms to the sky, clicking our castanets and stomping our feet. She taught me many things like climbing trees and swinging upside down. My days were full of adventure and fun. I told Maria, "I love you." I relied on her.

One day, Maria asked me, "Would you like me to teach you how to skip rocks by our creek?" I wanted to learn and begged Mama to let us go. She allowed us, providing Francisco escorted us. Señora Herrera made some food for us to enjoy. After eating, I got up to look at the butterflies flying in the air.

Giggling the whole time, I began to chase them, laughing. I caught a beautiful, bright yellow butterfly. I was thrilled. Wanting to protect it, I clutched it in my hands, ready to show Maria her gift. I opened my hands, giving the butterfly to her. She took it, smiled, and thanked me. Maria pointed out some pretty daisies. She said, "Please pick some for Mama." I later found out that the butterfly I gave Maria died. I accidentally killed it by clasping it in my hands. When Maria took the butterfly, she buried it. She didn't want me to know what I did. She knew I'd feel guilty that I crushed it. When I found out what I had done, I felt bad.

Maria and Francisco discovered they had many things in common, even though physically they looked very different. Francisco was fair, tall, and skinny. Maria was dark, short, and plump. He took great pleasure in tasting her food before she was ready to serve it. Maria would always say, "Francisco, no, no, no. It's not ready."

Francisco would answer, "I love tasting the food you make."

When Francisco walked, he did so with a strong, purposeful stride, back straight, and his head held high. On the other hand, Maria looked down when she walked, with rounded shoulders. They loved to take strolls together in the evening. When I was a little girl, I had the pleasure of joining them. We had many days by the creek together. It was that spirit of fun and adventure that attracted Francisco to Maria. He said, "I have never seen a woman behave as you do." They enjoyed being with each other. A friendship soon developed into love. My insistence on learning how to skip rocks got them together. They married at our estate. I made a bouquet of wildflowers for the bride, my wonderful Maria.

Listening to that part of the tape made me appreciate Francisco and Maria. They truly loved my family. I now understood why they took such a dangerous journey with Estrella and her family. They were all devoted to one another. I was eager to learn more about their travels.

The tape said that my family spent the day traveling ...

We were exhausted by midday because of the heat and decided to find an inn as quickly as possible. We found a place, rented rooms, and went to the dining room for dinner. In the dining room, we saw some sinister-looking men—Captain Rodriquez, with members of his army dressed in uniforms at the table. The captain kept looking suspiciously at Francisco. We ate dinner in silent reflection. After dinner, we retired to our rooms. Again, I had a troubling night. I dreamt of being captured and tortured by the authorities. They wanted me to give up my jewels, but I refused. Needing our gems to secure our future, I couldn't surrender them. Even the light of a new day could not ease my mind. I felt being caught was inevitable.

I needed to think about what I had just heard. My ancestor Estrella suffered nightmares as I did. We had so much in common.

I went back to the audiotape ...

I heard a scuffle in the hallway. The soldiers were beating Francisco. I began to cry. I left my room to investigate and saw Francisco taken away. I shouted at the guards to let him go. They turned and grabbed me. I yelled for them to let go of me, but they ignored me. Maria had wisely snuck back to her room to alert Jose about what had happened. Maria quickly ran to tell him.

I knew I needed a plan. Greed! I thought it would work if I bribed the captain with my pin. *I will tell the captain we are going to visit relatives for a wedding celebration, and he will get a token of my appreciation for expediting our release.* I decided I would give him the beautiful sapphire pin I was wearing. This pin had been in my family for hundreds of years. I wanted freedom at any cost.

The captain was a large man with an even-shaped mustache on the top of his entire upper lip. He was strikingly handsome and fit. His uniform was clean, and there was no smell of garlic and onions, like most people, because he disliked them. They upset his stomach. As for being well kept, he never liked being dirty. He was always neat and clean.

Much to my dismay, the captain wanted more than the sapphire to release my servant and me. He looked at the ring on my finger and said that he wanted that too. It was a bright, round ruby that I had received from my mother. The captain had one of his men yank the ring from my finger after I refused to give it to him. Smirking, he said, "Now it is mine." The behavior was appalling, and I was outraged by his disrespect. I had never experienced being so mistreated. I wanted to slap him across the face but thought I'd better not. I didn't know what the captain would do if I smacked him, so I did nothing.

I thought, *I must keep my composure! My beloved Francisco needs my help.* Since I was a child, he had loved and cared for Maria and me. The captain immediately released us after stealing the jewels. We returned to the inn, where the rest of our party was relieved to see us. The inn was one of the safe places on our map. As we packed, we thanked the Lord of Israel for our redemption.

Quickly, we left the region. We wanted as much space from that horrible experience as possible. We met our group at the inn, just like we had planned if detained.

Meanwhile, the captain was looking over his new prizes. The stones were magnificent. He studied the inside of the ring. Squinting, the captain looked at the ring again.

He saw that the inscription was in Hebrew. He knew Hebrew because he had studied to be a priest when he was young. "Oh, Dios (Oh God). Los Judios (The Jews)." He called for all his men to mount their horses and follow him. As we were crossing the river to safety, we heard the galloping of horses. My horse got stuck in the mud. I ordered Francisco to go ahead and tell Jose what had happened. I said I would meet all of them in Cadiz. "Please take care of the children." Jose turned his horse around when he heard the news, ready to go back for me. Then Francisco gently reminded him about my request to go forward. Jose reluctantly agreed. He feared for my safety.

I kept trying to get my horse out of the mud. I got off my horse and tried to lift one of its hooves to release it from the muck. I wasn't able to do that. I got back on my horse, waiting for the Captain to come.

I felt terrible for my poor family despairing over my inevitable capture. They proceeded to Cadiz with sadness in their hearts, for they were leaving me behind. Meanwhile, I began thinking of what to tell Captain Rodriquez. Slowly, he approached me with his men. I spoke to him, saying that we were meeting again. He said, "I didn't know that you are a Jew."

I said, "All I want is to get to Cadiz safely with my family. How can this happen? Then we will be on the ship to New Spain."

The greedy captain said, "I need you to give me all your gems." Pleading with him, I told the captain I had nothing with me, but if he took me to the ship, I would give my jewels to him. The captain agreed. So we left for Cadiz. We rode silently to the boat.

As we approached the port where Jose waited, I could see that my husband was outraged that the captain had captured me; he was stomping his feet angrily, back and forth on the road. Jose was furious! He did not like to see me as a captive. He shouted to the captain, "All I want is my wife! I'll give you what you want if you let her go." Then my husband asked Maria to pull the gemstones from the hem of her skirt and put them into a leather pouch. Maria kept a few jewels in her hem. Jose told Maria that we could not be without any wealth. For our new life, gems were needed.

The captain spat and pushed me toward Jose, calling out to me, "You filthy Marrano" (a derogatory term for the Conversos, meaning pig). I saw waves of joy and relief on their faces; they were exhausted by the ordeal of saving me. We boarded the ship called the *Santa Inés*. Jose threw the leather pouch to the captain. We could sail to the New World safely on board in peace. Or could we?

As I listened to the story, my love of research started to kick in. I needed to know more. I went to the library and devoured facts about

Spain during the Inquisition. I learned that this trip from Córdoba to Cadiz was usually a seven- to ten-day journey by carriage. They would have time to spare if everything went as planned before the ship sailed. The road to Cadiz was well maintained. The Romans built it, and the Moors made improvements. As a route to the port city of Cadiz, it was essential to have a well-constructed road. It was a busy port, and they needed a well-maintained road to get there.

I thought about the terrible situation my ancestors faced. I also imagined the fantastic sight before them as they approached the harbor in Cadiz—struck by the grandeur of a flotilla (a convoy of ships), the one hundred vessels set to sail. There were caravels and heavily armed galleons (ships that accompanied the convoy). In addition, there were supply ships. The lead ship was the *capitana*, or flagship, and the *admiranta* was the vice-flagship. Usually, the fleet would leave from Cadiz and sail along the coast of Africa until they came to the Cape Verde Islands. The convoy would split into two groups when they arrived in the Caribbean. One group was the Nueva España Floata, which went to New Spain, and the other, the Tierra Firme Floata, went to South America. I wondered if they could appreciate the magnificent sight after going through the difficulty of the kidnapping.

11

TO THE NEW LAND

Sailing to a life of newfound freedom felt exhilarating. We stood on the deck, facing the setting sun, smiling for the first time in weeks. We were ready to embrace life in a new land. Our sleeping quarters for the family were terrible, with rats scurrying around. The only safe place for us was the deck with the other families. A curtain separated each family. The conditions were appalling. I found relief by transporting myself someplace else in my mind. My thoughts were of happier times, beginning with meeting Jose. Thank God I had more joyful memories to focus on rather than the dreadful voyage.

I met Jose when I was fifteen years old, thinking he was handsome with his dark, wavy hair, deep blue eyes, and quick smile, especially when he looked at me. Our families were close friends, having picnicked together in the fields on the outskirts of Córdoba. Jose had always liked me, but I was timid around boys. I hid behind a tree and peeked out to see Jose looking for me. It became a game. I hid from him, and he hid from me. I loved it. We would laugh together about our little game.

The elders discussed with my parents and Jose's parents that we should wed. Everyone agreed before Jose and I even knew about the marriage. When my father told me I would marry Jose, I told him that he was too short for me! Mama explained that Jose was from the right family and shared the same beliefs. "This marriage is your duty. It's final!"

I cried myself to sleep that night and many other nights, but I could not dissuade my parents. One day, Jose came to our home to speak to me about my reluctance to marry him. My intended explained that this marriage was our duty to our community. Jose promised to be a good husband. Furthermore, he told me we would learn to love each other. We would make each other happy. Then Jose said what I longed to hear, "Will you marry me?" I told him I would marry him. I needed him to ask me, knowing he would be a wonderful husband. I also requested that Maria and Francisco come with us to our new home. "If they agree, will they be welcomed?" Jose would ask them together with me.

Seated at the dinner table, I asked my parents if they would allow Maria and Francisco to join my staff in my new home next to theirs. My papa said that would be fine. Both Jose and I invited Maria and Francisco to take a walk by the creek. I reminisced about the things we used to do when I was young and how much fun I had with them. I asked if they would join me as I began my new life as the lady of my own house. Without hesitation, they agreed. In one year, I would be married. There were many beautiful parties and celebrations. Maria and Francisco were busy training their replacements.

The wedding was magnificent. Everyone said it was the grandest fiesta of all time. The dignitaries of Córdoba were in attendance. I wore a beautiful gown embellished with jewels. On my head was a white mantilla. We had wine from Rioja, quail from the countryside, and fresh fruit and vegetables from southern Spain. Flowers, flowers from everywhere. I was excited by all of the attention I received. It was as if I was a queen, with Jose as my king. Our family priest, Father Diego, married us in the cathedral.

In addition to this grand celebration, there was another private ceremony under the chuppah (wedding canopy) in our hidden prayer room. Conversos were the only guests. We made sure to include our vows following Moses and Israel's laws. We recited words of love to each other. They were "Ahnei Dodi v'dodi lei" (I am my beloved, and my beloved is mine). Jose sipped some wine; I did the same. Placed under Jose's foot was a glass to commemorate the destruction of the Jewish Temples in Jerusalem. My husband smashed the cup with all of his might, making a loud shattering sound. All of the guests stood up and yelled, "Mazel Tov!" My parents presented us with a solid gold mezuzah about four inches long, with a large diamond mounted in the middle. We would place it on the doorpost of our new prayer room. Now it was time for my husband to go back to work grooming another member of our family for the vital position of head of the import-export business. That was the way people in his family learned how to run their company.

Jose had watched and absorbed the art of negotiating business deals from his father and uncles since he was a little boy. They had a traditional of bringing in relatives to run the family business. Our newly married cousin, Luis Gomez from Toledo, was selected to be an apprentice for Jose. He would visit and follow his older cousin Jose everywhere he went for years. Jose jokingly called him his shadow. Once again, Luis followed Jose, this time to learn the business. Now Luis would be living at the estate, learning from Jose every day. My husband was the perfect person to teach Luis. He understood how to be successful in business; he always said you must know what your customer wants. Jose had a great mind for business. He was a skilled negotiator, knew his product, and said just enough to make the sale. Listening more and talking less was his mantra. He wrote down facts about merchants, like the names of their wives, how many children they had, and anything they said to make the sale. He was an excellent notetaker. Jose was patient and encouraging with Luis, who learned the trade quickly. He would be a great leader.

What made Jose so successful was his attention to detail. At least once a month, he hosted customers for dinner. It was there they enjoyed spices from around the world. Before starting this business, Jose knew nothing about food and wine. He quickly became an authority in selling his products and making the merchants happy through his monthly dinner of the best quality food and wine. To help local vendors sell their goods, he invited them to our home for his customers to sample their products, such as oils, olives, and sherry wines.

Being a successful businessman, he financed shipping vessels as other Conversos had done before. The repayment for his investment was a percentage of the profit from the shipments going to New Spain and returning. The stakes were high, and the rewards were great. He doubled his family's fortune with his great intellect and winning ways.

Jose needed to pass the business on to someone responsible, and he chose Luis as his successor.

Cousin Luis was proud to show off his new bride to his family, Sofía, who would learn to run a large estate from me. I was happy to take on the task but found it challenging. We were very different women. Sofia had little sympathy for those less privileged than she. Over the next few days, I saw how badly she interacted with my staff. I wondered how I could show my new family member how to treat people with kindness. We took a coach to the convent the following day, where we greeted Mother Superior, who encouraged us to walk around the grounds. She wanted us to speak with anyone we wished. I introduced Sofía to Grace. With her children, she had recently arrived. There were horrific black and blue bruises all over their bodies.

Grace's face became distorted from the constant beating. Once a lovely young woman, she no longer was attractive, looking much older than her thirty-five years. Seeing this upset Sofía. It distressed her. On the carriage ride home, Sofía was quiet. She had never seen a woman beaten before. I could see she was sad. I began talking to her and reminded her we could have ended up this way. We were born into wealthy families that arranged for us to marry kind men. Grace wasn't as lucky. I told Sophia that she needed to be thankful for her life. Being charitable had changed my life. I hoped it would change hers. One of the many honors is to help those in need. Being generous had made me a better person, wife, and mother. I told her, "Jose taught me the benefits of helping others, and I showed him how to have more fun."

After we got married, Jose started to act differently. His outlook on life was very positive, and he smiled more. I began the day by jumping up and down on our bed to wake him, making him laugh. I loved it when I heard him say, "My life would be empty without you, the keeper of my heart." He would follow that by saying, "You are more beautiful than the stars in the sky."

While he dressed for work, I dressed for riding. I always made sure to look my best. For my eyes, I used charcoal to line my lids and darken my lashes, which was a fantastic trick to make my eyes appear more prominent. I powdered my lips and high cheekbones with red vermilion Jose got for me from India. Jose loved the way I looked. He loved everything about me—my eyes, laugh, smells, olive skin, and body. Riding was my favorite activity, and I began my day doing that.

People said I was the finest horsewoman in the country. At an early age, I loved riding and caring for horses. I went riding every day and developed a sense of what my horses needed. I developed a sense of what my horses needed. I lovingly brushed their manes, fed them carrots, rubbed their back, and spoke to them. Each time I entered the stable, the first thing I heard was the panting of the dogs, followed by the wagging of their tails. Then the horses would whinny, welcoming me. I loved going to the stable. My horse was ready for me to ride, so I quickly mounted him for my venture around the countryside. I felt free riding.

While galloping on my favorite horse, Blanco, the wind whipped my hair about in the early morning. Long and flowing, it bounced around when I rode my powerful white stallion. As I walked back from the stables, I passed the courtyard, marveling at the rectangular pond and hearing the water splashing from the fountain—one of my favorite places to lie down and read poetry. It was the most relaxing place on the property. I loved being the best horsewoman, and Jose loved it too.

I had the perfect husband for my ways; any other man would have made me feel trapped.

In Spanish society, husbands regularly beat their wives. I helped women who were in terrible marriages. There were many. When I found a woman mistreated, I arranged with the nearby convent to take the woman and children in to be cared for by the nuns. I also paid for them to go to another town where the woman could start a new life as a servant in a wealthy household without fear of being hurt. Jose encouraged my acts of charity.

To help me deal with the horror of the voyage, I transported myself to a happier place. It didn't last long. My daydream ended with a large splash of seawater on my face, with the taste of saltwater on my lips. I quickly snapped out of my fantasy world and was back to being on that dreadful ship.

There were stories of the New World spread among the passengers on the voyage. Who knew if they were true? I didn't want to hear the tales. I had no choice. The Garcia family heard about cheap land in New Spain and the northern territory. There were other stories as well. The Gonzalez family heard of wild Indians who captured women and enslaved them. Another tale told by the passengers was that the Indians scalped white people. The Indians saved the scalps as trophies. It sounded dreadful.

I laughed when I heard these stories and found it hard to get involved with the speculative chatter. Within the next few months, we would know the truth. I just wasn't feeling well. My stomach had been upset since we left Cadiz two weeks ago. I couldn't seem to keep food down. The salt air made it worse. There was water, water everywhere, day in and day out. All those aboard were craving land, any kind of land.

The voyage was tedious. The only planned activities were worship services and an occasional songfest. Sometimes there were cockfights and simulated bullfights to relieve the monotony. Many travelers brought books with them. We learned a lot about Judaism by reading Catholic accounts of the Old Testament found in religious texts on the ship.

As the days passed, David seemed to grow. A little over two weeks ago, he celebrated his Bar Mitzvah at thirteen in our hidden sanctuary in our Córdoba home. Now he was a seasoned passenger on a seagoing vessel to New Spain. Things had changed quickly.

The younger generation wasn't affected by their watery surroundings at first. The little children on board loved to be with David and Valentina. My children worked well together, keeping the little ones occupied. Parents were happy when they saw them involved with their little flock. My children made up silly games for the little ones to play. They played jacks with bones, leapfrog, tag, and their favorite, hide-and-seek. At times, David and Valentina had the children pretend they were monsters or ghosts. If the children made too much noise, disturbing the adults, they made up a quiet game. Mostly, David and Valentina played make-believe with the children. They were pirates at sea, teachers and students, and soldiers in the Spanish army. They would take a blanket and rope, make a tent-like structure, and then tell scary stories. David and Valentina were at their service whenever the children wanted to play.

As lovely as it was to see the children happy, the ocean voyage was horrendous, replete with scurvy, diarrhea, and lice. Maggot-laced food meant there was little to eat. The smells were awful. Not only were there the strong, foul bodily odors, but clouding our noses were the rancid smells of spoiled food. We often wrapped rags over our faces to reduce the stink. It was a miracle that we didn't get sick. Francisco and Maria took good care of us, fortunate as we were to have them.

Francisco was more than just a servant. He was a friend—a father. Francisco, my loyal servant, stayed very close to me. He had tended to my needs since I was a baby. No one knew me as well as Francisco, except Maria. When I fell off a horse for the first time, he was there to bandage me and quickly help me back on the horse. When I argued with my Mama, Francisco knew how to calm me down. He would tell me stories, not scold me when I was wrong. By the time the story ended, I would apologize to Mama. Always a lesson learned.

I needed to reflect upon all that my ancestors had to go through in order to get to the New World, so I stopped the tape once more. I concluded that I had many things in common with my ancestor Estrella. Just as she had someone calm her down, I had my abuelita. I looked in the encyclopedia to learn more about travel by ship in the sixteenth century. It was not surprising to know that sailing to the New World was uncomfortable. The vessel was a caravel, a small craft used by Spanish and Portuguese explorers. It carried supplies, such as nails and hammers used in construction, a church bell, and stylish clothing from Spain for the new residents. The ship had beautifully colored birds, monkeys, and other exotic animals not found in the Old World on the return trip to Spain. They also brought back precious metals. The vessel measured only ninety-six feet long, with a seventy-square-foot deck area. Everyone except the captain and senior crew slept on the deck because sleeping in the hold meant battling rats.

The tape said that everyone huddled together at night, wearing all the clothing and blankets they had brought. Despite that, they were still cold. The weather was brutal. The wind blew hard, especially at night. After many weeks at sea, everyone was tired, dirty, and eager for the journey's end. Though the *Santa Inez* was a small vessel, it navigated very well in the open sea. Even in a spring storm, the ship held up to the elements, the fierce winds, and the high waves.

My ancestor Estrella said that the trip was arduous. She had never been on an ocean voyage and didn't know what to expect. She might have rethought going if she knew how hard it would be. It was the same for the other passengers. The constant choppy, rolling water and the lack of sanitation on board were challenging to handle. A bucket was used for the elimination and thrown overboard into the ocean. Boys and men would pee through a hole in the ship's side. Only enough water was available to drink or cook. No one washed. Longing to be clean, this bothered all of the passengers.

I pressed the start button on the tape recorder again, looking forward to hearing what my ancestor was experiencing.

I knew Jose found it hard to concentrate on anything other than securing a future for our family. He wrote notes whenever he had an idea. Unable to sit still, he constantly walked around the ship. With most of our gems gone, there was little left of our fortune, which worried him all the time. He was sure that things would work out but was fearful until they did.

My Jose was unaware that David had something from his grandmother to help provide for our future. My son did not want to disclose that he had something valuable with him until he knew he could speak to his father privately. Finally, he told his dad that he had the gold mezuzah with a large stone, thinking it was a diamond. It probably would have helped Jose understand that money was not a concern. David had good instincts and felt it was not the right time to tell his papa since he didn't trust the captain and the crew.

Our ship's Captain Hernandez was a tall man with long gray hair pulled back and tied with a black ribbon. His face was wrinkled from long years of exposure to the wind and rain on the open sea. He had a large, muscular body with many scars on his face. Disagreeing with this man would be a detriment. We listened and did what he told us to do.

The captain and his men, all experienced sailors, had crossed the ocean many times. They encountered pirates on occasion and defeated them. No opponent was strong enough to overpower the crew of the *Santa Inez*. Captain Hernandez's reputation was so frightening that ships turned back and left it alone when a pirate's ship came close enough to read the vessel's name—until the day he saw a boat he didn't recognize.

12

TROUBLE ON THE HORIZON

When Captain Hernandez saw a ship on the horizon, he was curious about the vessel's name and its country of origin. He couldn't make out the country of origin on the flag because the ship was too far away. For the first time in his life, the captain could not decide instantly what action to take. He had two choices. He could fire cannons at the ship. The challenge with this plan was it could provoke an unnecessary fight, especially if the vessel meant no harm. Or he could continue sailing and avoid the ship. The issue with that plan was his craft was not as fast as others, which meant it was likely to be overtaken if it was a pirate ship. Both ideas were risky. For the safety of the passengers, he chose the latter move, which was a mistake.

The shipping vessel headed toward us was a galleon. like ours made to carry passengers and goods. Unfortunately, it brought neither. It was full of heavily armed pirates. It came closer and closer to the *Santa Inez*. Captain Hernandez was still unable to make out the ship's name even as he squinted his eyes to focus more clearly. He said, "Who are these people? What do they want from us?" He needed to decide if he should let the ship overtake them or fight quickly for his passengers' lives. The vessel was approaching swiftly.

What a relief, the boat was flying a Spanish flag, but in reality, it was a pirate ship. Many pirate captains of his ilk deceived others by raising their country's flag. Usually, our boat would have fired some cannons to scare the pirate ship away, but it got too close. The boat got so close that the pirate captain could board our vessel by jumping on our craft.

The pirate ship was enormous and under the control of the tempestuous Captain Benventura, a powerful-looking man—tall and muscular with deep blue eyes and a quick smile, whose long black hair shimmered in the sunlight. "Who is the captain?" he yelled. "Let him show his face."

Diego Hernandez hollered back, "I am here."

Captain Hernandez was a man of action and an experienced fighter. He ordered his men to board the pirate ship to keep the fighting away from the passengers. The sailors fought well. Praying to Saint Christopher, the protector of travelers, we gathered together, frightened and trembling. No sooner had we finished our prayers than the fighting stopped. Our prayers went unanswered. We lost three men from our ship, with the rest of our sailors injured. Now the enemy was boarding our vessel. We knew something terrible was about to happen.

When David and Valentina saw the pirate captain take over their ship, they quickly hid. David hoisted Valentina into a barrel. He whispered for her to be quiet. David hid behind the barrel. My little daughter pressed her eye into the knothole to see what was happening. She covered her mouth to muffle the sound of her cries. They both saw the massacre of some of our crew, praying to help them calm themselves. They did not leave their hiding place until the fighting stopped, and then they ran over to our family. They hid behind me so they couldn't see the fearsome pirate captain.

Strutting like a rooster, Captain Benventura surveyed his captives. The women hid behind the men. The pirate captain viewed the women with his leering eyes and pulled them out away from their families with groping hands. He selected my Maria as his conquest. He dragged her kicking and screaming by her hair to Captain Hernandez's cabin, the size of a closet with a door. We were frightened, knowing that death would await us if we fought. Maria began to scream out in pain. My eyes began to fill with tears as I searched for Francisco. Once our eyes met, I could see the same horror I was feeling on his face. Francisco could do nothing to save her. Captain Benventura laughed, relishing the sound of her pain. Maria's discomfort and degradation delighted the captain.

Upon her return to us, we saw rips in her clothing and bruises all over her body. Sobbing, she slowly crept to a corner, vomited, and sat down. I crawled to her and put my arms around her for comfort. My heart was breaking for her. The pirate captain looked down at me, then said, "You are next." My body began to tremble. I was petrified.

It must have been difficult for Francisco and the others to see Maria that way. What were they to do? The fear of rape and worse looming, they had to take the ship from the pirates. I thought, *Where is our captain? We need him now.*

Captain Hernandez had been knocked unconscious into the cargo bay. When he awoke, with his men massacred or injured, he decided that he needed to keep hiding. He was not a coward; he had a plan.

Diego Hernandez was an orphan from Seville, a town not far from Córdoba. His upbringing was rigorous. Sisters of Mercy had no mercy for the children who were wards of the church. Diego snuck out of the orphanage with the other boys to steal food from the local merchants. The boys had little food to eat at the orphanage. Invariably, the orphans got caught stealing and beaten with a switch. Even getting extra chores to do and many rosaries to recite, they continued their lousy behavior. After years of beatings and thieving, the sisters cast them aside. Thrown out of the orphanage at nine, Diego had to fend for himself. After years of stealing and dodging authority, this was easy for him. He knew how to survive.

Our captain found himself in a survival situation after the pirates took his ship. The captain had a plan to recover his vessel at this critical moment. He whispered to one of the children to tell me to meet him in the cargo hold. Carefully, I crept down the stairs. He pleaded with me, telling me that he needed my help to get his ship back.

Puzzled, I asked him how I could help. He instructed me to lure Captain Benventura to this side of the ship, next to the cargo door. "Once he is there, signal me. I'll take care of the rest."

Walking around the ship, I met with the other passengers and told them about the plan. We all prayed for spiritual guidance during this time of great need. We came up with the idea that we would start a fight among ourselves. Francisco would start the brawl. The women came to get Captain Benventura who was disoriented from drinking whiskey the night before. Shaken out of a deep sleep, he headed toward the fight.

I signaled Captain Hernandez, who opened the cargo hold, and he captured the pirate captain. All of this happened so quickly that the pirate crew could not understand what was happening. It seemed to be taking place in slow motion. I remember seeing one of the pirates moving his hand toward his sword, only to have it smacked away by the first mate. After that, he was punched unconscious. Another pirate grabbed a young boy and held a knife to his throat. Two passengers threw a barrel. I watched in shock as the barrel moved through the air, hitting the pirate in the head, killing him. He fell to the floor as blood slowly seeped from his head.

After the captain took his ship back, Francisco tried to tie the pirate captain's hands. The captain began to fight with Francisco and was about to kill him when Maria took a knife and shoved it into Captain Benvenuto's stomach. Maria shouted, "This is for you, you monster!" The captain grabbed his stomach, looked at his hand, and saw the blood gushing. He fell backward, crying out in anguish on the floor, and died. Francisco threw his body into the ocean. We were all happy to get rid of that dreadful pirate.

The rest of the pirate crew set sail in a rowboat. Their survival was doubtful, but there was a chance they would make it to shore alive. We left the pirate ship to wander the seas, becoming a famous ghost ship.

Injured, the surviving crew needed help to manage the ship. It was up to the passengers. Francisco and Jose helped Captain Hernandez and the others. In the meantime, I was having more difficulty keeping food down and was always tired. I knew something was wrong with me. At last, I realized I was having a baby. I thought I was probably six weeks into my condition. How glorious! What a blessing; another child would grace our lives. How awful! I didn't look forward to having a baby during a sea voyage.

The passengers were very excited about the news of my baby. Even Captain Hernandez was happy for me. He insisted on giving me the first mate's room for the remainder of the trip. Thankfully, since his room was on a different part of the boat, there were no rats. Not that the place was anything much, but it shielded me from the elements and gave me a little privacy. Most nights, Jose was a great comfort to me. My only love, Jose, hovered over me as though he was the mother of a newborn baby. We had time together during the rocky, sleepless nights at sea. When we first left Spain, the plan was to arrive in the New World, then find safe travel to Santa Fe with cousin Pablo. Luckily, cousin Pablo would be in Veracruz for business when we arrived. Our plan changed. We were so excited to have a healthy baby and decided it would be best for Jose to go on to Santa Fe without the family. He would find a new business and begin building our new home. While Jose was away, David, Valentina, Maria, Francisco, and I would live in Mexico City, where I had family. We felt this would be a safer place to have the baby.

Without a complete crew fit for service, getting the ship to its destination would be nearly impossible. The captain had to press the passengers into service. We wanted to help but didn't know a bow from a stern. The men learned how to reach the New World with Captain Hernandez's guidance. The men had no experience with seagoing vessels but quickly realized what they needed to do. There was no other choice.

Shortly after taking the ship back, there was a severe storm brewing. Large black clouds rolled into view, followed by jagged lightning strikes, filling the sky with loud thunderclaps. Fierce winds threw trunks, barrels, and food about the ship. The men tied themselves to the mast with ropes so as not to fall into the ocean. The wind whipped unmercifully, turning freshwater casks over and cargo everywhere. Barrels of water, chairs, and ropes cluttered the deck.

Many of the children were sick, vomiting, and frightened. The stench was intense. The storm contaminated the food and the drinking water. To make the children comfortable, David and Valentina made finger puppets to amuse the little ones. The stories enthralled the children. They calmed down within a few minutes, thanks to my children's soothing voices and smiling eyes. The voyage was bearable because David and Valentina helped with the children.

As the storm grew, I became ill. Maria tried to help but to no avail. I was feverish and kept shouting for Jose. Since he could not leave his post, Jose kept sending messages to me through Maria. "Keep fighting,

Estrella. You can make it. Estamos a las manos del Dio (we are in God's hands)."

In my delirium, I yelled to him, "I love you. I won't leave you. God will save us."

At last, I slept, though it was not a restful sleep. When I awoke, the storm was over. The sea was still. I started to feel better. It was like the storm had been a nightmare, except it really occurred. The only traces of it were the disarray of barrels and trunks.

Could there ever be peace for us? It was the fourth week of almost unbelievable conditions on the ship. There was little sanitation, privacy, food, or water. Some of the passengers had already died. "Oh, Dios, give us strength." Though the conditions were terrible, I felt that God would save us to observe our faith in peace. I felt safe in God's hands.

There were five families on this voyage. I suspected they were Conversos. I wouldn't dare ask, for fear of casting suspicion on my family. I was always frightened of new situations because I was scared of being identified as a hidden Jew.

Meanwhile, Jose was worried about our future. He had given away most of our family's gems in exchange for my freedom. Maria still had some in the hem of her skirt, as did the others, but not enough. My dear husband was troubled. What could he do? It would be months before he could send a message back to Spain about our plight and additional time to get funds back to the New World.

"Papa, what's the matter? Are you sick?" David saw how sad his father looked.

"No, mi *hijo*, my son. I'm worried about our future in New Spain. Since we gave most of our gems away, we have little to get us started."

"Oh, Papa. I've wanted to tell you something important, but there was never the right time to let you know. Abuelita Fuentes gave me the gold mezuzah with a stone in it. She hoped we could place it on the doorpost of our new prayer room. We can melt it down in exchange for anything we need in the New World. We will replace the mezuzah later," said David.

With tears in his eyes, Jose looked into his son's face with pride.

For the first time in weeks, Jose felt a glimmer of hope. It was possible to think of a future for our beloved family. "David, you have saved me from further worry. Why did it take so long to tell me?" Jose asked.

"I was afraid. But really, who would think that a young boy would possess such wealth?" asked David.

"You are right, son, once again. Thank you so very much," said his grateful father. Jose went to see me with tears in his eyes.

"What is it, Jose?" I asked.

"I've just learned how mature our son is, my dear," said Jose. "I am grateful to God for allowing us to have such a treasure in our lives."

I said, "I'm so glad that you feel that way."

That evening, I said my favorite prayer to God. "Shema Israel Adoshem Alohanu, Adoshem Ehad" (Hear, O Israel, the Lord is God, the Lord is one.) Jose said that it was time to sleep.

"Good night, my love. Golden dreams," I whispered to him.

My ancestors were so close and caring, just like my own family, I thought, smiling as I stopped the tape player again. I thought about their struggles and was hopeful they were over the bad times. Again I pressed play.

The land was sighted, and it was beautiful. The passengers on the ship could see green, rolling hills. There were dozens of people waiting on the dock with bright-colored clothing and sweet-smelling bouquets of magnolias and dahlia flowers. They were smiling and happy to see the passengers as we left the ship. We had finally arrived in the New World. It was the opposite of how the passengers felt on the voyage. Many of the children died during the final days of the journey. It was hard for David and Valentina to see their little bodies stretched out on wooden planks, ready for burial at sea. The spoiled food and water were too much for their little bodies to overcome. Some of the adults died too. Most survived.

After eight weeks, the ship had reached its destination, Veracruz, New Spain. We could put our worries away; we were in the New World. After stepping off the boat, the first thing Jose did was to bend down and kiss the earth. Then he said a silent prayer, "Deshame entrar, yo me hare lunar." (Let me enter. I will make a place for myself.) He promised the Lord to create a new home for our family. My husband had to send a message to our families. He shared the good news that everyone arrived safely and requested additional funds be sent to our family's home in Mexico City.

I had to stop listening to the tape because I needed to go back to the library. I didn't understand what life was like during this time. I needed to do more research. I couldn't believe this was a real story. At the library, I learned how slowly communications were between New Spain, today known as North America, and Spain.

My ancestors must not have been aware of the great dangers they still faced as Jews even in the New World. I uncovered a story about a high-ranking official in New Spain, Luis de Carvajal. He was the founder of the area named Nuevo Leon, one of the country's most extensive tracts of land. Luis de Carvajal and his family were also Conversos from Portugal. Practicing Judaism in New Spain, the authorities caught them. After warning them, they refused to give up following the laws of Moses and Israel. Nine family members were burned at the stake after an *auto de fe* (public act of penance) in 1596 in Mexico City. The Inquisition was in the New Spain! Other burnings happened as well. Communications were sparse, so few people knew about the burnings.

I prayed my family had fared better than the others. When I got home again, I wanted to learn more about my family's story, so I returned to the tape.

13

HEADED TO MEXICO CITY

Truly blessed, a smile washed over my face as I saw our family waiting for us on the dock. It had been years since we'd seen them. When Pablo and Jose saw each other, they embraced and cried. They were first cousins but grew up together like brothers. Pablo's jaw dropped when he saw David. The last time they were together, David followed Pablo everywhere he went, tugging on his pant leg for attention.

We decided to stay in Veracruz and rest for a few days after our exhausting, tumultuous sea voyage. While at the inn, I had one of the most delicious meals. The dish was called Huachinango a la Veracruzana, snapper Veracruz style, made with olives, tomatoes, garlic, onions, and herbs.

The next stage of our journey was to travel to Mexico City, 240 miles away. It was going to be strenuous. Francisco and Maria took extra care of me. They both shared our heartache when my three babies were born dead and wanted to take extra special care of me with this new baby.

The trip to our new home began. I did very well during the journey, despite how challenging it was for all of us to climb up the mountainside. The scenery was breathtaking. We had never seen such extraordinary sights, including different kinds of cacti. The children were not used to seeing sharp, pointy plants and cried, "Ouch!" when they touched them. That happened only once before the children understood to keep their hands off them.

The rolling clouds were so low that you could almost touch them. I laughed when I saw Valentina. She was so fascinated by how close the clouds appeared that she jumped up with her arms raised, trying to catch them. Then she ran to me and proclaimed, "I almost caught a cloud."

I asked her, "Could you please go back and try again?"

Valentina happily answered, "Of course, Mama."

Sadly, Francisco and Maria found the trip difficult. Mexico City is at a high elevation, surrounded on three sides by mountains. We learned that high altitudes affect some people negatively. They both felt the typical symptoms of mountain sickness—headaches, dizziness, swelling, vomiting, and lethargy. I took care of them traveling with me in the wagon. I held their heads when they vomited, giving them small sips of water when they could drink. After all those many years of serving me, I was finally able to do what they had always done for me. Besides my family, Mama and Papa, I loved them the most. Given a chance to show how I felt about them, I did.

Each night when we went to bed under the stars, we all said prayers of thanksgiving to the Almighty in our way. Before falling asleep, I silently recited the Shema, confirmation of the Lord's oneness. We traveled a long way for our newfound freedom, knowing that without God's help, it would never happen. We kept vigilant, not saying too much about ourselves to strangers, as in the Old World, having just learned practicing Judaism was a crime in New Spain. We always needed to be watchful of what we did and said.

The longer we traveled, the more seasoned we became in getting our bedrolls folded in the morning and making a fire for the evening meal. Of course, the guides helped. David was an amateur cartographer, a mapmaker in Spain. My boy was familiar with maps. As we traveled, he noticed errors, like the placement of a hill or the length of a river. David made corrections as we went. The guides called him *le cartografía pequeño* (the little cartographer), and they enjoyed working together. He listened to what they taught him, and in turn, David explained to them about maps. It was a good arrangement.

One of the leaders, Miguel Sánchez, was short and very muscular. He appeared to be a man of forty with big, dark brown eyes, a full mustache, dark skin, and an easy laugh. He lost his wife in a riding accident the year before and still grieved. With him were his two sons— Carlos, fifteen, and Tomas, nine.

On that fateful day, when she died, Rosalinda woke up early in a cheerful mood. The sun was shining, and birds singing—a perfect setting for a picnic. Rosalinda was on her favorite horse, Cesar. Suddenly, the horse slipped on some rocks and tumbled down the hill. Both Rosalinda and Cesar fell to the bottom.

Miguel and the boys rode down to help her. She was moving. Quickly, they dismounted their horses and rushed to her side. They tried to make her comfortable, but they saw she was severely injured. Rosalinda told them, "I love you. I will be watching over you in heaven." As they lifted her to bring her home, Rosalinda died. They buried her on the spot where she fell.

Miguel wanted no trace of that horrible day. He did not want anything that reminded him of his sweet Rosalinda, so he gave almost everything away. The only things Miguel kept were her silver candlesticks, heirlooms from her family. Originally from Spain, they were passed down through the generations. Tomas asked his father if he could keep a piece of his mother's jewelry. Miguel asked what he wanted. There was a favorite necklace of the Ten Commandments Tomas requested. Miguel complied. Tomas wore it close to his heart every day.

Miguel always brought his sons with him to guide travelers from Veracruz to Mexico City and back. We were fortunate with Miguel as our guide because other guides were not honest. Sometimes escorts robbed their passengers and left them behind. At night, while preparing for sleep, our guides sang songs of Spanish conquests and took turns as sentries to watch for prowling Indians. Their voices were pleasing and lulled everyone to sleep.

As the sun began to peek over the mountains, we would rise, eat breakfast, and start the day's adventure. We needed to take advantage of the daylight since it was too treacherous to travel at night.

Week followed week as we continued to climb mountains to our new home. David's confidence grew as he planned the day's course with Miguel and his sons. He continued to change the maps when necessary.

He was fascinated by them and planned to continue to learn more about cartography.

I surmised that it must have been very difficult for my family to travel up the mountain. It was hard for me to fathom the challenges they faced traveling by a horse-drawn carriage through rocky paths. Beginning at sea level, they headed into the mountains at seven thousand feet above sea level. David was absorbed by the subject of cartography. Abraham Cresques and his son Yehuda from Majorca were known for their outstanding contribution to the field. Most explorers used their writings to help them along their journeys. Map making was a valuable skill many Jews possessed.

We approached Mexico City, a city of sixty thousand people, wondering what life would hold for us. My thoughts were of having my baby and caring for the precious one. I hummed the melody my mother sang to me when I was sick.

Now recovered, Francisco and Maria redoubled their commitment to me. They anticipated the arrival of my baby as though they were the grandparents. David and Valentina were as full of adventure as I was in my youth. All of those wide-open spaces called to them. They knew they needed to stay with me until they were old enough to be on their own. Then they would soar like eagles, exploring different lands and cultures. Jose, anxious to get to the city, focused on settling our family. When he felt secure, he would continue his journey with Miguel and his sons, if they decided to join him.

Just as Jose was about to invite Miguel to join him in Santa Fe, Miguel thought my husband would be a good person to work for since he was ambitious and honest. He told me years later that he wanted to work with Jose. I thought, according to David's calculations, we were about a three-day ride to Mexico City, with rough roads ahead.

We were finally able to imagine an end to our journey. Surrounded by mountains, Mexico City unfolded before us. Glorious Mexico City! The home of the Aztec Indians, an ancient civilization conquered and destroyed by the Spanish. Mexico City rose from the ashes of the ruins of the Aztec capital Tenochtitlan.

We stood in awe. We were there. With the assistance of cousin Pablo, Jose secured a house for us here. It did not resemble our palatial home in Córdoba, but there was plenty of land to build if we decided to stay. There were five rooms. Miguel had asked me to take care of Tomas, as he had quickly become friends with David and Valentina. They loved the idea of having their young friend around. It would be easier if Tomas stayed with our family.

When our Mexico City home was in order, Jose, Miguel, Pablo, and Carlos planned to join the company going up to Santa Fe on the Camino Real, a series of old Indian trails. A Spaniard, Juan de Oñate, would lead a big expedition claiming the land for Spain. We felt traveling in a large group would be a safer way to navigate such a grueling trip. Miguel hired a doctor to care for the travelers. It would take around six months to complete.

When I was listening to the history on the recording, I remembered reading about this in my high school's library. I found this heavy book. When I put it on the table, it made a loud thud. I let out a little giggle and quickly apologized for the noise. After all, the library is not a good place to make noise. I learned a lot about the trails. Diverse groups of people traveled along the Rio Grande and met other groups from far and wide who were selling and trading supplies. They saw beautiful silks from China, spices from the southern part of New Spain, and the most delicate European lace.

There was a better chance of getting to their destinations safely by traveling with many people. Raiding Indians were discouraged from entering an encampment filled with many people. Avoiding unnecessary risk was the goal.

I read that Juan de Oñate was the leader of the expedition in 1598. It would be a difficult journey. He needed to blaze trails that could accommodate large wagons and large numbers of people. Seven thousand head of livestock, including oxen, beef cattle, donkeys, pack mules, goats, sheep, and hundreds of people comprised the wagon trains. There were many reasons for being part of the expedition. Some wanted to make Santa Fe their new home; some came for opportunities; others believed they might locate the Seven Cities of Gold. Most of those on our journey were peddlers. Since Santa Fe was a remote place, they could get higher prices. They were an adventurous array of people from all over the world. There were Asians, Arabs, Jews from Europe, and Americans from the eastern cities, such as New York, Philadelphia, and Pittsburgh. Included in the mix were some Conversos. The Wild West was an intriguing place. The sights, sounds, and smells must have been incredibly unique and fascinating. I can almost hear Estrella Gomez recount the stories of their adventures.

Miguel allowed Tomas to stay with our family while he went up to Santa Fe because his son was so happy for the first time since his mother's death. I treated him like another child. Miguel could hear laughter from his young son again.

No one knew how long it would be until we saw each other again, so it was hard for Miguel to leave Tomas behind. Carlos was also concerned about his little brother, but Tomas would stay in Mexico City. Once business flourished, they would return.

The night before they left, Jose held me tightly in his arms. Since we first married, we had never been apart. We loved each other so; we didn't want to let go. We talked until the sun came up. We laughed at the silly names we came up with for our child, like Pitasio or Herculano. We devised a plan for how Jose would find out about our baby's arrival. A couriered message would be sent to my love when I gave birth. Usually a cautious man, he was making the most significant decision. He was taking a chance without knowing the outcome. So many people depended on him that he could not fail. He prayed to the Lord for guidance.

With everyone assembled, it was a spectacular sight to see. After many delays, the expedition was finally going to Santa Fe. It was a bright, shining day. All the travelers were smiling as they moved forward, eager to start their new lives in the northern hills of New Spain. Juan de Oñate led the pack, complete with priests, doctors, soldiers, miners, and peddlers from many lands. Two hundred mules carried two to four hundred pounds of goods each. They traveled between twelve to fifteen miles each day. Up at dawn, mules packed, Miguel and the others were ready for the day. Everyone was gathering in the center of the city. For the first time, a Spaniard was leading an expedition to Santa Fe, which was a great undertaking. Jose and his group were in the center of the pack, an excellent position. If Indians attacked either at the beginning or the end, my loved one would be safe. Was I certain?

From what I read in reference books, the food of choice was *flamenquines*, pork rolls, *maíz* tostado, dried corn, pa lamb *tomaquet*, bread rubbed with tomatoes, olive oil with salt and pepper. Corn was eaten every day. They carried pinole, ground maize, prepared by cooking soaked corn kernels. It was allowed to dry and was then roasted in an earthenware dish placed over the fire, stirred continuously to avoid being burned. The corn would burst open and resembled popcorn called *esquitas*. The women would use *mano* and *metate*, pestle and mortar, to ground the popped corn into pinole. It was easy to make these dishes on the trail. Combined with water, it made a quick drink. Added for more flavoring were cinnamon and sugar. Jose must have eaten the dried corn, pinole, and pa amp tomaquet but probably just played with the flamenquines since he wanted the others to think he was eating the pork. Not eating pork was a sure sign that he was a practicing Jew. Fortunately, the Indians did not like pork either. They would go hungry rather than eat it. What a relief to know that he was not the only one not eating pork. They ate desert plants and their favorite chili peppers. As a midday meal, they ate dried beef from butchered cattle.

The crowd of well-wishers waited until the entire group was out of sight. They then went back home. Most of the women were weeping as they watched their families leave. I was no exception. I cried so hard that the baby began kicking. That made me stop instantly.

Slowly, David, Tomas, Valentina, and the others walked back to our new home. How could we get along without Jose and Miguel? In silence, we returned. We did not know when we would see our loved ones again. It would probably be at least a year.

Another trail master was Leonardo. He led many expeditions in the west to far-off places, but this was the first with such a large group of people to Santa Fe. His wife, Isabel, and children stayed in Mexico City. Leonardo's wife taught me about running a household in the new west.

She was a kind soul despite the great tragedies she suffered. We quickly became friends. We were both married women who had to take care of families independently. With Jose gone, I was in complete charge for the first time. Isabel had been on her own for a few years. She knew how to handle things as they came up. Isabel, Leonardo, and their children had to flee Spain because they were found to be secret Jews and were lucky to escape with their lives. Sadly, Isabel's parents were captured and burned at the stake. This tragedy shaped how Isabel lived her life. From that day forward, she dedicated herself to putting more good in the world with acts of kindness.

We had a lot in common. We were excellent singers and horse riders and loved to needlepoint. I marveled at the beautiful blanket Isabel had wrapped around her on a walk. The pattern and colors were exquisite. I was stunned to learn just how talented my new friend was; she had made the blanket. Isabel offered to teach me how to weave. I was thrilled to use a loom and quickly mastered the craft. This helped me keep busy so I wouldn't think of Jose all of the time.

On the trail, Miguel and Jose were able to learn more about each other. Both were from Spain, and both held secrets they could not reveal to each other. Miguel spoke of his late wife and told Jose he couldn't bear to keep anything belonging to her except for the candlesticks from her mother. Jose asked to see them. As Miguel was about to show them to Jose, he realized they had Hebrew writing on them. Before he could take them back, Jose saw the writing. Miguel was so frightened he pulled out a knife, ready to kill his friend for discovering his hidden past. Jose said, "It says SHABBAT."

Miguel put the knife away, smiled, and said, "Shalom Aleichem" (Peace to you).

Jose replied, "Aleichem Shalom" (And peace to you.) The men embraced, feeling relieved they could trust each other.

Back on the trail, Jose thought of me. He wondered, *How is my lovely Estrella feeling?*

I felt fabulous. Time had passed so fast since Jose left, and I was now ready to have the baby. I could hardly wait and secretly wished for a healthy girl. We also spoke about our beloved Spain, though we were forced out of our homes because we were secret Jews.

Reading these words felt so familiar to me because it was my history too. I was separated by centuries from my ancestor, yet certain things are so universal and transcend time, like how to deal with heartache. I knew I could not have faced my divorce alone. It was my friends and family who helped me move through my pain. Just as Estrella had to deal with being separated from her parents, her country, and her husband, all while pregnant, I'm so happy my family could find such wonderful, giving friends to help them through the challenges they faced. I continued to listen. I could understand my ancestor's devotion to her servants as I listened to the words from another time. Estrella Gomez continued …

The love I felt for them was as deep as I felt for my parents, but it was hard to deal with their constant attention. "Doña, do you need an extra cushion?" asked Francisco.

"Can I get you something to eat?" questioned Maria. I was going mad with all of this care. Sometimes I would go for a walk to get away from them. Francisco and Maria would run after me with a rebozo, shawl, to put on so I wouldn't get a chill. They kept a close watch over me, like doting parents. I was annoyed with them, but since I loved them so much, I put up with it, knowing they wanted the best for me.

I longed for my mother and wanted her to see the new baby. I wanted my mama to sing lullabies to my child as she had done with David. I needed her to tell me everything would be all right. I remembered my mother's sweet singing voice. Sadly, it was becoming a faint memory. Thankfully, Isabel became my guide.

The activity that I loved the most was riding. I would venture through the countryside to breathe the fresh air and clear my mind. I relished the time that I had alone with my thoughts. Sadly, I could not ride now but looked forward to it after my child's birth.

I explained to my servants what to do each day. After that, Isabel and I would meet for breakfast and discuss topics like childbirth, child-rearing, and prices of commodities that were important to know. When we composed our poetry, we would walk out to a clearing in the woods, sit under a tree, and share our newest writings. Isabel and I helped each other in so many ways. It felt like home to me.

One place that didn't feel that way was the kitchen. It was like being transported into another world. The beauty and freshness of the food before me were a feast for the senses whenever I entered Maria's domain. She had quite a reputation for her outstanding cooking, instructing her assistants on how to prepare the most delectable meals. Her kitchen was a busy place. Women moved swiftly around, pots bubbled with sauces and soups, and a roaring fire with delicious-smelling loaves of bread blazed in the oven. Hanging from the ceiling were bundles of drying herbs, including rosemary, basil, parsley, cilantro, and thyme.

Everyone around asked to be seated at our table. Visitors from Veracruz, including dock workers, merchants, and others, stopped at our home. My dear Maria began to understand how to cook with ingredients found in the New World. She had brought capers, grapes, and olive plantings from Spain and would combine them with foods, such as tomatoes and dried salmon, from New Spain. She escorted me to the heart of Mexico City, the marketplace, to find and select the freshest ingredients for our meals. There were many sights and smells that were almost overwhelming in the market. Those nearby sold their goods in the center of town. They would hear news from newly arrived passengers from Spain. Sometimes I received a letter from my parents, which always made me smile.

It was here I also received word about Jose's journey north. He was happily progressing with the mine near Santa Fe. They settled in Pablo's home and immediately began looking for a mine to buy, renting some horses to scout the area. There were abandoned mines near town that no longer held silver. Rumors floated around about a silver mine owned by a man who wanted to go back to Spain. Anton was old and wished to die in the land of his birth. He had never hired anyone to work his silver mine, doing all the work himself because he didn't trust anyone. Jose was interested in buying the mine and asked Anton what he wanted for it. Anton asked for a lot of money. Jose tried to negotiate with the old man but soon realized that Anton didn't really want to sell. Out of curiosity, Jose went to the assayer's office to see if Anton's mine had been productive. He was told that the mine had produced high-quality silver in the past, but in recent years, because Anton wouldn't hire anyone to help him, there was very little silver found. This information made Jose more eager to buy the mine. He decided to go back to ask Anton once again if he would sell. When the group got back to the mine, Anton couldn't be found. They looked around for him everywhere. Then they heard a faint cry, "Help, help!" The men searched and found him at the bottom of a hill. They helped him back to his home and bandaged his broken ankle. Jose asked again if Anton would sell him the mine. It was then that Anton consented to sell. Jose decided that Anton needed to stay on at the mine to help them find the silver veins. Jose vowed to Anton that he wouldn't be alone anymore.

On the way back to Santa Fe, Jose spotted a large piece of land on a small hill. It was stunning. As the sun was setting, he could faintly see Santa Fe in the distance and unusual plants called cactus. He liked how he felt on the land. He began thinking about the design of the house he would build. It would resemble his home in Córdoba. A land grant was given to him from the Spanish government. He was anxious to begin the building but wanted to wait for me for my thoughts.

Carlos and Miguel were hard workers and an asset to Jose's company in the mine. Jose was doing well and hoped to join the next caravan back to Mexico City. It was likely he would be back when the baby was an infant.

I was thrilled with the news and began to sing songs I learned in Spain.

Jose looked forward to seeing his son, now a little taller than his father. As a proud father, he knew David showed competence in managing people, just like on the ship. Children loved him because of his approach to them. Everyone loved doing their best for him.

Since coming to live with us, Tomas and David had become inseparable, with Valentina following after them. Where David went, Tomas was soon to follow. David was a good role model and taught Tomas everything he knew. In time, they would learn from each other. They helped with the household chores and were quiet and respectful of their elders. Time kept slipping by, both growing up. Tomas was excited since he heard that we would all go to Santa Fe when Jose returned. He missed his father and brother and looked forward to going home.

14

JOSE, MIJO

I was about to have my baby. It would be any time now, so I no longer ventured far from my home. It would be safer that way. Since Isabel was a midwife, I felt confident that my delivery would be easy. The weather was changing, and I liked it.

I could smell fall in the air with the leaves gently floating to the ground. I listened to the sounds they made as I walked, enjoying the crunch of the broken leaves. Suddenly, temperatures dipped. Walking outside was comfortable. I loved the cool night air and pretended to be a bird flying off into the sky, using my rebozo as wings. As I was running toward a small hill, I lost my footing and fell. I cried, "Oh no! Maria and Francisco will be mad at me." I wasn't hurt. Francisco and Maria insisted that I lie in bed and rest from the ordeal. Normally, I would have protested.

Nevertheless, I decided to lie down in bed, listening to them instead of ignoring their advice as I usually did. Just as I was getting comfortable, my water broke. Maria raced to get Isabel. She had been taught by a *partera* (midwife) to deliver babies. Isabel came quickly and told the others that it would be a while before the baby was born. My pains were about ten minutes apart, thankfully. I was doing well. Suddenly, they began to come faster, every three minutes. It was hard regaining my strength between the pains. I had forgotten how miserable I was when David was born fourteen years before. Isabel spoke encouraging words to me. She softly told me about the joy I would feel just as soon as the baby arrived. I was groaning, saying, "Jose! Jose, my love, I need you."

Isabel urged me, "Just a few more minutes, my dear."

Isabel warned me, placing a stick wrapped in cloth between my teeth, "Don't push yet." It was hard not to push. A few moments later, she said, "Now it's time to push. No! Stop, Estrella! The cord is wrapped around the baby's neck!"

Isabel directed Maria, "Move the candle closer so I can see better—and bring the blankets." Isabel worked fast to save my baby. Then she looked up at me and grinned. "I did it. Now push. I can see the head. I need one more big push, Estrella. Felicidades por tu nueva bebe. You have a girl."

"I am overjoyed. Just wait until Jose sees her. She looks like him," I told my dear friend.

Isabel quickly took the baby, cleaned her, and wrapped the precious bundle in a blanket. Then she gave her to my waiting arms. I looked at the baby and said, "Since you look so much like your father, your name is Josephina Isabel Gomez." Isabel cried when she heard the baby's second name was in her honor. There were tears of joy in the Gomez home that night.

The moment the baby came into this world, Jose felt it happen and knew I was doing well. I heard that if people were very connected, they could sense things that happened to the other one. I knew it was true. He had about two weeks to wait until the caravan would start their journey back to Mexico City. My husband would meet his new child with renewed enthusiasm, spend time with David and Valentina, and return to my waiting arms. It was a new beginning for our family.

Meanwhile, David took Valentina to play in the field to keep her busy. Valentina ran with her hands out, ready to catch butterflies, just as I did as a girl. She grabbed one and ran to David to proudly show him what she found. Valentina happily told him there was a present for him. Then she opened her hands, and the butterfly flew away. Just as she was about to cry, David thanked her. He explained that the butterfly went home to take care of its babies. Valentina was happy again. My David always did an excellent job comforting others, just like his father. It would be nice to see them together again.

Since he was familiar with the El Camino Real, Jose knew what to expect on the trail. He decided he would be in the front of the caravan to be the first to see if Indians or animals threatened the travelers, a courageous act on his part. He was always watching out for the safety of others.

Toward the journey's end, he noticed smoke coming from a small home near the trail. As the expedition approached, they did not see anyone in the house. When they looked around, they saw the burnt body of what appeared to be a man. Lying beside him was a little boy about seven years old. He, too, was severely burned but still alive. Jose thought of his children and bent over to hear what the child was trying to tell him. The small boy muttered. He was drifting off from the pain, crying out for his mother, gasping for breath. "Mama ... don't take her ... the Indians." Jose's and the young boy's eyes met. They connected. After speaking those words, the little boy gave Jose his rabbit's foot and died. The men in the caravan buried the father with his son in the same plot, said some kind words over their bodies, and resumed their trek to Mexico City.

The experience badly shook up Jose and some of the men in the caravan. They knew that they needed to avenge the deaths of those innocent people. Jose decided to take a few men to kill the Indians and rescue the kidnapped woman, whose name he found out was Romina. Leonardo, a caravan leader, did not like the idea of the men leaving the caravan but could not convince them to stay. Leonardo yelled at his friend, "Jose, this will be your death. Please don't do this." He grabbed him by his shoulder, saying, "Think of your family."

Jose replied, "I am thinking of them. If anything happened to them, I would want someone to help."

Leonardo compromised with Jose. "Then please take a scout with you. Taza is the best. I'll ask him to go with you. He will know how to track the Indians." Jose thanked him and agreed.

The men could follow the Indians' tracks on the trail, making good time. The footprints were fresh and deep. It didn't take long to spot the kidnappers. A plan was set. Jose, Taza, and the others waited until dark before they approached the site. There were about fifty sleeping inhabitants in the Indian village. Taza crept into the settlement and searched around, peering into the huts. At the end of the community, there was a tiny hut hidden away from the rest. He quietly walked in and saw the captured woman. Romina was sleeping in the dwelling by herself. He approached her and placed his hand over her mouth, telling her that he was there to rescue her. She screamed, not believing him, bringing the Indians out of their quarters with their weapons. The Indians began to fight the strangers with their bows and arrows. Romina tried to get away from Taza because she did not know if he was a friend or foe. Taza held her tightly and pulled her to the horses, where Jose was waiting. Jose told her to come with him, handing her the rabbit's foot that her son had given him. Seeing that, she began to cry. Romina trusted that Jose was there to help her. Trying to run up a hill with Jose, she moved very slowly. All of a sudden, an arrow struck Jose in the back. They continued running until they reached the horses.

Again the whooshing sound of another arrow flying through the air—it lodged in Jose's back. Romina helped him on his horse. As they began the ride back to the caravan, another arrow pierced him. They were back on the wagon train hours later. Jose went directly to a waiting medical wagon attended by a young medical doctor from Europe named Doctor Alejandro De Grazie. Jose was severely hurt and in and out of consciousness. The doctor was able to stop the bleeding after he excised the arrows from Jose's back. "My darling Estrella, please come to me," Jose cried out in his delirious state.

Then Doctor De Grazie applied poultices to the wounds. The doctor took out a small bottle of laudanum, medicine to relieve pain made from poppy seeds. Jose was severely wounded and sweating, his body burning hot to the touch, which was a bad sign. The doctor was worried because the wounds looked inflamed. Jose rested in the wagon, where he remained during the long trip to Mexico City. Several times a day, the doctor attended to his wounds.

Romina would not leave his side. He was her guardian angel. It was her job to protect him, as he had done for her. She would hold his hand and tell him how wonderful he was. "Soon, you will be with your family," Romina reminded him.

His sleep was fitful as Jose groaned in pain, continuing to call out for me. "Darling, please do not cry. After I'm gone, Miguel will take you to our new home in Pueblo. You will marry him and live happily with him."

"Do not say such things, Jose. You will take Estrella to your new home yourself," Romina scolded Jose.

He responded, "No, no, I will die."

Romina wiped his head with a damp cloth and tried to reassure him that he would recover from his wounds. When he fell asleep, she was relieved. The reality of his situation was agonizing to witness. Later, Romina told me that each day, my love went in and out of consciousness, sleeping most of the time. His wounds seemed to improve. However, there was still a concern.

They were within a two-day ride from Mexico City. One of the men who had befriended Jose decided it would be better for me to see my love as soon as possible. He quickly rode to find me at our residence. The first person he saw was Tomas, who led him to the house. From the look on this stranger's face, I immediately knew something was wrong. "Where is Jose?" I questioned. "Tell me!" Before he could reply, I started yelling that I knew he was dead.

"No, he is not dead, but he is wounded. It would be better for everyone if you went to see him alone, without the others. Leave the children with Francisco and Maria," the man advised, hurrying me along. He wanted to get back to Jose quickly.

I stopped to tell Isabel what had happened. Isabel asked to go with me, saying that her grandfather was a doctor in Spain and had taught her many healing ways. She showed us his medical bag, telling us that she knew that she could help. I was glad Isabel came along, as she said, "I know that I have a calming effect on everyone, Estrella. I can help."

The ride to the caravan was only one day away since it was heading toward Mexico City. We would meet the next day. It was a hard ride. In the distance, the expedition was in sight. At last, we caught up with it.

Sweat dripping down my back, I quickly jumped off the horse and ran around the caravan, looking inside each wagon to see if I could find Jose. Someone shouted, waving his arms, and yelled, "He's here, he's here."

Breathing so hard, I could barely catch my breath as I dashed to the wagon. Jose was stretched out, covered with blankets, looking pale and exhausted. I leaped into the wagon. Gently, I cradled his head, bent over, and kissed him softly on the lips. "I am here, my love. You can get better now."

Jose opened his eyes and said, "I dreamed about you, Estrella. Are you real? Am I still dreaming?"

"Mijo, my love, I am here with you. I am real." I sobbed. "We are together again."

Jose was so happy to see me that he began to cry. "Why did God do this to us?" he said. "Now, see what has happened? My death will destroy our family." He cried.

"Hush, mijo," I said. "Your work is to get well now. Everything will be all right. Just pray and stay alive. I will take care of everything." I sang, "Las estrellas en los cielos. Uno y otro hacen una pareja. No existe mayor estabilidad que la de nosotros dos." (The stars in the skies. One and one make a pair. There exists no greater steadiness than like that of the two of us).

Jose smiled when he heard the song. He had sung it to me many times to express his feelings. It made me feel cared for and loved. I could see that Jose was worried and in great pain. It was hard for him to stay awake with a furrowed brow and a sweaty face.

"You must be in charge right now," he said. Jose slept all day. Everyone worried because he did not wake. When he breathed, there was a slight movement. He looked peaceful. The wagon was getting closer and closer to Mexico City. Jose would see David and Valentina and meet his new baby daughter, Josephina. I was anxious for him to see them.

When we entered Mexico City, David was the first to reach us. He hopped on the wagon and approached his father. "Papa, it is so good to see you. It has been such a long time. Wait until you see the baby! She is beautiful. She looks just like you, Papa."

There was no response. David took his father's hand in his and stroked it. He sat there for what seemed to be a long time. My son looked at his father and smiled. David was happy to see him even if he couldn't reply.

I was excited to show Jose our little daughter. Maria placed our darling daughter next to him in the wagon. Jose opened his eyes and gazed at Josephina. He said, "She is so beautiful. Thank you, Estrella, for this wonderful gift."

I smiled with tears and said, "I'm so happy that you like our daughter. I had to call her Josephina since she looks like you. The baby even has your blue eyes."

Lifted carefully out of the wagon, the men placed my love in the back bedroom of our home. It was a very long night as the family watched over Jose. Sleeping most of the time, he looked peaceful.

At dawn the following day, Jose opened his eyes and looked over at his sleeping son sitting on a stool beside his bed. Jose grinned and softly said, "Good morning, mijo."

Nearly falling off the stool, David yelled, "Papa!" Running into his father's arms, they embraced. I stood at the door, watching. I felt such relief.

"Did someone get shot with arrows?" Jose laughed. "I feel great. I can't wait to get out of bed and dance with my wife."

I laughed and said, "Yes, my love, we will have many dances, but how about something to eat for now?"

Jose nodded. "I'm so hungry, Maria. Can you make me some food?"

She said, "Of course, Master." Maria ran to the kitchen. In just a few minutes, she brought a beautifully arranged food tray, including fruit, cheeses, juice, jams, and freshly baked bread. Also on the tray were white flowers in a bright blue vase. Maria smiled. "The flowers will bring good luck." Jose ate with gusto and smiled at Maria, thanking her.

Later that morning, Doctor De Grazie came to see his patient. He was greeted at the door by Maria. "Good morning. Can I help you?" Maria inquired.

"Yes, my name is Doctor Alejandro De Grazie. I am here to look after Jose."

"Oh yes, doctor. I am Maria. I take care of the family. Come in, please. Right this way." Maria took him to Jose's room.

The doctor looked at Jose's incisions and saw that they were pink and warm, showing some improvement. He cleaned the wound and applied more poultices to the areas. Jose also had more color on his face. Pleased, Doctor De Grazie said, "Maria, I would like to speak with Doña Gomez."

Maria quickly ran to find me. "Yes, Doctor, how is Jose doing?" I questioned.

"I'm happy to report Jose is doing better. Since I'm here, I can look at anyone who needs medical attention. May I see the children?" he suggested.

"Well, thank you. Yes, is the kitchen a good place to see them?" I asked.

"That would be fine." He found them to be in perfect health with good appetites, which pleased him.

As the doctor was leaving, Maria stopped him at the door. "I have a plate of food for you, Doctor. Please stay and eat."

"Thank you. I cannot say no to you. Your food smells wonderful." The doctor sat down at the table and ate. He had missed home-cooked meals.

"Please come again," Maria said.

The doctor told Maria that he would check on Jose before he left as a precaution. He walked back to Jose's room, removed the bandages, and was surprised. The incisions were looking better. He was relieved, telling Jose to get some rest and he would see him in the morning.

Jose smiled. "I am feeling better. Thank you."

I waited outside the room, nervous about finding out how my love was doing. I bit my lower lip as the doctor approached me. He told me that my husband was a remarkable man and doing very well. The doctor smiled and said, "I am happy to report, your love has a long life ahead of him." Then he said he would be back tomorrow to check on him.

After the doctor left, Valentina came into the room with a glass of water, afraid to get too close to the bed. Jose motioned her over. He told her to join him in the room, happy to see her. He wanted to know how she was. Tears began to flow down her face. Our little daughter was scared. He was calling her "my sweet Valentina."

"I'm fine, my dear," he said. "What do you think of your little sister, Josephina? I think she will be brave just like you, her big sister. I am proud to have two wonderful daughters." Valentina was pleased. She had never heard Jose call her his daughter. They laughed together. As Jose fell asleep, Valentina quietly left the room. It was my turn to be with Jose.

I slowly joined my husband in bed with our baby in my arms. Jose and Josephina both slept so peacefully. For the first time in a long time, I took a deep, relaxing breath and drifted off. When I awoke, I heard laughter coming from Josephina. I opened my eyes and laughed as I saw Jose playing with our baby. He was trying to fit her little hand in his mouth. Josephina squealed with delight.

My dear husband and I remarked about the joy we felt having our sweet little Josephina. I saw how tired he was, so I told him to rest as I left the room. He was fighting to keep his eyes open. I stood up and said that I would bathe our little one, telling him, "I will be back soon."

Jose slept as Maria made dinner. Coming into his room with a tray of food, Maria had made one of his favorite meals. The feast included roast lamb paella, a Spanish rice dish, seasoned with Spanish saffron and olive oil. As Maria was leaving, Jose insisted she sit with him.

He began to speak to her, praising Maria for her cooking, saying that her cooking had always been his secret weapon for selling spices. Without her delectable meals, my husband would not have done so well in business. He told her that some customers were delighted when they received an invitation for dinner at Casa De Gomez, the Gomez house. He asked her if she remembered when he was trying to sell cardamom. She said that she did; she had prepared a feast using cardamom in every dish. He laughed, telling her that his customers were so impressed with the meals they doubled their orders. Maria smiled, telling him it was her pleasure. Those spices contributed to making her a better cook. Jose talked about his ideas for the future. He told her he had big plans for his next business and needed his secret weapon again. There were plans to host many dinners at the new Casa De Gomez. "There will be a need for the delectable food your staff will make for my customers, who will be so happy they will have to buy more from me."

Maria laughed. "Of course. Please allow me to leave so you may rest." He took her hand and thanked her, then fell asleep.

David stood in the doorway, watching his father resting with a big smile. He thanked the Almighty for bringing his Papa back to him. Jose stirred, opened his eyes, looked out the window, and then motioned for David to come closer. "Yes, Papa. Do you need something?" asked David.

"Yes, my son. I want you to know how proud I am of you. I know it was not easy to be the man of the house. Thank you for taking such good care of your mama and sisters."

"Papa, it was my pleasure. I love you. Please rest now. I'll check on you later," David said.

Throughout the evening, David stopped at the doorway of his father's room. When he saw his eyes open, again looking out the window, David cheerfully asked, "Papa, do you want to play a card game?"

Jose nodded. "Yes, it has been too long. Let's play!" For the next several minutes, they played by his bedside. David let his father win, which made them both happy. Jose enjoyed winning. He was tired. He told David he would see him later and win another game in the morning.

It was dawn the following day when David came back to his papa's room. David wanted to play another card game with him. Jose's eyes opened as he gazed out the window. David walked in and waited by his bedside. He stared at his father, watching his chest rise and fall as he took breaths. David felt a calm wash over him. He gave his papa a big smile and then said, "Today is going to be a great day." Suddenly, with no warning, David realized his father's chest was no longer moving. He shook him and yelled, "Papa! Papa! Please be all right. Say something!" Jose did not move. His eyes were still open, staring toward the window. David screamed, "No! Help!"

The family rushed in. Francisco began to shake Jose. He gasped, then gently closed his master's eyes, saying, "He's gone."

Nothing was said. No one moved for a while until Josephina began to wail uncontrollably. Maria left the room to soothe the baby. Valentina sat on the floor holding her baby doll, crying. David stood mute. His face was red as hot tears streamed down. Francisco quickly brought a chair for me, took my arm, and helped me sit down.

"Everybody, leave! I need to be with my husband." As they all left, I locked the door. I walked back to the chair and sat down. I began to speak to my love. "Jose, I know this has been hard on you, but you will recover. You are so strong and young. We have many years ahead of us. Please speak to me." I stroked his cheek and bent over and kissed his lips, but he did not move or kiss me back. Then I pleaded with him. "Jose, please say something." The silence was deafening. At that moment, I knew he was gone. I sat in silence. Then I slowly walked to the door, unlocked it and left the room.

15

LIFE ANEW

Francisco and Maria prepared the house for the mourning period. They covered mirrors and placed low stools in the sitting room for the mourners. The burial would be quick. I spoke to Francisco, asking him to make the arrangements. He found a local priest to officiate at the funeral. After the attendants left the burial grounds, David and Pablo arranged a secret service only for family and trusted friends, following the tradition of our ancestors. *"Yesgadal, v'yesgadash, shamay rabo …* glorify and sanctify. It is the prayer for the dead. There was a water pitcher outside the cemetery to wash our hands to separate life from death. People spoke kindly about Jose. Dr. De Grazie expressed his deep regret for not saving him. During the week of mourning, no one spoke until the mourners spoke. All sat quietly.

I spent most of my time in bed. All I could do was cry and sleep. Maria and Isabel checked on me several times a day. They asked me to go for a walk, listen to poetry, let them brush my hair, have something to eat, and play with Josey. I simply said, "No."

Then I began to boil with anger. All I saw was red. I started to rant. Doctor De Grazie told me Jose would live. He lied to me. There was no consolation for me. I railed against God. How could he be so cruel? How could he have returned Jose to me and then quickly snatched him away? *No, I will not believe in him. God does not protect us. God only deserts us when we need him the most.* No one thought this would happen. It looked as if Jose would recover, but it was not to be. I began to wail.

How could God play such a terrible trick on us? "Why, God? Why did you do this to me? I have always believed in you. You have forsaken me."

Maria and Francisco tried to soothe my troubled mind but could not be of any help. I hid in my room, only to come out to eat meals. I didn't even care for Josephina. Fortunately, Francisco and Maria took care of the baby. After a few weeks of hiding, I began to come out of my room to take care of Josephina. I began to sing the songs my mother sang to me. I even bathed the baby. Slowly, slowly, I returned to my old ways. Once again, I took care of my children.

Meanwhile, we stayed in Mexico City. I would take walks with Maria and Francisco in the evenings. In time, I went riding in the countryside. I was getting stronger each day. Finally, one day when I was in the middle of my ride, it began to drizzle. I lifted my head to the sky and smiled. Smelling the rain exhilarated me. I got off my horse and started whirling around with outstretched arms. Uplifting songs came to my lips. "Quiero ir al mundo madre, tengo que salir." (I want to go into the world, Mother, I have to leave.)

That evening, I dreamt about Jose. When I saw him, I was sad and confused. He held me in his arms as I cried on his shoulder. I looked at him and asked him how he could be there. I knew he was dead. He smiled and answered that everything would be fine. He promised me that he would always be with me. I cried and asked him how. *Why? I can't do this without you, my dear one. Jose, why did God take you from me? I will never forgive him.*

Then Jose held my hand, looked deeply into my eyes, and repeated, "My love, if you want God to forgive you, then you must forgive him." He reassured me that everything would be fine. He pleaded that I must trust him. The following day, I woke up feeling lighter. I felt a strange warmth inside. Since Jose's passing, I once again believed everything would be all right in my heart. This feeling gave me comfort. I looked up and thanked Jose for coming to me in my dream. I was whole again. Smiling, I thought, *I will be devoted to my children and work at the mine.*

I told the family that it was time to go home to Pueblo at breakfast that morning. "Let's take the next caravan." Everyone was astonished. They thought it would take me longer to be interested in life again. I had rediscovered my will to live.

The caravan to Santa Fe would be leaving in another month. The plan was to meet with the family in Santa Fe and then arrange transportation to Pueblo. I needed to look at the mine, find lodging, and build a new home. Once again, the Gomez family would need to pack all of our belongings and start anew. Perhaps this time it would be our last stop.

While packing, Maria and Francisco had time to reflect on the past few years. They were eager to tell me what they had talked about. So much had happened, both tragic and triumphant. The best part of their journey was being with Josephina, nearly two years old. Beginning to see the world through her eyes, they felt young again. She was bright-eyed and full of life. Francisco often thought his life had meaning for the second time, caring for this child. It first happened to him when I was born.

Josey responded to Maria and Francisco in the same way. Constantly held, my daughter didn't need to cry. Maria did a lot with Josey on her hip, and she became an extension of her body. Francisco and Maria devised a way of securing the baby with an oversized scarf around her middle. Maria's routine was to supervise all the household duties, such as meal preparation and cleaning the house, with Josey attached. She thanked God that Josey was still small. When Maria got tired, she allowed other servants to care for her precious Josey.

While I mourned the loss of my husband, his doctor, Alejandro De Grazie, was also coping with the horrors of the expedition. From Italy, he had attended medical school in Bologna. The doctor was hopeful and happy when hired to join the trip. It would be his chance to see the west. As a new doctor, he would also be caring for patients independently. Doctor De Grazie had changed dramatically over the past year and a half. At the end of the journey, he was devastated by the number of patients who died.

Once he reached Mexico City, the doctor needed to take some time off. He rented a small room. For several weeks, he stayed in his dark room, unable to stop replaying the suffering and death he saw firsthand. One traveler mistakenly took a wrong step and plunged off a cliff to his death. Doctor De Grazie delivered three stillborn babies and lost two mothers in childbirth. There was so much suffering, blood, broken bones, and vomiting. Then his last patient from the expedition, Jose, was recovering from his wounds and expected to live. Suddenly, he died. It was all too much for the untested new doctor.

Thankfully, he received a letter from Italy. In it, his father told him about an opportunity to care for patients in a small town called Pueblo. It was beautiful, covered with deep green grass, with one hundred families strong, situated on a hill, conveniently located near Santa Fe. This request helped to lift his spirits. He knew what his father meant when he wrote about the town having people like us. It meant they were Jews. Once again, he was ready for a new challenge and gathered his belongings.

Packing was easier this time since Maria had become an expert at it. It was saying goodbye to our friends that would be hard to do. In a short time, we had all made many friends. A quick goodbye was the only way to handle leaving. Isabel had become like a sister to me. On the day we were to leave, I had the servants prepare food baskets for all of my friends and then deliver them. My friends came over to the hacienda to thank me for my thoughtfulness. We hugged and kissed and said our goodbyes.

Though El Camino Real was more traveled, it was still tricky. With Tomas in tow, David and Valentina walked alongside the oxen. To them, it was an adventure. Making a game of counting people brought them hours of fun. There were thirty-two priests, forty-nine peddlers, twenty-six miners, fifty-one children, twenty-five Indians, and thirty-four soldiers with the accompanying women. They quizzed each other about the numbers in each group.

I was very determined to begin my new life in Pueblo. I even thought I would enjoy digging in the mine. I could tell that my family thought working in the mine did not befit a woman of my stature, but they said nothing. If I did try to use a pick, I would find out how hard it was. They felt that I wouldn't do the work, so why think about it.

There was no deterring me. Walking every day carrying Josey was building up my muscles for the work in the mine. With my added strength, I could be helpful to the men when they were trying to steer the oxen on the trail. I felt satisfied with myself and determined to accomplish my goal. Little by little, I was doing what I wanted.

Until the accident, everything was going well. Under the loving care of Francisco and Maria, Josey was flourishing. Carrying Josephina, Maria tripped and fell in front of an ox. It stepped on her foot, crushing it with its enormous weight. Maria pushed the baby away so no harm could come to her. Francisco swooped up Maria and brought her to the side of the road. She was crying out in pain.

She said, "Don't worry about me. Is the baby all right?"

Francisco consoled her. "We have taken care of Josephina. Maria, how can I help you?"

"Wrap my foot and give me a sleeping potion, Francisco," urged Maria. "If I am sleeping, I won't feel as much pain," she said.

Francisco ran to me and told me what had happened. I asked if anyone in the caravan had a sleeping portion. One man stepped forward. "Please allow me to help. Do you remember me? My name is Dr. Alejandro De Gracie. I cared for Jose."

I was stunned to see the doctor again and answered, "Of course, Doctor De Gracie. Maria is hurt."

He went to Maria and spoke softly. Maria seemed to relax with his words of comfort. He skillfully wrapped her foot and put a sleeping potion into some water. "This should help," the doctor reassured her. I came by to see how Maria was doing. She seemed to be more relaxed after seeing the doctor. Maria told me how kind he was to her and said how handsome he was, with a twinkle in her eye. Maria told me she invited the doctor for dinner once our house was ready. I could tell my Maria was woozy.

Riding an ox was uncomfortable for Maria. She needed to have her leg up, so Francisco devised a way to raise her leg by tying a rope around the ox's neck and Maria's leg. He also fashioned a chair with sides so she could sleep sitting up. It worked. The pain subsided with the help of the sleeping potion.

The journey was slow and laborious but uneventful. There was time for me to think about my life with Jose. I was grateful for our time together. I had a good life with him. I wanted it to last forever, but it was not to be. The children, I had to think of the children. They were the future and needed care. I knew I could do it because I was not alone. Maria and Francisco would work with me to take care of everyone.

The caravan arrived safely in Santa Fe. Dinner that night was at Pablo's home. I felt so much love from my family. Josey was the star of the evening. Everyone took turns cuddling her, remarking how much she looked like Jose. Pablo said, "He was like a brother to me. I can't believe I'll never speak to him again." It made me miss him more. I knew how happy my husband would have been to see everyone together. My children were delighted with their cousins. We stayed another two days and then continued our journey home.

Our new lives were about to begin as we approached Pueblo. After trudging through the wilderness, we could rest our weary bones. I had Francisco secure lodging for us all. I was ready to start building our new home in the exact place where Jose had imagined it. Tomas, David, and Valentina were anxious to see Carlos since it had been over two years. They could hardly believe their eyes. This incredibly handsome, tall, and well-built young man stood before them. Carlos looked nothing like the boy they had last seen. What a difference hard labor had made. He worked with Anton to make the mine successful. Carlos gave the business direction, which was what it needed.

The time was right for a celebration. Good food and good wine were the order of the day. Platters of hot, steaming tortillas wafted in the night air. Sangria quenched our thirst. The well-wishers enjoyed an abundance of roasted lamb and pig, just not pig for us. Tears of happiness and sadness came and went, with the fiesta lasting into the late hours of the night.

The next day, no one stirred. Even Josephina didn't wake until late. Carlos and Miguel talked about the progress in the silver mine. Carlos spoke about how invaluable Anton was in getting the business going again. They had hired some Indians who, when they were there, worked hard, but they averaged working two days a week. There was a need to hire more workers.

The mine was producing large quantities of high-quality ore. The assayer was surprised at the amount they were able to extract. Anton seemed to blossom working with Carlos. It was as if he had a grandson to give all of his knowledge. Many nights, they talked about ways to get the ore out faster. Anton also taught him how to tell if the assayer was cheating. He showed him how to cook food and wash his clothes. They became very close. All three men worked well together.

A nervous Doctor Alejandro De Grazie was about to meet the elders in another part of town. Even though the elders knew the doctor was coming to their village, they were suspicious. He knew they wanted him to prove that he was a practicing Jew. They wanted him to show that he was circumcised. In front of the community leaders, Doctor De Grazie refused their request but was willing to say a prayer. They agreed to that. Dr. De Grazie began. "Shema Israel adoshem alohanu adoshem echad." (Hear, O Israel, the Lord is our God, the Lord is one.)

The elders were satisfied with the recitation of the prayer and welcomed Dr. De Grazie into their midst. They found a comfortable hacienda for his medical office and residence. As soon as he unpacked his things, he promised to open his office. He was pleased with the arrangement.

Soon it was time for Miguel and his sons to leave. Needed at the mine, they packed up their equipment and provisions, returning to work. I couldn't stop worrying about Tomas. He had become part of my family. I didn't feel the mine was safe for such a sweet young boy. I asked Miguel if Tomas could stay with us for a while. Grudgingly, Miguel agreed. It touched him to know how much I loved his son.

Miguel was lonely. His heart belonged to his beloved wife, who Tomas resembled. He desperately wanted a mother for his boys. I remember seeing Miguel watching Tomas and me together. There was such joy in his eyes. The next day, he asked me to be his wife. I recalled how Jose said Miguel and I should marry in my husband's feverish dreams. Miguel bought me a new rebozo to make sure I would be warm when we went on our walks.

He was happy that I settled in his community and spent a lot of time introducing me to the townspeople. He even found some from Córdoba who knew my family and were familiar with my husband's family. Each extended sympathy to me for Jose's death. He had been a legend in his time, always remembered for his willingness to help others. If there was a need for money, Jose gave them money. If they needed a letter of introduction, Jose wrote the letter. Every wish had been granted. His family had a reputation for helping hidden Jews whenever they were asked. While I was thinking about Jose and his generosity, Miguel was becoming impatient, waiting to know if I would marry him. One of the problems was we were still in love with our deceased partners. Comparing Miguel to Jose was a losing game. My husband was meticulous about all of his ventures, cultured and refined, while Miguel was a good worker and tough. Their worlds were different.

16

TO OUR TOWN

Following my dear husband's instructions, after years of careful planning and preparation, the hacienda was ready. A long road led to the large, arched front entryway with bright red maple trees lining the path. Then there was a grand red door with our family's crest proudly displayed. Red was our family's color. Domed openings were aligned with ornate wrought iron. It was a magnificent sight to see. When the door opened, a large sitting room appeared with a vast opening, shuttered when it was hot. It faced a glorious, rectangular-shaped garden with a pool and fountain in the middle. All year long, there were flowering plants filled with all of the colors of the rainbow. Behind the hacienda was a creek with a stone footbridge. As I crossed the bridge, I could hear the babbling of the water as it moved past the boulders. I loved the sound of birds chirping as they bathed in the creek. All along the garden were bedrooms to accommodate the family and guests. The thick walls were white, made of adobe, with exposed wood beams. The roof was covered in red tile, resembling the tops in Spain. All through the house were arches to resemble a Spanish-style hacienda. Marble floors imported from Italy graced the house. The dining room was large enough to accommodate thirty guests.

There was plenty of work for all to do taking care of such a grand estate, the land, and the animals. Francisco and Maria were in charge of securing staff. I was delighted with our new Casa De Gomez and felt welcomed in Pueblo.

There was a pleasing similarity to Spain. The buildings, clothing, food, and smells were reminders of our homeland. One of my favorite songs went like this: "uno tarde de verano, pase por la morería, Y vi a un a mora, lavando, a los pies de un fuente fría. Yo la dije mora bella, Yo la Dije: Mora linda." One afternoon in summer, I passed through the Moorish quarter and saw a Moorish maiden washing at the foot of a cold fountain. I said to her, "Lovely Moor, beautiful Moor." My love of Spain would forever be in my heart. I vowed to keep the memories of Spain alive. Our children would know of her charm, language, food, and customs and the generosity of her people.

I was grateful for all of Miguel's help, but I could not commit to him. After dinner, before his return to the mine, we walked outside into the cool night air. "My dear friend, I cherish you and want you to know that I am indebted to you for your kindness. I lost my husband a year ago and cannot love anyone else just yet. If I can ever love again, I will think of you."

My words saddened Miguel. He spoke softly to me, saying that he could wait for me; he cherished me too and only wanted to make me happy. "Until we meet again, *vaya con Dios*, go with God." The villagers were there to say goodbye to Miguel. As sad as it was, my family quickly adjusted to life in Pueblo. There were many fiestas. We celebrated El Dia De Ester, Saint Ester's Day in the spring. I loved this holiday because, as legend tells, Ester means Morning Star, a translation of Venus. I loved that Ester and Estrella both meant star. Everyone did their spring cleaning and dressed up in new clothes. A prayer was said, thanking God for the holiday. We ate *empanaditas*, a special dessert made in the shape of a crescent, filled with pumpkin and apples, then fried in oil and served alongside nuts and fruit. As a secret Jew, Ester was important to us.

Things were going along smoothly until one day while David was riding his horse, Oro, meaning gold, he stumbled upon some rattlesnakes. The horse was frightened and reared its legs in the air. Unable to stay on Oro, David fell. When he landed on the ground, he heard a loud crack and couldn't move his arm. With difficulty, he caught up with his horse and managed to get back on. When he arrived home, I ran to him. I called out to Francisco for the carriage. Then immediately, we took him to Doctor De Grazie.

Things changed for me that day. When Doctor De Grazie saw David, he came out to help him. I placed my hand on my boy's back, and then the doctor put his hand over mine to help steady David as we carefully moved him out of the carriage. In that brief moment of contact, I felt something I hadn't felt in a long time. The doctor set his arm and tended to his wounds with great compassion. Dr. De Grazie spoke to David, telling him he knew how much he loved riding, but he had to refrain from it for quite a while. David nodded in agreement with his doctor and thanked him for his concern. The good doctor had asked me to hold David's arm as he straightened it. Overcome with anguish at seeing my son cry out in pain, I cried too. Dr. De Grazie thanked me for helping him and asked me to sit down as he went to get some water for me. When I took the water from him, our hands met, and once again, I felt a connection to him. With tears in my eyes, I told the doctor how much I appreciated his kindness. Then I asked how much I owed him. He answered that he was happy to be of service and would check on David at home. The thought of his visit excited me. When we left, Dr. De Grazie thought for the first time, *This may be an enjoyable place to live.* Doctor De Grazie was an honored guest in our home.

Maria was delighted to see Doctor De Grazie at our door. She asked if he was there for the dinner she promised him. He answered that he was there to see David, requesting if he could come for dinner another time. "Thank you, Maria." Teasing her, he said, "I heard about your excellent cooking. Your meals are talked about as far away as Italy."

Maria laughed. I said to her, "You like the joking from the handsome doctor."

She asked me, "Can we invite him for dinner on Friday?" I nodded yes. She smiled broadly and told the handsome doctor, "There's always a special meal."

"I can hardly wait until then," he replied.

Maria woke early on Friday to collect herbs from the garden. This evening, she would make a magnificent dinner in honor of Doctor De Grazie. Maria planned the menu, hurrying to the marketplace to buy the freshest fruits and vegetables. She would serve polenta (corn mush), lamb stew with tomatoes and olives, roasted chicken, sweet peas, and a fresh apple cobbler for dessert.

The man of the hour arrived with flowers for Maria and me. We thanked him, put them in vases, and then placed them on the Shabbat table. He asked me to call him Alejandro. "Of course," I said. "I'd be happy to address you as Alejandro if you call me Estrella." We smiled and nodded to each other as we sat down at the festive table. White linens graced the table.

I left the table. In the back room, away from everyone, I placed a lace head covering on my head. I motioned with my hands to gather in the light of the candles. I recited the prayer over the gleaming candlesticks my mother gave to me on my wedding day. *"Baruch atah Adoshem elhanu meleh ha'olam ...* Blessed art thou, God, King of the universe ..." I closed the window shades while the candles burned brightly and placed them in a large clay pot so others could not see their light. Everyone was in high spirits with good food and conversation.

Surprised to see his favorite dishes, Dr. De Grazie enjoyed every savory morsel of the polenta and a perfectly juicy roast chicken with saffron and lemon. He had not eaten those dishes since he left Italy and was happy to have them again.

After dinner, the doctor and my family went into the sitting room. Francisco offered him brandy. Happily, he swirled the goblet and took a sip. He spoke softly to me, saying he enjoyed the evening. He told me that the food made him miss Italy even more.

"It is a beautiful country; you need to see it, Estrella."

I replied, "I would like to visit sometime."

The doctor continued telling me that his grandparents spoke so lovingly about Spain. "It has always been a dream of mine to see Spain one day."

I responded by telling him that there is no other place like Spain. "It is too sad to remember a place that we cannot call our home. It will always be my home in spirit." As I spoke, tears began to stream down my face. He gently brushed away the tear that fell on my cheek with his hand. I moved away from him. I was beginning to have feelings for this stranger from Italy. I could tell that he felt a stirring too. Just then,

Josey appeared in the doorway, wearing a silk nightgown with a pink ribbon in her hair.

My angel demanded a kiss from everyone. Happily, I turned my attention to my daughter, telling her that I would kiss her. Maria came into the room and held her hand out for Josey. She said to her, "It is time to go to bed."

Josey disagreed. She blurted out a loud no.

Maria asked, "Why not?"

Josey explained, "I need a kiss from everyone."

Dr. De Grazie asked, chuckling, "Does that mean me too?"

Josey nodded. "Yes, I mean you too," said the little one.

"All right, come here."

And with those words, she ran to him and jumped on his lap. Putting her little arms around him, she gave him a big kiss with a hug and said, "I love you." I gasped hearing these words.

My daughter instantly liked our new doctor. He returned the hug and said that he loved her too. He called her Jaffa. She was puzzled hearing that name, telling him that her name was Josey. Doctor De Grazie smiled back and said, "You are to me." With a questioning look on her face, she asked what it meant. He responded, "It means pretty." With a giggle, she thanked him. He told her that she was most welcome. "Buenos notches" (good night). Maria once again held out her hand for Josey. This time she took it. Maria put her precious child to bed and tucked her in, wishing her sweet dreams. Her little princess smiled back.

At this time, David came in with a chessboard, asking Alejandro if he wanted to play a game. It had been a long time since either one of them had played. They enjoyed the competition. My sweet David whispered to me, "I let the good doctor win."

Alejandro suggested that we take a walk in the moonlight. There was a full moon that evening. Francisco ran after us with a rebozo, handed it to me, and followed closely behind. As we strolled along the creek, the doctor told me how delightful my daughter was. I smiled and thanked him. I told him that she was the light of my life. He said, "It looks like she is the light of everyone's life," smiling at me.

I nodded, saying, "She is pure joy to us all." Whenever I sang to her, she enjoyed the music and began to sway her hips from side to side, clapping her hands and stomping her tiny feet. Then she raised her arms to the sky and danced the flamenco. Dancing was in her blood.

"You called her Jaffa. Is that a Hebrew word?" I inquired.

He answered, "Yes, it is."

I urged him not to call her that. "We must keep our Jewish identity a secret. Things are different here than in Italy. In Italy, Jews practice our faith but live in ghettos locked at night. My little girl is too young to understand how to keep a secret." Alejandro pleaded with me to accept his apology, saying that he was sorry, thanking me for reminding him and saying that he would be more careful in the future.

I was glad Francisco insisted I wear my rebozo because the night air was cold. The stars were bright and shining. It was as if they were twinkling just for us.

We walked silently. Then we began to speak to each other. I told him, "I find you to be a kind man, a devoted doctor doing the best for your patients."

He said, "I find you to be a loving mother with many talents, like managing a large estate." He was in awe of my independence.

It was getting late, so we went back to the hacienda. As we headed back, I began to fall over a rock, losing my balance. Thankfully, Alejandro acted quickly and caught me in his arms. As he held me, we gazed into each other's eyes for what seemed like a lifetime. Nervously giggling, I thanked him for helping me.

We returned to the parlor, where my servants had prepared a roaring fire along with hot tea and *biscochitos* ready for us to enjoy. "What are your plans for yourself?" he asked.

"For myself, I want to help our people wherever needed."

He leaned toward me. "I mean for you, Doña Estrella Fuentes Gomez, as a person."

I was nervous and looked away before saying, "I want to run my household and business."

"All right, Estrella. I know this is hard for you. I will ask you outright. Do you want to marry again? Do you want a father for your children?"

With a broad smile, I said, "Yes, with all my heart. Just not now."

That was all Alejandro needed to hear. He asked, "Would you consider me?"

I responded lovingly, "Yes, I would. But I am still too much in love with my departed husband."

I was excited about the prospect of having love back in my life. I promised myself that I would not compare Alejandro to Jose. The love of my youth was Jose. The love of my adult life could be Alejandro. It was unexpected. It was thrilling. I never thought it could happen to me again. Life is full of twists and turns. In this sleepy town, I wondered whether I could find love again.

We spent every evening together, taking walks in the moonlight, finding out many things about each other, accompanied by Francisco and under the watchful eye of my beloved Maria. Some evenings, the new doctor would be summoned to someone's home to attend to a patient, and other times he would read stories to my girls. He loved telling them folktales. We all grew to love our charming doctor from Italy.

Alejandro was the eldest son of a wealthy merchant who worked in Murano, Italy, but lived in the Venice Ghetto. His family had initially come from Granada, Spain. When the Christians took Granada from the Moors in 1492, his family fled to Italy. They spoke Ladino, a language started after families left Spain, a combination of Hebrew and Castilian Spanish. They sang songs of the golden land of Spain and practiced their Jewish traditions. Though separated by distance, hidden Jews kept in touch with other Jewish communities throughout the world by courier. That was how Alejandro's father found the need for a doctor in Pueblo. International business was a specialty for Jews since traveling was a part of their work. Sending secret messages under the noses of governments could be easily accomplished.

It was a way of life for the various communities throughout the world that were isolated. Couriers brought news of family and friends in faraway places. When Jewish communities were in trouble and money was needed for food, shelter, or freedom, members of the nation of Israel, all Jews, helped one another. No one else would. The Fuentes and the Gomez families often dug deep into their pockets to help their brethren.

I read about Murano in the encyclopedia. The city my ancestor spoke about was familiar to me. Murano, Italy, was the glassmaking capital of the world. The industry began in Ur, Mesopotamia, around 2400 BC and became a Jewish craft. When the Romans dispersed the Jews from the land of Judea, the trade went where they went. Glassmaking was profitable in Spain. Before and after the Inquisition began, the Jews left for many other lands. They had established foundries in Morocco, Egypt, Holland, and Italy. Venice was the center of Italy. In 1292, the Council of Ten in Venice proclaimed that the glassmaking industry move to Murano, an island off Venice. The reason given for the move was to protect citizens from the fires that spread from the foundries. There were two reasons for the action, and they had nothing to do with protecting the populace—to keep the glassmaking secrets away from other countries and to gain control of the glassmaking industry.

One evening while taking our stroll, Alejandro told me that he loved my children and me. He sang a Ladino love song. "Create a ti, es suvir en las nuves, En mounds y yega solo la imagination, Kererte a ti, Es bolar en Los siglos, En la luz radiante del dia ke nase. Kererte a ti, Es bivir en verdad." ("Loving you is like rising to the clouds, in worlds reached only by imagination. Loving you is like flying in the sky, in the radiant light of a dimming day. Loving you is living.") Hearing that song sung to me by this kind doctor made me fall in love with him.

A courier handed Alejandro a message when we returned to the hacienda. The letter said that his father had a weak heart and was dying. He wanted his son to return to Venice as soon as he could. There was a long tradition in his family of making glass. It was something that a father passed down to his son. Alejandro had been taught the art of glassmaking work for a few years. He did well but had little interest. He preferred to be a doctor. His father accepted his son's decision, though he was disappointed.

Hearing of his father's imminent death, Alejandro told me he had to return to Italy. He begged me to marry him before he left so we could go together. I refused. I told him, "You need to be with your father now. I promise we will have our time when you return." My love understood and said that he would return as soon as possible because he loved and needed me. I sighed, saying, "Until we meet again."

The thought of Alejandro leaving for Italy frightened me. We had only known each other for a brief time, but he had become an essential part of my life. I worried he would find someone in Italy and not return. When he left, I pressed a piece of gold in his hand before he rode away. I told him that God would protect him when he gave the gold to charity when he reached his destination. He smiled and waved goodbye.

Alejandro's leaving was difficult for me. It was as if there was a hole in my heart. I tried to keep busy but found myself daydreaming about my love. I began to write poetry once more, praying to the God of Israel to keep him safe and return him to me.

He was gone for a month. I had no word from Alejandro, which made me nervous. No couriers came to my home. I could not wait any longer. I had a letter sent by courier to Santa Fe, where it was forwarded to Mexico City. Someone there would be going back across the ocean to Spain. Taken to Italy, the letter would reach Alejandro. The letter said the following:

> My dearest darling,
>
> Much peace and health, my most beloved Alejandro. May God grant you and your family good health until one hundred twenty. First of all, you shall know that I am well, as are the children; I hope to hear the same of you and your loved ones.
>
> I did not know how much I would miss you, my dear one. I now am sure of my love for you. I will be devoted to you all the days of my life. Return to me as soon as you can leave your family. I wait for your return, as do the children. I am not whole without you. *Los matrimonios se hacen en el cielo*; marriages are made in heaven.
>
> Forever,
> Estrella

I wanted him to see how much Josey was growing. She made up stories and acted them out with puppets Maria made for her. She acted like her brother and sister did when they were on the ship. After dinner each night, my darling would perform her plays. All the neighbors came to our hacienda to view Josey's latest production. As she continued her art, costumes and scenery became more elaborate, with the help of her beautiful big sister, Valentina. I was delighted by the antics of my creative children.

Meanwhile, David and Tomas wanted to join Miguel and Carlos at the mine. Now sixteen years old, David wanted to be a man. I had to learn to treat him that way. I couldn't think about the boys leaving me. I kept postponing the inevitable, especially with Alejandro away.

I knew it was time to let the boys go. On David's seventeenth birthday, I announced that both could work in the mine. David joked, saying, "That was a real birthday gift, Mama." The thought of their new adventure thrilled the boys. They quickly prepared for their journey. Maria and Francisco cried as they helped the boys pack. Since my son's birth, they had been with David, and they had grown to love Tomas. Now it was time to say goodbye. They prayed that God would bless them and keep them from harm, sobbing. The boys also found it hard to leave, but the adventure called to them.

17

WORKING THE MINE

Ready for the venture of a lifetime, Tomas and David would follow the map Miguel had left for them. The trail had many twists and turns. As everyone said their goodbyes, Francisco insisted he go with the boys. He told me, "I am afraid for their safety."

I said that one of the younger men could travel with the boys. Francisco smiled and said, "I want to go with them." Tomas and David were relieved to have Francisco on the trip because they were frightened too. There were many stories told about Indian ambushes on the trail. Also, they knew they would eat well. Francisco spent a lot of time with Maria preparing meals. He had picked up a great deal of expertise in the kitchen. I blessed and wished Francisco and the boys a safe journey.

As they were leaving, I pressed a letter into Francisco's hand and asked him to please give it to Miguel for me. Taking the note, he smiled. As was the custom, I gave each of them a piece of silver to give to charity at the end of the trip. I had given Jose money for charity when he left for Santa Fe. He got to his destination and gave the money to the poor without any trouble. I asked Pablo to provide Jose with money for charity when he came back to Mexico City, but he forgot. I never let someone I love leave without money for the needy.

The trail to the mine was rocky. Though it was easy for the boys, Francisco had difficulty navigating the terrain. They arrived safely, as fortune was on their side.

Anton, Carlos, and Miguel greeted them, happy to see they had made the trip without harm. Francisco gave Miguel the letter. He walked away and immediately opened it. His big, wide grin slowly turned to a frown. The letter said the following:

> May the Lord in heaven grant you good health all of the days of your life.

> To my dear friend Miguel,
>   When you receive this letter, Francisco, David, and Tomas will have just arrived from an arduous journey. Please give them food to eat and a comfortable place to sleep and ask someone to escort Francisco home, as he is old and I fear for his health.
>   I will always have a special place in my heart for you, my Miguel. When I was at the very lowest point in my life, you were there to help me through it. I will never forget your kindness. I can promise you my friendship, for I found love with someone else. May you also find someone to love.

> With great fondness,
> I remain,
> Estrella

I could only imagine Miguel standing there, thinking about his dashed hopes for happiness with me, needing some time to absorb the message. I'm sure Miguel thought the letter would say I would marry him. He would be shocked that it turned out differently. We didn't fit together.

Seeing Tomas, David, and Francisco put a smile on Miguel's face. The boys had changed so much. Francisco was a welcome addition since he was an excellent storyteller. The following day, they took a grand tour of the mine. Production immediately went up when the boys joined the Indians. They were terrific workers whose work ethic inspired others.

Sleeping accommodations were not adequate. There were only two bedrooms; the boys took one, and the other was for the men. Miguel decided to build another bedroom for Anton. He was old and needed his rest. Some days, he was too weak to work at the mine. He had lived alone for so long, and he needed his privacy, though he enjoyed the company of the men. After a long day at the mine, they pitched in to build the room for Anton.

Francisco needed to return home. He missed everyone but especially the little one, Josey. Francisco loved telling her stories and couldn't wait to see her again. She felt the same way as he did. They were always together.

The journey back to Pueblo could be dangerous. Miguel arranged for some of the workers to accompany Francisco, who thought it was ridiculous to be so concerned but conceded. The thought of traveling alone did scare him. He never liked to admit being afraid of anything. My trusted servant liked having others around when on the road. Thankfully, the trip back home was uneventful.

Francisco was sure that Josey had grown three inches. Maria was pleased to have her husband back. They had missed each other. Josey and Valentina greeted Francisco with a song they had made up just for him.

While Francisco and the boys were gone, there was a flood on our ranch. Around the house were bags of sand to absorb the water; it didn't work. The flood destroyed our garden and most of the sheep. Carcasses were everywhere. I had an idea. "Let's use the wool from the sheep to weave blankets," I said to Maria. I had learned how to spin yarn from Isabel in Mexico City. Happy to help the town's women make their own money, I could teach them how to weave to sell their wares in town. They could create designs of their own. I was proud of myself for thinking of this idea. Now we had to work making the looms and spinning the yarn.

Then a courier returned. He had brought a letter from Alejandro:

May the Creator of the world, our heavenly Father, bestow life, health, and peace upon you. To you, my dear Estrella,

159

I was so happy to hear from you, my dear one. I am afraid that I have sad news to share with you. My pious father, Avraham Yitchak, has departed this world to be with the Lord in *Olam habah* (the world to come). I fear that I must stay in Italy for some time to take care of his affairs. I will not be able to bring my mother back with me. She is in deep mourning and is not well enough to take the long journey. I am afraid that you will forget me. I pray to the Lord that this does not happen. I will return to you, my love. The distance cannot separate our love. When I look up to the heavens, I see your face in every star. You are my star, Estrella.

May the Lord protect you from all trouble. These are the thoughts and prayers from one who loves and honors you.

Forever yours,
Alejandro

I read the letter and looked up to heaven. I wanted the note to say that he would be coming back soon. I was disappointed. I asked God, "Why do these things always happen to me?" I cried. Thank God I had a new venture to keep me busy. Otherwise, I would have gone mad. Getting the business going would keep me from worrying about Alejandro. The more active I was, the happier I was.

Now it was time to get to work. I needed weaving looms to make the blankets. Men in the village made the equipment with available supplies. The wood came from the forest behind the town. Within a month, the looms would be ready for production. The wool would be sheared from the dead sheep and prepared for weaving. All the women were excited to learn the weaving process. It was hard work. When the first loom was ready, we put together the wool to be dyed. The yarn was placed in a bucket and left to soak for two weeks. Dirt and a pail of water produced the color brown. Berries mixed with water became red. Cactus made the color green. From flowers, various colors appeared, including yellow, orange, and purple. Some of the wool didn't have to be dyed.

Our *ovejas*, sheep, from Spain were naturally spotted. The white fleece was soft, and the black was rough. They had their unique patterns, which the weavers duplicated. The women knelt at their looms, weaving the many strands of different colors into the desired pattern. The local Indian women had been weaving blankets for many years. I asked them if I could use their blanket designs. They happily consented. As the village women became more adept at weaving, they came up with their own creations. It was as if there was an explosion of creativity. We were so busy that life became hectic.

The next time the caravan came to the village, I gave a peddler from Santa Fe many blankets to take back with him to sell. The business succeeded beyond our expectations. Even little Josey loved weaving. The workers made a smaller loom just for her. She loved making blankets for her dolls. It was so much fun watching her weave the blankets. You could not talk to her when she was working on her loom. She was busy focusing on her work. Josey would stomp her little foot every time she made a mistake, then go back and fix it. As she learned more, she too became a designer, creating patterns. Valentina had her loom and enjoyed making her blankets as well. She liked to make baby blankets. Becoming an expert, Valentina loved working with bright-colored yarn.

I was not happy. I missed my love, Alejandro. Why did I have this ache in my heart? I still thought about Jose, my first love. My mind raced back to our lovemaking, and I yearned to be loved that way again. We had so many beautiful plans for the future. I thought about all of this and sighed. What was the point? When he died, I died. Yet there was still hope for the future, just no longer with Jose. Alejandro would return to me. We would have a good life together. I prayed to God to let him return.

In the meantime, each day, the women worked hard at their looms. In time, they would have enough for another trading trip. The excitement of going to Santa Fe was contagious. We would bring our blankets to the plaza in the center of town. The merchants would sell cloth, ribbons, spices, and jewelry. The Pueblo Indians brought pottery, baskets, and chilies to trade. There were even times when the French trappers would come to sell their pelts from the animals they had killed in the forest.

The town had a mixture of Indians, Spaniards, and Mestizos, a mixed ancestry with a white European and an indigenous background.

I loved how stimulated all my senses were here. I smelled the food roasting over firepits, felt the fine cloth, heard the different languages, tasted various foods, and saw of all of these things; it was fascinating. The time had finally come to sell our blankets in Santa Fe. All the women involved in making the blankets were going to the marketplace. Josey was tall and willowy. She ran like a gazelle. My daughter was lovely to look at and bright. She was eager to sell some of the doll blankets on the plaza. The women wore full skirts and brightly colored, loose-fitting blouses, Santa Fe style. Rebozos covered their heads, and they wrapped them around their shoulders since it was cold outside. It would keep them warm while sitting out all day. We set up and waited for customers to come. We could hardly get our displays up before crowds of people circled our stands. The comments were complimentary. One woman said, "I've never seen blankets like these." Another lady said, "I must have two of these beautiful blankets." Still another said, "Look how tight this weave is. How warm it will be this winter." Even Josey sold all her doll blankets within thirty minutes. She decided that the next time, she would make twice as many.

We sold all the blankets except the ones with earth tones. All of the bright and cheerful ones were gone. The people only wanted reds, oranges, blues, and greens for their blankets. Who knew? Now we did. Next time, we would bring more colorful blankets to sell.

We all slept at the inn in town and headed back home in the morning. We were thrilled, hardly able to wait to tell everyone when we got home. What a satisfying feeling! Starting a business was good for the women in the village and our families.

While in Italy, Alejandro wrote to my father, asking for permission that we wed. I also wrote to Papa, requesting his permission, and eagerly awaited his response. After several months, I finally got the answer I had been praying for. My Papa granted permission for Alejandro to marry me. I was overjoyed with happiness.

Alejandro had not returned. I reassured myself that my love would get home as soon as possible. The distances were great, the roads difficult and dangerous. I had to be patient. Patience was not one of my qualities.

A courier came with a letter from Alejandro. This time, it was from Naples.

> May the merciful Lord bless you and keep you safe.
> My dear Estrella,
> I am writing my last letter to you. I will board the ship here in Naples and port in Veracruz in about five weeks. I will then journey by caravan to Santa Fe. I will ride home and begin our life together.
>
> I long to see you,
> May God be with you,
>
> Mi Amore,
> Alejandro

I began to calculate. How much longer did I need to wait? The letter, written three months ago, said my love would return in ten months. That meant only another seven months. *Only seven months! I better keep myself very busy. If I don't, I will go out of my mind.* In the meantime, I helped the women make more yarn for their blankets, which took a long time.

There were ten women making blankets. Many more wanted to weave, but there were not enough looms. The men were making them as quickly as they could. They also had to take care of their fields and livestock. They were able to finish a loom in about three weeks. It seemed as if the whole village wanted to be involved somehow. The money raised would go to a meeting place where we could gather.

I wondered if it was time for Alejandro's return. Suddenly, as if by magic, the time passed. Any day now, my love would come through my door. Each night before going to sleep, I prayed that this would be my last night without him.

18

MI AMORE

I dreamt that Alejandro had returned, appearing at my doorstep. Opening the door, I jumped into his arms. A long embrace followed. It was exciting to feel his lips on mine. Nothing else felt so good. I could still feel the kiss after our lips had parted. Each night, it was the same dream. I thought, *Tonight my dream will come true.* I fervently wished.

As the sun was rising, a small band of travelers arrived. They were tired and weary from their long journey. They had traveled far. In the group was a dashingly handsome man. It was Alejandro. He, too, had been dreaming of me, his love. The first face he wished to see was mine. I was going to be his wife. He had received word from my papa, consenting to our marriage. There was no time to waste. Alejandro knew that he would not be complete without me at his side. We had already lost years while he was away in Italy. I missed him terribly. He had to tend to his father's business and help his mother adjust to life without her husband.

I ran to the door when I heard the knock. The long months of waiting for my love's return melted away. I cheered when I saw my sweetheart. That was all that mattered. He was home. Francisco, Maria, Valentina, and Josey were standing next to us, waiting for their turn to greet Alejandro. Josey could not wait any longer. Finally, she pushed her way in between Alejandro and me. She began to tug on Alejandro's pants. "It is my turn to kiss Doctor De Grazie, Mama!" she shouted.

Alejandro swept her up in his arms and hugged her. He said, "Oh, so sorry, my dear. And how is my darling? My, my, aren't you tall? You are as tall as Maria—well, maybe a little shorter. Could it be—yes, it is true? You are more beautiful than when I left."

"Dr. De Grazie, you are so silly," Josey said with a giggle. Josey kissed Alejandro on the cheek.

All of the others circled him. Our family exchanged warm greetings. We were all thrilled he had returned. He had gifts for everyone. Francisco got a hand-blown glass figure of a horse. Waiting for David was a beautiful, hand-tooled saddle, and for Tomas, a leather belt.

For the women in his life, Maria received a hand-embroidered apron. A beautiful blue and gold bracelet for Valentina. For Josey, there was a gold locket. For me, his wife-to-be, was a diamond tiara.

It was a special day because we were fortunate to celebrate Josey's birthday and Alejandro's return. The ladies of the village had prepared all day for the Fandango. They made tortillas on the *horno* (an outside oven) and baked biscochitos for the party. Before the guests arrived, the family enjoyed our tradition of pulling the birthday girl's ear eight times. One for each year and an extra pull for good luck. Josey was beaming with all the attention, giggling and laughing with each tug.

Maria had made beautiful white dresses for Josey and Valentina for the festivities. Sewn onto the sleeves and the neckline were colorful ribbons. The bodice was loose. My angels enjoyed twirling around in their newly created dresses. They felt like they were flying. I asked Alejandro to come to my room to see the dresses. Josey asked Dr. De Grazie, "What do you think of my party dress?"

He said, "You and Valentina will be the most beautiful girls at the party." Valentina blushed and thanked him for the compliment. Josey smiled.

Many of the town's people were at Josey's party. Dressed in brightly colored clothing, their faces bright and shiny, the children were excited about the celebration. Parties were fun. There were games and sweets for everyone. The children all got a turn at hitting the piñata. The clay pot was filled with money, nuts, oranges, and wrapped candy. Each child was blindfolded. The others would sing, "Dale, dale, dale, no preidas el tino porque si lo predre el camino. Hit, hit, hit. Don't lose the knack. Because if you lose it, you'll lose the way. You've hit it once.

You've hit it twice. You've hit it thrice. Now your time is up." The blindfolded child swung at the piñata with a pole. When the pot broke open, all the children rushed to get the goodies.

Listening to the tape brought a smile on my face because I had played this game when I was young. Kids now used piñatas as toys. It was all part of the excitement of the fiesta. I didn't know it had such a long history. The Spanish Conquistadors brought the game to the New World. They learned the game from the Italians. Marco Polo saw it in China and brought the game back to Europe. I couldn't believe how much history a child's game could have. What an exciting tale. I wondered what else I would learn.

On the tape, I heard that Alejandro helped Estrella host the birthday party. The villagers were happy to see him again. Their doctor had been missed and was not expected to return. It was a sleepy little place without the excitement of Europe.

Alejandro loved the village and the people. He especially loved me. Nothing but death would separate him from his love, except if I did not want him. The music played a lively song. He said insistently, "Marry me. I want you always."

I replied, "Yes, my love. When?"

"How about today? There is a well-known saying about love by philosopher Isaac ben Judah Abarbanel. The phrase is that love turns one person into two and two into one." I agreed with him.

I told him that I needed time to prepare for the wedding. "I'll need to tell David, Miguel, and all of the others so they can be with us."

"Let's send a messenger today. Francisco, could you please ask around if anyone is going to the mine."

He agreed. "I'll be glad to, Doctor," replied Francisco. Guillermo was going past the mine.

I quickly ran into the hacienda to find a paper and a quill with ink. With a flourish, I wrote the following:

> May the good Lord bless you all the days of your life,
> my dear son. I never thought that I could find such

happiness in my life again. After your father's death, I felt there was no hope for love and joy. I was satisfied to have you and your sisters to take care of all the days of my life. Now, I have the pleasure of inviting you to share my joy at my upcoming wedding. Alejandro and I would like you to walk me down the aisle at our wedding. In two weeks, we will be married. My happiness will be complete with you by my side.

Your loving mother.

I wrote another letter, this time to Miguel.

May the Lord of Israel bless you and keep you out of harm's way, Miguel. You are my dear lifelong friend. When my wonderful husband died, you were my companion. I needed your strength to get me past the worst tragedy of my life. Now, I would like you to be with me on one of the happiest days. Alejandro and I have found that we love each other and wish to marry. I hope you can set aside your feeling of hurt and join us on this happy occasion. You will be forever in my heart.

With great fondness to you always,
Estrella

Francisco brought the letters to Guillermo, who would be leaving for the mine in the morning. Now that the dining was over, it was time to dance. Alejandro and I danced with the guests. A slight chill in the air kept us comfortable as we danced. Alejandro and I spoke to all of the guests at Josey's birthday party between dances. We said nothing about our upcoming marriage. Tonight was Josey's night. We did not want to take any attention away from her. There would be time enough to tell everyone, starting tomorrow.

The next afternoon, after everyone had recovered from the fiesta, I began to tell people that Alejandro and I were to be married. The first people I told were Francisco and Maria. They both began to cry. They were so happy for me. They had prayed it would happen. Maria asked if she could oversee making the dresses for Valentina, Josey, and me. I thought that would be a lovely gesture, so I asked if she could include red around the neckline and wrists. It was the girls' favorite color. I told her that I would need one more dress for her. My second mother, Maria, was surprised by my revelation and cried happy tears. Then I started to cry, and we embraced.

There was an outpouring of well-wishers. Everyone wanted to be part of the wedding preparations. It would take two weeks to construct the building, which was quite an undertaking. The villagers were determined to do this for their doctor. Food preparations were taken care of by the women. Everything was in order.

Now it was time to tell Josey and Valentina. Both Alejandro and I asked the girls to take a walk with us. The sun had just set over the mountaintops. As it faded on the horizon, we told our girls we would be married. Valentina was excited and happy for us, but Josey said nothing. There was no smile on her face. I asked her if she would like the doctor to be her papa. Josey was pouting. "Oh yes, Mamacita," she cried. To the doctor, she said, "I thought you would marry me."

Alejandro smiled and said, "My dear Josey, we are all family. Josey, I want to be your papa."

I pleaded, "Please be happy for us."

My little daughter asked again if he was sure that he wanted to marry me. Alejandro replied that he was sure of it. Josey sighed and smiled, saying she thought she would like him to be her papa. Alejandro smiled, giving Josey a big hug and a kiss on her cheek. Our new little family walked back to the hacienda.

When I tucked Josey into bed that night, I sang my little daughter a lullaby I had learned from Alejandro that his mother sang to him as a child. It went like this: "Durme, Durme mi Angelico. Hijico chico de tu nación. Criatura de Sion, No conoces la dolor. Por que no canto yo Ah! Contaronlas mis alas. Y mi Boz amudicio Al! Edmundo de dolar. Sleep, sleep, my little angel. The little child of your nation. Child of Zion, You don't know sorrow. You ask me why I am not singing. They cut my wings. And my voice became silent. Oh, what a world of despair."

I tiptoed out of the room and joined Alejandro on the veranda, who was sitting with Francisco. Alejandro first looked around to see if anyone was near. Then he whispered, "I heard you singing to Josey. You have a lovely voice, my dear. Could you sing a song for me?"

"Of course, I will, my love." I asked if he had something special in mind. He replied quietly, asking for "La Shana habaha b'yerusalaim" ("Next Year in Jerusalem"). I told him that I would be happy to sing that song.

After I sang the song, Alejandro said to me that he loved the way I sang and that the piece was beautiful. Then he sweetly said, "You are the light of my life." I smiled at my husband-to-be.

Early the following week, I received a message from David:

> May God bless you, my mother and Alejandro. My hope is for you to have a long and happy life together. I am most honored to walk you down the aisle on your wedding day. Carlos, Tomas, Miguel, Anton, and I will see you soon.
>
> Your beloved son,
> David

I was so happy to hear from David. I began to dance through the house. I kissed Maria and Francisco as I passed by them. I swept up my daughters and started dancing with them.

The wedding day was getting closer. It looked like the community room would barely be completed in time. The men were working feverishly to get the project done. David and the others would be there in a few days to help out with the finishing touches for the wedding. The women planned and prepared the food for the blessed event.

The days leading up to the wedding had lots of activities as our guests arrived. Alejandro was the perfect host and provided lodging and meals for everyone, with a flair for the most exciting day in his life. Alejandro prayed, "Dear God, thank you for giving me the most wonderful woman. I promise to love and honor her every day as long as I live."

It was the night before the wedding. I was not able to sleep much.

I thought of my mother and father. They would be so happy for me. I would have liked them to be with me on my wedding day.

When I dreamt, it was about Jose. I remembered how silly I was with him. I thought of the fun we had together. Making him laugh was a joy. I remembered our lovemaking. Life was happy, so innocent for us then. I wondered whether I was doing the right thing by marrying Alejandro. "Jose, please send me a sign that he is suitable for me," I pleaded. Suddenly, I was floating in the sky. I felt uplifted. I could see my son, daughters, Maria, Francisco, and all the guests. They were looking up at me, wondering why I was in the sky. Holding my hand tightly, flying alongside me, was Jose. I asked him if I was destined to be a lonely, hidden star all of my life, not able to practice my faith openly with my family. Jose looked into my eyes and said, "One day, you will be free to be what you want to be with your family and community." He promised to always love me. "Go to Alejandro. He is a good man. He will take care of you and the children. Go with God." With those words, Jose let go of my hand. I floated down to Alejandro, waiting for me on the ground. I softly said to him, "I am ready to be your wife. Jose told me to marry you." Alejandro smiled. He took my hand and kissed it. He said, "I will always take care of you." When I woke up, I had a big smile on my face. It was time for my wedding.

On my wedding day, I woke up with my daughter Josey smiling at me, inches away from my face. She jumped on the bed and told me it was time to get up. Valentina ran over to the bed and picked up Josey. "Sorry, Mama. Josey's excited. Good morning."

I laughed and grabbed Valentina's hand. "I need hugs from my girls." We all giggled in bed together only for a moment. Then the housemaids came in with bath salts, clothing, jewelry, and makeup. It was time to get ready. My wedding gown was magnificent. I covered my head with a mantilla (head covering) made of the most delicate lace, topped with the diamond tiara Alejandro gave me when he returned from Italy. The silk gown had pearl petals sewn on the bodice. The ruby necklace given to me by my mother graced my neck. Maria said that I was more beautiful than at my first wedding. That was the way Maria spoke to me all the time.

Valentina and Josey both had red roses in their hair. David had a red rose fastened to his jacket. Out of the corner of my eye, I noticed how Carlos gazed at Valentina with a smile. I knew he was struck by how beautiful my girl was. It was true Valentina was a beauty, but what made me beam with pride was knowing how kind she was. I thought it was sweet. It reminded me of how I would look at Jose when we were young and first falling in love.

We were married by our local priest at our local church and then had carriages waiting to take our family and friends home for the wedding celebration at the hacienda. It was fit for royalty, complete with fireworks and imported wines, cheeses, and silks. The aroma of roses and citrus filled the air. Our staff lovingly prepared roasted meats.

We danced and drank bottle after bottle of imported wine and local favorites like tequila. Candles filled the yard. The fountains babbled as the music began to play. Then I heard the clacking of the castanets and saw our guests dancing the night away. I immediately jumped up to join in the celebration dance. David, Valentina, and Josey all joined me as we danced and laughed until the wee hours of the morning. We dined on delectable, sweet treats expertly prepared by our community. Everyone had a wonderful time. The only bitterness to this beautiful, sweet celebration was that my beloved mama and papa were not with me.

After the celebration, we had a more intimate ceremony honoring our Jewish faith. In front of God and everyone, Alejandro and I became husband and wife under the laws of Moses and Israel. Engraved inside our wedding band was a Hebrew inscription saying, "I am my beloved, and my beloved is mine." I had heard those words spoken to me at my first wedding. Jose had recited this age-old saying to me under the chuppah. I was happy to see those words on my wedding band as a constant reminder of the love I shared with Alejandro. It brought hope to my heart. Alejandro crushed the glass with his foot. Everyone yelled, "Mazel Tov." We kissed and stood smiling at each other under the chuppah.

I was thrilled that things had gone so well for our family and friends, with no incidents of Indian attacks, deaths, or the Inquisition following them.

My husband and I walked hand in hand to our home. After heartbreak and disappointment, we were hopeful that our lives together would be filled with joy. What did God have in store for us? Whatever would come our way, we would make it work. Time would give us the answers. Meanwhile, we were happy. That was all that mattered.

I sighed when I finished hearing my ancestor's story. There was nothing more. I hoped that they walked into the sunset of their lives content. Estrella's story had a profound impact on me. I had a hunger to know more.

19

WHAT'S NEXT?

I sat on the floor with my research strewn all about, yellow legal pads filled with my chicken scratch writing, photos, recipes, books, maps, pens, and highlighters. Everything I had learned about my family in the last couple of years was in front of me, including the wooden box Abuela had given me. A little voice told me I had to share this incredible story of perseverance and faith with others. My family had an exciting journey. However, I didn't know if there was enough for a book. I felt as if my world was getting bigger, with so many doors opening before me, yet still, there were many unanswered questions. Those same doors that had opened immediately slammed shut and locked.

The phone rang. Consuela told me, "There was a massive flood on our land. No harm came to any person or animal, though the ranch was in complete disarray." She had never seen anything like this before. The winds were so strong it felt like a tornado. There was a lot of damage to the ranch. The storm uncovered what appeared to be a cobblestone pathway under a massive amount of dirt and grass. The trees that had graced the area were all blown away.

I asked my sister, "Do you want me to come home to help out?" She said it wasn't necessary since I'd be home soon anyway.

My dad called the city to have someone inspect the area. He thought the cobblestones might be an important discovery. The city worker was amazed at what he saw. He thought it might be an ancient road. A team of archaeologists came, led by Dr. William Munoz. As they excavated the site, they were shocked to learn it was an old road. It appeared to be more than four hundred years old. The timeline made sense, as it coincided with my ancestors' arrival. The local and national papers covered the thrilling news. Historians and archaeologists were excited about the discovery and swarmed our property to see it for themselves. It was a sensation.

I had an epiphany. I thought my ancestors' trip from Spain to the New World was fascinating. Others might think so too. My first step was finding a literary agent. Together we came up with a proposal to present to my bosses. In it, I laid out my strategy. I would write a different type of travel column for the magazine. The articles would include fun facts about food, music, culture, and sights to see, with a twist. It would cover my family's history in those places. I planned to retrace the route traveled by my ancestors, starting where their journey ended.

Beginning in New Mexico, the first stop would be in my hometown of Pueblo, then to Santa Fe. Next, I would arrive in Mexico, visiting Mexico City and Veracruz. Finally, I would conclude the travel series in Spain, seeing Cadiz and Córdoba. These travel articles would eventually become a book.

I was a bundle of nervous energy, shaking my foot uncontrollably under the table before the meeting with my editors. I wanted to do this assignment and was thinking of all the angles. I presented my ideas with financial data showing circulation increases when magazines included travel articles. A few weeks later, I was relieved to hear a resounding yes to my proposal. My bosses thought it was a good idea. They had faith that I would make the series a success. For the next couple of months, I was busy preparing for my assignment with a flurry of activity. My team and I worked on obtaining travel documentation, scheduling interviews, corresponding with historians, hiring travel guides, and finding attractions.

My initial call was to the Pueblo Historical Society, run by a classmate and dear friend, Lucinda Martinez. She was happy to help. After the shocking discovery of the cobblestone road on our land, I wanted to find out more about the origins of the ranch. Lucinda researched land records from the archives and found documents. My ancestor Jose Gomez received the land from the Spanish government in 1600 as a land grant. I didn't realize our family lived on the same property for nearly four hundred years, though there were changes in the hacienda itself. What a revelation!

I took a cab from the airport and ran to the entrance of our hacienda. I burst through the door and yelled, "I'm home!" There were hugs and kisses all around. My parents arranged for a big party to celebrate Julio, who had just graduated from medical school. He had taken my grandparents' advice to do something that would benefit others. Soon he would begin his residency in, of all places, LA. It made me smile. Just as I was leaving for my big assignment, I finally got my wish to have family live near me. Hopefully, we would have some years to enjoy each other's company. It would be wonderful to have Julio nearby.

My brother loved to tease me about how competitive I was. It made me laugh, as I was not in the same league as Julio. He had to be number one in everything. If he wasn't the best, he took it personally, as evident with his rival classmate he called Ms. Know It All. She called him Mr. Arrogant.

Julio and Jojo battled class after class for the top-ranking spots. They continually fought to be the best. Jojo was usually a little faster at getting her hand up, which infuriated Julio. They were equally annoyed when the other got more attention and praise from their professors. Their constant complaints drove their roommates crazy. This childish behavior went on for several months.

They couldn't stop goading each other. The two geniuses couldn't even look at each other without saying something annoying, like when they got their tests back. Julio proudly showed his paper to Jojo, admiring the perfect score he got. Jojo said, "Congratulations," and then showed her paper with a score of 102 percent. She had received extra credit for answering the question on the back of the test. Julio's face turned purple. He hadn't seen the additional credit question. He hated that she got a higher score, even two percentage points.

Around this time, Julio's roommate, Harry, started dating a sweet girl named Cici, who thought it would be fun to go on a double date together with her roommate. Since Julio was not seeing anyone, she offered to set him up. Julio reluctantly agreed because Cici was an excellent cook. She promised, " I'll make your favorite dish, huevos rancheros, if you accept the blind date." It was worth being fixed up for a good meal. He might have consented anyway. Julio, Harry, and Cici waited outside the restaurant for Cici's friend, who was running just a few minutes late. When she appeared, Julio's jaw dropped, just as hers did. His date was none other than Ms. Know It All. Jojo greeted Julio as "Mr. Arrogant" and nodded to him. The two of them immediately started to argue with each other. Again acting like children, they feuded about who should order first.

Cici and Harry watched them bantering back and forth as if they were watching a tennis match. They felt so lucky going to dinner and seeing a show for free. Jojo and Julio both realized how immature they were acting and laughed. The tennis match ended.

The four of them had a great evening. At the end of the date, they all hugged good night. Since the two brainiacs impressed each other, they decided, "We should join forces and create our own study group together. After all, we are the brightest students in our classes. No one else could beat us." From that point on, they took turns answering their professors' questions. Their rivalry turned into affection, which later turned into love. Now Jojo is my little brother's fiancée. Their fights were a ploy to get to know each other. The arguing stopped immediately.

The other reason to celebrate was the launch of my travel series. I was thrilled to learn more about my family's background. Lucinda came up to me and said, "I made a copy of your home's land purchase." It was chilling to get a piece of history in my hands. What a find.

Since the party lasted to the wee hours of the night, we got up late the next day. Consuela and I strolled along the creek behind our home. I told her more about our family's journey so long ago. She was excited and had many great questions to ask the historians. I suggested she join me on my trip. She said, "I can visit Spain with you." It would be great to share this adventure with her.

As we were walking on our land, we made an exciting discovery—a giant boulder with a large crack down the center. Studying it, I saw what looked like letters, but it was very hard to see. Fortunately, I had my camera with me and adjusted the lens to get a closer view, snapping many pictures.

When we got back, I called Dr. Munoz and said, "Please come back to our hacienda. We found something else of interest." He came back and saw the writing was faint. He brushed the area and applied some chemicals to the stone. Suddenly he discovered the letters V-A. I recalled Jose and Estrella had a daughter named Valentina. Later, his team of archeologists confirmed my suspicions. The letters had been chiseled into the stone almost four hundred years ago. I thought my family might have put her name on the rock.

As Lucinda continued to dig through the records, she made more connections to Valentina's name. A marriage document from 1612 said Valentina Gomez De Grazie was wed to Carlos Sánchez. Valentina married Miguel's son, who she had known most of her life. Miguel managed the silver mine bought by her father, Jose Gomez. There was no mention of the marriage on the audiotapes, but I hoped they were happy.

Valentina's name appeared again on land purchased by Carlos Sánchez and Valentina Sánchez in 1630. An orphanage was built, dedicated to Valentina's parents, Don Jose Gomez, Doña Estrella Fuentes Gomez De Grazie, and Dr. Alejandro De Grazie. The charitable nature of the family deeply touched me. Valentina loved her parents so much that she endowed an orphanage in their memory, being grateful they took her into their family. She followed the family motto of *faith, family, future*. It was an oath she took very seriously.

As I typed the story for my editor, my fingers could not keep up with my thoughts. It was the fastest story I had ever written. I wanted to get it to my editor quickly. I was grateful that my fax machine was working because, at times, it was on the fritz. A few days later, I anxiously called my editor to see what she thought of my article. She was just about to contact me and told me she loved it and couldn't wait for more. I felt so proud of myself that I thought I could do anything.

After the successful finds in Pueblo, I was eager to go on to Santa Fe. I went to the New Mexico History Museum, which included the Palace of the Governors, built in 1610. Before my arrival, the staff had gathered some material for me to view. There was no information on

Jose and Estrella Gomez, but there was for Pablo Gomez. My ancestor Pablo had done very well with his business and community. He was a contributor to the Palace of the Governors. That was such exciting news. One of my ancestors was instrumental in laying the foundation of this lovely city.

As I walked down the Palace of Governors, I found it hard to believe I was walking in the exact place where Estrella sold her blankets. She had been a successful businesswoman at a time when women were relegated to the household. To this day, Pueblo is known for its unusual woolen blankets and other woven goods made by the town's women and sold in Santa Fe. It was also here where Jose first experienced the city's beautiful sights at the Fandango after his arrival.

It is a beautiful city full of people from all walks of life. There's a lot to see and do there, especially in the summer. It houses the Santa Fe Opera in a magnificent venue, with top operatic performers. There are many museums like the one that houses the works of Georgia O'Keeffe. My staff and I stayed at the stately La Fonda Hotel in the center of the town.

I decided to take a walking tour around the city with my team, to familiarize ourselves with the area. We came across a beautiful adobe home that became a museum. We entered, paid the admission, and were fascinated by the relics of colonial New Spain in the home. The docent was an older woman whose family had lived in the house for many generations. She loved talking about her family's history. They had been there since Juan de Oñate came in 1598. It was the same journey that my ancestor Jose Gomez had taken. I wondered if they knew each other. We asked her if she knew of any Jewish people in that caravan. Angela smiled and told us that there were Jews on the trail. "One of my ancestors was in the procession. He was Jewish. There are a lot of people here today who have Jewish ancestors." She told us that many practiced Jewish customs, like lighting candles on Friday night, then putting the candles in a ceramic container so their neighbors could not see the reflection of the light. Some people never ate pork. The fasting days, such as the Day of Atonement and others, were observed on different days. She told us that she kept those customs too. She wove a tale that proved Santa Fe still has descendants of Conversos. It was hard to believe that some traditions prevailed after not practicing their faith for five hundred years. It was time to go on with our trip. As I continued to retrace my ancestor's journey, my next stop was Mexico City.

The professor at the university was Dr. Barbara Weiss. She did not find land records, but there was a baptismal record for Josephina Gomez in the documents, who was the child of Estrella and Jose Gomez. On my way back from the university, I took a tour of the magnificent Mexico City Metropolitan Cathedral situated in downtown Mexico City. I imagined my family witnessing its construction because it took over two hundred and fifty years to complete. I was amazed by the grandeur of the cathedral. Many architects designed the building since it took so long to complete, each putting their mark on the cathedral. Mexico City is and was the country's economic and cultural hub.

Attractions abound in the city filled with museums. The Palacio de Bellas Artes features art nouveau and art deco style of architecture, complete with marble floors. Diego Rivera designed the murals. I saw a tribute to his wife at the Frida Kahlo Museum, also referred to as the Blue House. This house was where Frida lived.

Next, we went to Veracruz. It is an important port city, not your typical tourist stop. Attractions are the Aquaria de Veracruz, an aquarium featuring sharks and dolphins, a Wax Museum, and a place called Malecon, where vendors sell snacks and souvenirs.

There is a magical element found in Veracruz not heard in other places. Music fills the city. Tunes are heard everywhere, at the beaches and stores, walking down the street and by homes. Sometimes it is accompanied by singing and dancing. The fandangos are the road to peace, the people say.

The concierge at our hotel recommended a restaurant frequented by the locals. They served a delicate signature dish of the area, Huachinango a la Veracruzana, red snapper Veracruz style, using local fruits and vegetables, such as tomatoes and chili peppers, and Spanish ingredients like olive oil, garlic, and capers. I know from the tape that my ancestors had eaten this dish and wondered if they enjoyed it as much as I did. I wanted to learn how to make this tasty fare. It reminded me of when I went to New Orleans, where I tasted the very best coffee that I had ever had in my entire life. What made the coffee so delicious was the added ingredient of chicory. I excitedly bought a couple of pounds of coffee to take home. When I got home, I couldn't wait to go back to the memory of New Orleans with a cup of my chicory coffee. I anxiously poured a cup, lifted it, took a deep breath, and then drank it. I was confused, so I tried it again. I took a deep breath, smelled it, then took a sip. It didn't taste the same as it did in New Orleans. I didn't understand why it tasted different. Was it the water? Perhaps it was the experience of being in a new place and being on vacation. Thinking of coffee made me want some.

El Gran Café de la Parroquia is the most famous coffeehouse in Veracruz. Its signature drink is *lechero*, which consists of espresso coffee mixed with steamed milk. When customers request a refill, they rattle the sides of their glasses with their spoons. As you enter the coffeehouse, you hear the clinking of the spoons, which continues from the early morning till late at night. Everyone wanted another taste of this famous coffee.

I was curious about what our next stop in Cadiz would reveal. I was very excited to see my sister, Consuela. I met her at the airport with a big sign saying SISSY, my nickname for her. On my head was a chauffeur's hat, and I wore driving gloves on my hands. She ran over to me with her arms outstretched and gave me a huge bear hug. Following slowly behind her were two exhausted men lugging two massive suitcases apiece. I laughed and said, "Oh, I see you packed lightly for this trip. I wonder how our driver is going to find room for your bags in the car." She was Ms. Flirty, thanking the two men who helped her, giving them her signature two-handed handshake while looking into their eyes. Consuela had a way of making everyone around her feel special. Now my trip to Spain would be complete. My sweet sister was with me.

The port in Cadiz was and still is the most important port in Spain. We immediately went to the dock, where we bought churros, fried dough covered in sugar and spice, from a street vendor. They were delicious. As we ate the tasty, sweet treat, I thought about David and Valentina enjoying this delicacy, since it has a long history in Spain.

I knew a little about the ship my ancestors took to the New World. It was the *Santa Inés*. The ship's manifest at the Maritime History Museum showed the names of my family: Estrella Gomez, Jose Gomez,

David Gomez, Valentina Gomez, Maria Santos, and Francisco Santos. The notable tourist features are the Castle of San Sebastián, a long stone causeway that runs from the city's northwestern edge, and the classic Moorish-style Gran Teatro Falla, a magnificent concert hall. Another successful venture for me and my team.

Cadiz was a great experience; unfortunately, the flight delays and canceled reservations we experienced at the airport were not pleasant. We were supposed to fly into Córdoba and arrive in the morning. However, we wound up at the airport for an extra twelve hours and arrived in Córdoba late that evening. I was stressed, but instead of getting upset, I closed my eyes and slowly counted to ten. Then I transported myself to a happy place. After that, I was ready to get started making phone calls to reschedule appointments I had made.

20

WHERE IT BEGAN

Looking forward to learning more about the city of my family's origins, I was in the town my family had called home for hundreds of years, Córdoba.

As we passed through the town, I saw the flag of Spain flying on the roof top of our hotel, which was a converted castle. The grounds of the hotel were beautifully manicured.

Barely containing my excitement, I felt like a movie star returning to my hometown. Consuela and I smiled and started giggling as if we were little school girls who got to stay up late. It was a place of so much grandeur and rich history.

We had a luxurious suite. On the large, terraced balcony, we saw the river, cathedral, churches, cafés, shops, and museums. The breathtaking sights seemed to stretch out for miles. I was struck by how magical this place felt; the town's lights twinkled in the moonlight. I couldn't wait to explore and had no idea how I would sleep that night. I wanted to take in all the sights immediately.

Before I did anything else, I needed to confirm my appointment with the professor I had been corresponding with for months. We had a meeting arranged for tomorrow. We chatted briefly. I laughed at his jokes about traveling. When I got off the phone, Consuela began to tease me, saying, "You like the professor!" There's nothing like having a family to keep you grounded.

Eager to meet me, Dr. Emilio Gutierrez told me that I was from a well-respected, distinguished family with a long history in Córdoba. He had done his PhD dissertation on Córdoba's influential leaders during the Middle Ages. Our family was among those he studied. Many buildings bore their name. The Gomez family had significantly impacted the city in the arts and sciences. There was evidence everywhere I went, so much so that there was a park named in their honor.

When we met the next day at his office, Dr. Gutierrez showed me baptismal records and gave me copies to keep. The documents bore the names of Estrella Fuentes, Jose Gomez, and David Gomez. I said, "Dr. Gutierrez, it is thrilling to see these documents and to have copies of them."

One of the most outstanding features in Córdoba is the Mosque of Córdoba, a tribute to Muslim architecture that later became a cathedral where many powerful families of the time worshiped and were baptized. I was excited to see it. "Where is the Cathedral? Can we visit?" I queried.

Emilio smiled and nodded. "I would love to take you there. We can go tomorrow morning. Do you have dinner plans this evening? There is a famous restaurant I'd love to take you both to."

At dinner, the professor was charming. We talked about family, history, religion, and sports until the wee hours of the night. When I first spoke to Professor Gutierrez, I hadn't realized how attractive and young he was. I never pictured him to be anything but old and bald. It's hard to imagine how someone looks from writing or talking on the phone. As the night wore on and the wine flowed, I got tipsy. I began to stand up and lost my balance, sitting back down immediately. The professor chuckled and said, "Please allow me to help you." When he held my hand, I felt something I hadn't felt since the early days of my relationship with Jeremy. I was attracted to this fine young man.

The following day, as we drove to the cathedral, I saw the lovely Guadalquivir River and gazed at the Morena Mountains in the distance. Rows of barley, wheat, corn, olives, and sunflowers blanketed the landscape. Many different types of fruit and nuts are also grown in this region, like almonds, oranges, and vegetables. These were some of the things we saw on our way to the records office.

We discovered additional documents that surprised me. One was the land purchase for the hacienda, and the other for an orphanage called Valentina Gomez Orphanage. She had been living on the street before my ancestors took her into their home. I remembered listening to the tape, where Estrella asked her husband to do something for all the young children without a home and families. He said he would. There was no mention of this on the recordings. I told the good doctor I knew my abuelita would have been delighted to know that Jose had built an orphanage.

Dr. Emilio Gutierrez promised to take us to see the hacienda and orphanage area. Sadly, they no longer existed; we arrived at an empty lot. We walked around the site and looked for any traces of the former home. Although we found nothing, I was very impressed with the charitable work of our ancestors. My crew, which consisted of me, my sister, the driver, and a photographer, were then invited to Dr. Gutierrez's classroom, to take pictures, and sit in on a lecture on Spanish history. The passionate professor spoke with enthusiasm. Listening to him speak was riveting. When the class was over, we could see the chalk dust all over his jacket as we approached him. I chuckled a little to myself, thinking about how much chalk dust he must collect in a semester. His students came up to him to let him know how much they enjoyed his lecture. As they approached him, his students clapped. I had never witnessed anything like that before. He was beloved. We needed to see one more special place.

After the lecture, we visited Córdoba's Synagogue, built in 1391. The professor thought it was a private synagogue for a wealthy patron. It was tiny, containing only two rooms filled with documents about the Jewish community of old. It was a lovely reminder of the vibrant community long ago when three important religions flourished harmoniously. Next to the synagogue was a statue of Moses Maimonides, a famous rabbinical scholar still revered to this day. I think the figure serves as a reminder of the Golden Age of Spain when different faiths lived side by side.

Visiting Córdoba connected me to my ancestors in a way I hadn't expected. I found myself daydreaming about their lives when they lived in this inviting city centuries before. I knew my connection with this place would not end. I had to come back. It was especially hard to say goodbye to Dr. Emilio Gutierrez. He promised to visit in America. He said, "I want to get to know you, Estrella."

I told him, "I feel the same way."

Our final destination was to visit my beloved family in one of the most enchanting cities, Barcelona.

First, we traveled to the Abby Montserrat, which houses the *Black Madonna*. Legend is that if a woman touches or kisses the hand of the Madonna, she could become pregnant. She is called the Fertility Madonna. Another tourist attraction is *recortadores*, an alternative to bullfighting. Those who participate do not maim or kill the bull. They do daring tricks like bull leaping and flips. It is a fascinating and delightful to watch the show.

Since our family is so familiar with the art of the flamenco dance, we could not leave without seeing a show. We saw a young girl of nine dancing her heart out. She was one of the finest flamenco dancers I had ever seen. Full of passion. The music was so enticing that I wanted to get on the floor and join her. It was hard to resist, as were all the delicious foods Barcelona offered.

I've always enjoyed trying new foods, and I love being able to taste many different things, which is why tapas is so great, because it gives people the opportunity to do just that. Tapas are served on small plates and are suitable for tasting various food or sharing with others.

Not original to Barcelona, tapas have become very popular. You can see tapas bars everywhere.

Another unique sight is a sport called castell, which is climbing a human tower. A strong base is needed to avoid toppling over. If the column falls, there are many injuries. As many as two hundred people can participate in this exotic event, with participants as young as four years old from everywhere. In 1980, it became more popular with the addition of women.

My daring sister kicked off her heels and climbed up two levels of people to be part of the tower. She cut in line ahead of others waiting to join the tower. Consuelo was oblivious, blinded by her enthusiasm, smiling as she climbed. Despite her faux pas, the very same crowd booing her for cutting in line cheered her on as the tower grew taller.

That was a beautiful thing about my sister. Her joy for life was infectious. She always found a way to win people over.

We shared how excited we were to see our family in Barcelona. Aunt Mia was at Abuelita's funeral in 1978, comforting our family. The last time I saw both my aunt and uncle was in 1974, just before my abuelo died. They were fortunate to see him when he rallied before his death. He was thrilled to see his daughter Mia again, returning to life when she came into town. It was delightful to see them for something happy instead of a funeral. Fond memories popped into my head.

I remember my mom and her sister sharing stories about growing up together. They would laugh so hard, tears flowing down their faces, recounting the bubble fight they had with Abuelo. As Consuela walked into the family room, she immediately ran to get her camera when she saw the two sisters together. She took pictures of the sisters asleep on the couch with their heads cocked in the same direction. After taking the photos, Consuela ran to the kitchen and grabbed my hand, wanting me to come with her. I didn't know what was happening, but I understood when I saw my mom and Aunt Mia sleeping. We could barely contain our laughter, watching them napping. We brought the pictures to share with our cousins, who howled just like we had when they saw the photos. It was good to see all the family. They had visited us individually, but this was the first time we were with them all together. Both Consuela and I invited them to visit us. We planned to have a reunion in the next three years. We had to decide where it would be. Maybe we would pick a city in Europe, so no one would have to play host. It's more fun to go somewhere you've never been before anyway. We had time to figure that out. There was the old synagogue in Barcelona that I was curious about.

Aunt Mia asked us if we wanted to see the old Jewish quarter named El Call to see Barcelona's Ancient Synagogue. I was surprised that she was interested since she only spoke of our Jewish connection once at the funeral. Since Abuela's funeral, my dear aunt began learning more about Judaism. Long ago, the chief rabbi in Barcelona was Shlomo ben Avraham ibn Aderet. He served the congregation for fifty years until his death in 1310, during the Golden Age of Spain, when three religions lived in relative peace. So revered, Rabbi ibn Aderet was known as the

Rabbi of Spain, writing Talmud, religious commentaries. A synagogue was named after him.

After 1492, the synagogue was no longer used for prayer and became a hospital for treating rabies after the Jews left. Now it was open to the public for viewing. The beautiful stained glass window was a tribute to the community. Barcelona's Ancient Synagogue, no longer in service, was filled with information about the history of the city's Jews. Aunt Mia knew some Converso families that had stayed in Barcelona since the Inquisition. They were practicing Catholics but still lit candles on Friday night. Some Israelis came to live in Barcelona in the last few years, so there was a small Jewish community. It was nothing like the community that existed in the Middle Ages when Jews were persecuted or thrown out of the country.

I said goodbye to my family and charming Spain. I did get some answers to my questions but still needed to know more. Though I'd been to Spain before, this time it was different. I looked for my family's past in a place where I felt I belonged.

On my way home to LA, I kept thinking about all I had learned during my trip by retracing my ancestors' steps. I understood and felt love for Spain, this enchanting place, just like my family. The sights, sounds, and smells were home. I had a longing to connect with my family and hometown more often and vowed to do so.

I began to frequent Santa Fe often to learn more about my culture. It was a fantastic opportunity to spend time with my family since Pueblo was close to Santa Fe. I was happy that my parents and uncle kept a lot of the traditions alive from my grandparents; however, there were some notable changes.

Instead of having the ruckus game night every month with too much drinking and smoking, we had a morning walk followed by brunch. At brunch, guests enjoyed many healthy salads and fruits and my mom's famous creation, the blue corn waffle utilizing the fresh corn growing on the ranch. I think my grandparents would've been happy for this healthier outlet for celebrating time together.

I also joined a group in Santa Fe that helped Anousim, Hidden Jews, discover their roots. We discussed any new information we found about our families and shared resources at our meetings. Attending with me were my mom and sister. I spoke at a conference, telling the audience my story of discovery. I addressed the struggles my ancestors and I faced. Afterward, I suffered from nightmares again. Speaking about my Jewish past was still hard for me. It dredged up many unhappy memories. I wondered if it would get easier with time. Three women from the conference became my friends.

I met and bonded immediately with Yasmin, Isa, and Carla. They knew that I was on an emotional roller coaster. Whenever I needed to talk about things, they were available to listen, and when asked, they would offer advice. It helped me to know that I was not alone. Sometimes they invited me for a Shabbat dinner. They would sing songs about Shabbat. The melodies were familiar to me. They sounded like the melodies Abuelita had sung to me.

Yasmin, one of my new friends, was a performer. She was learning Ladino from a local woman. When the Spanish Jews left Spain, a new language began called Ladino. It is a combination of Hebrew, Castilian Spanish, and any other language spoken where they lived. They spoke Ladino in many countries, including Turkey, Tunisia, Morocco, and the New World. She was a descendant of Turkish Jews. One evening, I saw her perform, which dazzled me. She had a unique way of combining interpretive dance with the melodies of ancient songs. Soon, Yasmin began to perform regularly at Bar Mitzvahs and other Jewish celebrations. Yasmin was tall and lean, and she moved her arms and legs with the grace of a ballerina. Soon, my friend became a local celebrity in the community, even having a TV show in town.

Isa, another new friend, learned that her feeling of being different all of her life was grounded in reality. She found out that her family celebrated Jewish customs as she studied the faith. Isa wrote poems expressing her feelings of alienation. She wove words magically to communicate her feelings. Many people approached her to express their deep sorrow after hearing her poetry, since it was relatable.

There was Carla, who observed the celebration of the holidays. She became my closest friend except for my sister. Carla was the most outspoken of the group. Her road to self-discovery and Judaism came after taking a comparative religion class in college and stumbling upon the fact that her family had many of the same practices as Jews. She asked her family to admit they were Jews. Her family warned her to drop the subject. If she kept on talking about it, they would disown her. Sadly, Carla could not let it go, and her family disowned her.

Carla found out she was part of a Converso family from the southwest portion of Texas, where people only married others from three nearby towns. They were all Converso communities. No one had told her of her Jewish roots. Her family always said they were not Mexican but were descendants of Spanish nobility. They felt superior to the Mexican people.

Since she no longer had a family, she found friends to be her family. She even changed her name from Christina to Carla. Like me, one of the holidays she celebrated as a young girl was St. Ester's Day. It was a favorite celebration. Mysteriously, the holiday disappeared. Anousim felt a kinship with Ester because she had hidden her Jewish faith. After discovering that Ester was not a Christian, there were no longer any St. Ester's Day celebrations, even though the Anousim revered her.

There were many Conversos in the past who had returned to the faith of their forefathers. Rabbi Shimon Duran wrote a prayer in the fifteenth century especially for those returning to their faith. "Our G-d and G-d of our fathers bring success to your servant … and bestow your grace upon him. Just as you moved his heart to return in complete repentance before you so may you plant in his heart love and fear of you. Open his heart to your Torah and guide him in the path of your commandments that he may find grace in your eyes. So may it be, and let us say AMEN." It was the persistence of the Crypto Jewish women who kept the faith alive. They are heroines of this story.

Carla and I began taking classes from a rabbi to learn more about Judaism, considering ourselves to be sisters in faith. I trusted her, so I told Carmen when I decided to know more about my ancestors. Though she felt complete as a member of the nation of Israel, she still felt a tug in her heart when she could not join her family in celebrating their Christian holidays. It pained me to know that her family broke contact with her. I knew I'd feel terrible if that happened to me. My family was accepting of our newly discovered faith. *Wait a minute. Am I ignoring my dad's reaction?* Something was different.

I said, "Papa is everything okay? You're not mad about anything, are you?"

He reassured me, "Mija, everything is wonderful. I get to see my lovely Star more often. I love your visits."

I pressed him. "I love seeing you more too, but it seems like something is upsetting you. I think I know what it is. Every time I talk to you about what I am learning through my Jewish studies and discussion group, you change the subject. Or you tell me that secrets belong hidden, and I shouldn't look into the past. Is something upsetting you about Judaism?"

He responded, "Oh, mijo, no, no, no. If you know me, I don't understand a lot about history. Everything's fine."

I said, "Papa, we've always been so close. I know something's bothering you. Can we talk about it?"

Papa took a deep breath. I could hear a slight tremble in his voice. "You know I've never really felt worthy of your mama. Hearing about her family and all the wonderful things they did for their community reminds me that my family is less accomplished than hers. You, your siblings, cousins, aunts, and uncles have this shared new history that I have no part in."

I kissed him and said, "Papa, how could you think you are not part of this family?"

Sniffling, he smiled and said, "Mija, I'm just a silly old man."

I responded, "Papa, one thing that I have learned about this religion is that it is inclusive. Judaism teaches people to respect and love each other for what they have in common and what is different. Why don't you go with Mama and me to the next meeting of Conversos, so as not to exclude you?"

Ever since my abuelita told me we were Jews, my life had been in turmoil, filled with happiness and pain. There were still so many unanswered questions. I lost my husband to prejudice because he hated minorities. My road to discovery also helped me realize we just didn't fit together.

Then I discovered my ancestors' journey with their noteworthy accomplishments in Spain. I felt a sense of pride. I felt proud that my family tried to observe as much of their faith as they could remember. They were so committed to Judaism they risked their lives to practice.

Next, I met many lovely friends whose struggles resembled my own. And finally, I met a wonderful man who wanted to know who I was. It feels right to be in a relationship where I can be true to myself even though an ocean separates us. Time will tell if anything more comes of our relationship. New love is always exciting.

I'm still trying to unravel the story of my family's past and how it relates to me. I do believe I am on my way to finding the answers. As my life reveals itself, I've learned to take the bitter with the sweet. The Inquisition lasted more than three hundred and fifty years. Many Conversos were tortured and burned at the stake because of their unfaltering attachment to Judaism. In the last few years, both Portugal and Spain have granted citizenship to those who can prove they are descendants of family members once living in those countries, in an attempt to apologize for the Inquisition. The last victim, Cayetano Repoli, a teacher, was hung in Mexico City in 1826. The royal María Cristina de Borbón officially abolished the Inquisition in Spain in 1834. Appalled by the grueling tortures imposed by the Spanish and Portuguese, the founding fathers of the United States added freedom of religion to the First Amendment of the Constitution so no one would be punished by the government for their religious beliefs.

Sadness swept over me, knowing the one thing that my ancestors never found was a place where they could practice their faith freely. After traveling thousands of miles and risking their lives, they still did not find the religious freedom they longed to enjoy.

FAVORITE SPANISH RECIPES

Spanish Hot Chocolate

Serves 4

Ingredients
4 ounces bittersweet chocolate
4 cup of whole milk
1/4 teaspoon cornstarch
1/2 tablespoon fine sugar to taste, or up to 3 tablespoons

1/4 teaspoon chili powder to taste
nutmeg (optional)
vanilla (optional)
cinnamon (optional)

Preparation

Heat the cornstarch with the milk until dissolved.
    Mix the sugar into the mixture.
    Put pot on low heat on the stove.
    Add chocolate and mix thoroughly.
    Add spices.
    Place hot chocolate back on stove to heat.

    Enjoy.

Bischochitos

Ingredients for the wet mixture. Place in a separate bowl to be creamed with a mixer.

Makes 36 cookies

1/2 cup shortening (cut into pieces)
1/2 cup butter (cut into pieces)
3/4 cup white sugar
1/4 cup brown sugar
1 teaspoon vanilla extract
1 tablespoon Grand Marnier or orange juice
1 egg

Ingredients for the dry mixture. Place in a separate bowl.

2 1/2 cup or 312 grams flour
1 1/2 teaspoons cream of tartar
1 teaspoon or 4 grams baking powder
1/4 teaspoon or 1 gram baking soda
1/2 teaspoon or 2 grams salt
1 1/2 teaspoon or 6 grams anise seed

Add the dry mixture together with the wet ingredients and stir until thoroughly combined. Spice mixture for rolling the cookies in before baking to taste. (Typically, it's a sugar mixture consisting of white sugar and cinnamon. However, I feel adding more spices enhances the taste of these cookies.)

Add these ingredients to taste:

white sugar
cinnamon
cardamom
allspices
ginger

cocoa powder
cayenne powder

*Important note: Spend time creaming together butter, shortening, and sugar mixture longer than you think. I recommend doing this for 3 minutes. When baking cookies, this step is rushed, which impacts the taste.

Spanish French Toast (Torrijas)

4 servings

Ingredients

1 cup milk or cream
2 eggs
2 tablespoons honey or maple syrup
1 teaspoon vanilla extract
1 teaspoon cinnamon
1/2 teaspoon cardamom
pinch of salt
6 slices of stale bread

Preparation

In a large bowl, add all the ingredients together except the bread.
Next, soak each piece of bread, making sure to completely cover it
in the mixture.
Using a nonstick pan heated to medium, add butter or a nonstick
cooking spray.
Place the bread in your pan. Bake until it is golden brown on both
sides.
Plate and enjoy with more butter, cinnamon, and power sugar. This
also pairs well with a mint berry salad.

Mediterranean-Inspired Salmon and Farro Dish

Serves 4–6

Ingredients

1 1/2 pounds of salmon
8 ounces grape tomatoes
3 ounces marinated artichokes
2 shallots
2 ounces sundried tomatoes
1 tablespoon butter
1/2 teaspoon paprika
salt and pepper to taste
2 tablespoons olive oil
lemon slices to juice over salmon
1 cup farro
3 ounces sliced almonds
fresh herbs like parsley for garnish and taste

Preparation

Farro is a delicious, nutty-tasting, high-fiber grain from the Mediterranean region. It can take on the flavors of the ingredients used in the recipe. If you cannot find it at the store, you can always substitute it with quinoa or rice.

Anytime cooking a grain, it's always important to impart as much flavor to it as possible. Here are some great tips to accomplish this. Toast the grain in a lightly oiled pan until it has a pleasant nutty smell, which takes around 3 minutes on medium heat.

After that, it's time to add the liquid. Instead of adding water, why not add some broth? This is a wonderful way to bring the grain to life. Bring the liquid to a boil, drop the heat to a simmer, and cover with a lid, taking 20 to 30 minutes. Remember when cooking grains to let them cook without stirring them. When done, take the lid off. Add the sliced almonds and mix them in. The farro will be perfect and ready to serve.

When selecting vegetables to go with a fatty, rich piece of fish, it's important to add acidity, like there is in tomatoes, to help balance the richness of the salmon.

Start with the shallots and a little bit of oil. Cook them for 5 minutes over medium-high heat. Stir as needed. The goal is to tenderize and sweeten the shallots. Next, add the artichokes, grape tomatoes, and sundried tomatoes and cook for another 5 minutes. Set aside.

Cooking in a cast-iron skillet gives you the ability to cook at higher temperatures for more extended periods. It's excellent for creating a nice crust on your food. Season the salmon with salt, pepper, paprika, dried oregano. The pan should be lightly oiled with some olive oil. Start with one side. Do not turn before it's ready. The pan should be on medium-high heat. Sear the salmon for 3 minutes. After you flip the fish, add some butter to the top of the fish while cooking it on the second side. Cook on the other side for an additional 3 to 4 minutes.

Important note: Food safety is essential, so use an instant-read thermometer at around 120 to 125 degrees. The ideal internal temperature should be 125 to 130 degrees. You may take the salmon out of the skillet slightly before it reaches the desired temperature since there will be additional carryover cooking time.

Now that the salmon is ready, it's time to serve and enjoy. Plate your dish with a nice portion of the farro, vegetables, and the salmon. Then sprinkle with fresh lemon.

Gazpacho

4 servings

Ingredients

6 large tomatoes, chopped
2 cans of crushed tomatoes
1 red onion, finely chopped
1 cucumber, peeled, seeded, chopped
1 red or green bell pepper, chopped
2 ribs celery, chopped
1 to 2 tablespoons chopped fresh parsley
2 tablespoons chopped fresh chives
1 clove garlic, minced
1/4 cup red wine vinegar
1/4 cup extra virgin olive oil
1 tablespoon freshly squeezed lemon juice
2 teaspoons sugar, or more to taste
salt and freshly ground pepper to taste

Preparation

Place all ingredients in a large bowl. Blend the gazpacho to the preferred texture. You may use an immersion blender or regular blender.

Ladle your soup into bowls, topping with one ice cube in each bowl and whatever you wish for a garnish. Some great options for garnish are tortilla strips or crackers and a dollop of sour cream.

Modification: If you would like a slightly sweeter and more mellow flavor, you may sweat the onions, a process of reducing the amount of water in the onion for a few minutes on the stove before adding them to the blender. This allows you to get a more concentrated flavor.

Sweet Corn Waffles

Serves 4–6

Ingredients

1 cup all-purpose flour
1 cup fine yellow cornmeal
1 teaspoon kosher salt
1/3 cup sugar
1 tablespoon baking powder
1 cup corn kernels from approximately 2 ears of corn, kernels grated on the large holes of a
box grater
2 large eggs
1 1/2 cups buttermilk, or whole milk mixed with 1 tablespoon white vinegar
1 teaspoon pure vanilla extract
1/2 cup (4 ounces) unsalted butter, melted, plus more for greasing the waffle iron
salted butter, for serving
maple syrup, for serving

Preparation

Stir together all of the dry ingredients.
   Stir wet ingredients together.
   Mix the wet with the dry ingredients.
   Butter or spray oil on the waffle iron.
   Heat the waffle iron to medium.
   Place mixture in the waffle iron.
   Remove waffles when they are golden brown.
   Add butter and maple syrup.
   Enjoy!

DISCUSSION QUESTIONS FOR BOOK GROUPS

1. Why were women responsible for telling the younger generation about their Jewish past?

2. How did Converso groups keep in touch with other communities around the world?

3. Why was it important to distinguish between Old Christians and New Christians?

4. What are the parallels between the lives of Estrella Gomez De Grazie and Estrella Schmitt?

5. Kat and Jeremy are clearly anti-Semitic, which becomes blatantly apparent when Estrella reveals her heritage. Do you believe that Jews today face this type of anti-Semitic reaction?

6. Prior to the Inquisition, were Jews safe to practice their faith in Spain?

7. How did the Inquisition impact the lives of the Jews in Spain after 1492?

8. Why did the Conversos risk their lives to practice Judaism?

9. If you were in this situation, what would you do?

10. What are the similarities and differences between the Inquisition and the Holocaust?

ACKNOWLEDGEMENT

I'm grateful to the many family and friends who helped me over the years with my passion project including several writers groups that helped me along the way .I especially want to thank my sister and brother-in-law, Hetty and Zack Davies, who were with me the entire time I was writing, and my beloved daughter Rachel who was the biggest supporter of this book. My friends Sander Nassan and Kathleen Darrow were helpful in the editing of the manuscript and encouraging me. Thank you to authors Danny Siegel and Miriam Ruth Black, who gave me writing tips.

REFERENCES

Brooks, A. (2002). *The Woman Who Defied Kings: The Life and Times of Dona Gracia Nasi*. Paragon House.

Gitlitz, D. (1996). *Secrecy and Deceit: The Religion of Crypto-Jews*. University of New Mexico Press.

Gitlitz, D. & Davidson, L. (2000). *A Drizzle of Honey: The Life and Recipes of Spain's Secret Jews*. St. Martin's Press.

Hordes, Stanley, *To the End of the Earth: A History of the Crypto-Jews of New Mexico*.

Le Porrier, H. (1979). *The doctor from Cordova: A biographical novel about the great philosopher Maimonides*. Doubleday & Company, Inc.

Umansky, E. & Ashton, D., Eds. (1992). *Four Centuries of Jewish Women's Spirituality: A Sourcebook*. Beacon Press.

Jewish Heritage Alliance. *Women of Sefarad - The Crypto-Jewish Women of Sefarad*. Mar 7, 2021. https://jewishheritagealliance.com.

Jewish Heritage Alliance. *Women of Sefarad - Doña Gracia*. Apr 20, 2021. https://jewishheritagealliance.com.

Jewish Heritage Alliance. *Sefarad Hidden Legacies Uncovered*. Feb 1, 2022. https://jewishheritagealliance.com.

Jewish Heritage Alliance. *Sefarad: Secrets of the Inquisition. The Life & Times of Luis de Carvajal the Younger.* May 2, 2022. https://jewishheritagealliance.com.

Jewish Heritage Alliance. *Sefarad - The Untold Story that Changed the World: Part 1.* Aug 2, 2021. https://jewishheritagealliance.com.

Jewish Heritage Alliance. *The Converso Comeback - In the Footsteps of Hispanic Crypto-Jews.* Jun 5, 2020. https://jewishheritagealliance.com.

Jewish Heritage Alliance. *Sefarad... To Be or Not to Be.* Dec 20, 2021. https://jewishheritagealliance.com.

Jewish Heritage Alliance. *Sefarad... Hiding in Plain Sight.* Feb 21, 2022. https://jewishheritagealliance.com.

Jewish Heritage Alliance. *Sefarad - The Untold Story That Changed the World Part II.* Aug 24, 2021. https://jewishheritagealliance.com.

Israel Explained: Through the Lens of History; Class #3 (*Ottoman Empire & Occupation*). Created by Laureen Lipsky, CEO & Founder, Taking Back the Narrative (www.tbtnisrael.com)

Printed in the United States
by Baker & Taylor Publisher Services